Can't Catch My Breath

SARAH SUTTON

Golden Crown Publishing, LLC

ALSO BY SARAH SUTTON

WHAT ARE FRIENDS FOR

OUT OF MY LEAGUE

IF THE BROOM FITS

CAN'T CATCH MY BREATH

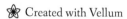 Created with Vellum

To my parents,
who are seriously superheroes.

One

'd never experienced loss before my dad died. The closest I'd come to death was when my pet hamster died when I was seven. On paper, the two wouldn't even be comparable. The death of a small rodent shouldn't have come close to the death of my father.

I will say this, though: I cried more for the hamster.

Which makes me sound heartless. And a little psycho.

But I couldn't be sad, couldn't even *think* about Dad. If I thought about him, if I fully acknowledged what had happened...I just couldn't.

So, I locked it away. All thoughts of the accident went into a box sealed shut with superglue and duct tape and lots of staples. *Do not open.* If I caught my thoughts wandering down that road, I'd take in a sharp breath and push into a different direction. There was no other option.

Like now, as I stared at Greenville High for the first time in over a month, I forced myself to think about anything but the accident.

Despite the rapid beating of my heart and the patches

of ice on the pavement, my footsteps were sure as I made my way across the student parking lot. Snow settled perfectly over the ground, not yet paved away from last night's fall. The building loomed ahead of me, cars driving around it to drop kids off left and right. Just a few weeks ago, I'd been dreaming about this very day, waiting for it to come.

Yeah, I'd been dreaming about going back to school. Like a nerd.

Facing high school hadn't ever been a source of anxiety. I was a rare breed of human beings that loved high school. Thrived off it. The people, the conversations, the home-work—busy, busy, busy. That was why I was in yearbook, chair of the dance committee, a straight-A student. That was all right up my alley. And after an entire month of being starved for connection, I was desperate to return to the people, the conversations, the homework, the *busyness*.

I'd only have to fight my way past the *I'm so sorry*'s and *Is there anything I can do*'s. All eyes would be on me, at least today. Maybe after the first day back people would grow bored of the girl whose dad died.

I took a deep breath in, held it for five seconds, and then let it out. A mental reset.

You've got this, Addy, I told myself, stepping around a large chunk of ice. *You're going to fall back into your new normal and everything will be all right.*

I hadn't even made it inside the school before I heard someone call my name in all its alliterative glory. "Adeline Annabelle Arden!"

And then something slammed into me. Or *someone,*

because arms wrapped around me, holding me tight. A mouthful of vanilla-scented red curls clued me into who was trying to strangle me.

"Vesta," I said, greeting my best friend, but the word came out choked. "You're crushing me."

I mentally assessed how I must've looked to her. My outfit was hidden behind my red-and-white checkered coat. My fair hair hung straight, not an inch frizzed or out of place. I'd spent enough time this morning with the straightener to make sure of it. I hadn't put on makeup at all the past month, but today I'd layered it on, focusing as much concealer as I could underneath my eyes. It felt both refreshing and suffocating to look put-together again.

"And *I* can't believe you're here!" she screeched back, loosening her death grip. "Why didn't you tell me your first day back was today? I would've baked cupcakes or something!"

Of my two besties, I'd known Vesta the longest. We'd gone to preschool together and had been best friends since. Mollie, best friend number two, hadn't started at Greenville until last year, but we were already a close knit-trio.

I let myself bask in the hug for only a moment, afraid I'd cry if I clung to her any longer. Pulling away, I gave her a beaming smile, one that felt foreign on my lips. "I wanted it to be a surprise. I mean, it's the first day back from winter break—of *course* I'd be starting today." It was the most animated I'd sounded in a long time.

Vesta's fiery curls were wild today, looking as though she'd tried to coax half of her hair up into a bun, but it seemed to have a mind of its own. It curled every which way, catching the morning breeze. "Well, it is a nice surprise," she said at last, still sounding unsure whether she could believe my cheer. After a month apart, it seemed she couldn't read my cues. She reached over and wrapped her arm around mine, tugging me toward the building. "I just wasn't sure if you'd be back so soon...you know, since after...well, we haven't really talked."

Deep breath in. "Oh, I haven't been talking to anyone, really." Which was the truth. I hadn't spoken with her or Mollie since I'd texted them "Merry Christmas." They'd texted back—flooded my phone—but I just couldn't figure out how to respond.

And Bryce...it'd been a bit since I'd spoken to Bryce. Granted, he hadn't called or texted either.

"But that's because I was in the land of no cell service," I continued as we walked inside. Almost immediately, the heat of the building shook off the outside chill. "We were in Rickett Falls with my mom's parents for almost the entire month. Apparently the falls around that city make cell reception impossible? No clue." The rehearsed speech just fell from my lips easily; I guess practicing in the mirror really paid off. "We got home on the second, and Mom and I just hung out. We both decided it was time to get back to normal."

About all of that was true, except for the part about Mom and I "hanging out." We'd barely spoken a word to each other since we left Rickett Falls.

Vesta followed me to the junior lockers, and I did a good job avoiding eye contact with anyone in the halls.

Look confident, happy—no one will want to bring down the mood.

I pulled the lock off the metal door, popping it wide. There was a mirror magnetized to the door, and I debated on ripping it off. At the very least, I made sure not to glance at my reflection.

"Well, I'm so happy you're back," Vesta said, watching as I unzipped my coat. "I've really, really missed you."

"December was rough," I told her, shrugging off my coat. I tightened the tie around my neck, the familiarity oddly comforting. All of my ties and skirts had collected dust over the last month while I lived in sweatpants, but it was nice to have one thing familiar. "Definitely the worst ever, but I'm just so ready for things to go back to normal, you know?"

When Vesta didn't immediately answer, I looked up to see her watching a boy step into the hallway, and I recognized him immediately. Bryce Jacob Calhoun: football player, treasurer of the student council, future valedictorian. He didn't look any different from when I'd last seen him a little over a month ago, with his short dark hair and baby blue eyes.

We hadn't been officially dating, but before everything happened, I had a feeling he'd been about to ask me that special question. Seeing him now stirred a familiar flutter of anticipation, but after being dormant for so long, it almost felt uncomfortable.

He and I had crossed paths romantically in a game of Lip Locker—it was a game that Greenville kids usually started at parties where two people were blindfolded and sent into a closet to kiss. Like Seven Minutes in Heaven, but you didn't know who you were kissing.

I'd never played the party game before—because *ew*, kissing someone you didn't know?—but Vesta had pushed me into it.

When I found it was Bryce I'd been paired with, I'd been over the moon. A cute, sweet guy who was a good kisser? Sign me up.

Bryce's eyes now caught on Vesta's red hair first before shifting to mine, realization lighting up their depths. It only took him a few moments to cross the hallway. "Addy," he said in greeting, though the word was nothing more than an exhale. He came up on the other side of Vesta, expression a mix of surprise and something else. "You're here."

"In the flesh." I let out an awkward half-laugh, clutching my planner tighter to my chest. "How was your break?"

"Uneventful," Bryce said slowly, slipping his hands into his pockets. The longer he stared, the more I realized what that "something else" in his eyes was: pity.

It was almost a mirror of the expression Vesta had worn outside. Great—I'd have to avoid the awkward sympathy stare from my friends, too.

So I made sure my smile was still in place. "Are you doing anything today? Maybe we could all go to the movies? There's a new horror flick that looks really cheesy." And cheesy horror flicks were my *favorite*.

Bryce, though, looked less than excited. "Mondays are my late tutoring days, so I can't today."

"Besides, Addy, you're the only one who likes scary movies." Vesta chuckled from beside me.

Yeah, everyone else thought stupid romantic comedies were God's gift to humanity. Apparently the cheesiness in those movies was acceptable.

Bryce jerked his thumb against his backpack strap. "Well, I should head to my locker before the bell. I'll...see you two at lunch?"

Vesta was the one to pipe up. "Yeah, absolutely. We'll see you then."

With one of those awkward forced smiles, Bryce headed off toward the senior lockers. He didn't look back.

Once he was out of earshot, I lowered my voice. "That was weird, wasn't it?"

"He's probably just tired. It's hard to get back in the groove after a break, especially winter break. It's like coming out of hibernation."

I could see through her excuses easily. Bryce may have been tired, but there was no missing the look in his eyes. *Your dad died, and I don't know how to be around you.*

I sucked in a deep breath, pushing that thought from my mind before I could linger on it. "It's okay." Once I gathered the rest of my supplies, I shut the door. "So, fill me in on everything I missed. Don't leave anything out."

Vesta jumped on that like a dog on a bone as we walked to her locker. "Jackson broke up with Trish, *again*. She's already with some guy who goes to Hallow now, so I think they're done for good. But I always say that, don't I? I'm sure Jackson will find someone new within a few days. Jordan—the senior—broke his collarbone at a party and it was so gross. You could practically *hear* the snap. Someone even said they saw the bone poking out from his skin."

I grimaced at the mental image. "Were you there?"

"Duh! Jeremy's New Year's parties are, like, tradition."

Vesta wasn't wrong. Jeremy Rivera, a guy who'd graduated last year, always threw a New Year's Eve party. He must've come home from college to keep the spirit alive.

I, however, had been stuck at my grandparents' house, ringing in the new year with no cell service and one parent short.

"Anything new with Mollie?" I asked. "With *you?*"

"Not really." Vesta shrugged, jostling me with the movement. "Same old, same old."

After we stopped by her locker so she could ditch her stuff, we got to our first period classroom, and she let me walk in first. I tried to tell myself not to look up, not to look around at the almost full classroom, not to look anywhere but where my empty assigned seat should be, but it was impossible.

Especially when conversations ceased around me, every head swiveling in the direction of the classroom door. Even our psychology teacher, Mr. Walker, seemed surprised by my presence, his fingers pausing their typing on the keyboard.

It was a very disconcerting feeling, knowing that everyone was looking right at me.

I made my way toward my assigned seat, smoothing down my A-line skirt. Blood pumped too harshly in my ears for me to make out the whispers of conversation around me, and I couldn't help but wonder if they'd been whispering about me.

With shaking hands, I flipped my bullet journal open, the sight of this week's spread immediately pacifying my fraying nerves. My yellow dotted journal kept a set of weekly to-dos, my habit trackers, goal trackers, and a monthly spread. Like a planner, but mega specific to *me*. Many people who did bullet journals made the month one whole cohesive theme, but I liked to shake it up by week.

Since this was my first week back to school, I made it academic-themed—pencils, pads of lined papers, things like that. Next week, I'd probably do a blue color theme, and then the week after, I'd do snowflakes.

I'd started this bullet journal at the beginning of the school year when my other ran out of room. There was something nice about starting fresh, and I wished that my journal had been used up *now*. If I flipped through, I knew I'd find past to-dos and events that involved Dad.

I traced out another pencil in the top corner as I took a deep breath, forcing my thoughts to empty.

"Good morning," Mr. Walker said as he came to the front of the room, waving a sheet of paper. "I know today's our first day back from break, but since this semester is almost over—let me say it again, to the seniors in the back. The semester's *almost over*—we can start the big one. Yes, that means it's going to be a nice chunk of your semester grade."

I flipped to the monthly spread, ready to jot down the due date of this "big assignment." I wasn't too concerned. I had an A in this class for a reason.

"Here in psychology, we take a look at people's thought processes and examine their mental faculties. This past semester was focused on examining others—celebrities, political figures, and even TV show characters—so this final assignment, we're going to do some research on people closer to home." Mr. Walker's eyes connected with mine as they roamed over the room, just as I resumed my straight-backed position, hands folded over my planner. "The peer interview partner assignment has finally approached, ladies and gentlemen, and I have your interview pairings here. I'm not going to be allowing time in class for this, so it's up to you to find time with your partner. It's going to be due the Thursday before the Snowflake Dance. I want it hand-written, at least two pages. That way none of you can mess with the font size or the margins. I know how your brains work."

I wrote down in all capitals PEER INTERVIEW, jotting down the due date. One thing that tripped me up, though, was that Mr. V had said *pairings*. Meaning he'd already stuck us together with partners. I knew I wouldn't have gotten lucky enough to be paired with Vesta, but I honestly wasn't sure if there was another student I'd want to have to spend two weeks interviewing. Or, most likely, one week interviewing—the second week would be spent drafting that report.

"Greyson Clemon and Kristen Veracruz," Mr. Walker called out. "Yvonne Buckley and Ella Garrett. Vesta Upperton and Kyle Casey."

Figures. My best friend was with another easygoing,

charismatic person. All kinds of unfair. She'd get someone like him, and I'd get—

I'd been looking at Mr. Walker, and I saw the moment he scanned the next pair of names, saw the moment he came up short. "Addy Arden and..." He paused, looking like he visibly swallowed. "Vincent Castello."

Time stopped.

My whole body seemed to freeze, an iciness sweeping through my veins. It was like I'd fallen into a lake of water in the middle of winter, instantly turning into an Addy Arden popsicle.

I'd never thought about Vincent Castello before, at least not for any longer than five seconds at a time. He was a partier, definitely *not* my crowd. He didn't party like Vesta partied, with a few sips from a red cup. Word was he did drugs. Had tattoos. I mean, he had a *lip piercing*. I'd never even looked him in the eye.

Until now.

While holding my breath, I glanced behind me and almost immediately wished I hadn't.

He wasn't looking at me, almost like he refused to. His dark hair hung in his eyes, lips turned down into a frown— even from here, I could see his silver lip piercing, and it made my heart skip a beat. That rumor was true, so what else was?

Just as quickly as I'd turned, I flipped back toward the front, slipping lower in my seat. Whether Vincent looked over at me or not, I had no way of really knowing, but there was no shaking the feel of eyes on the back of my head.

It wasn't just this assignment that made me panicked. It

was the fact that his dad was Carlo Castello that complicated things. A lot.

A sticky, hot feeling unfurled over me. If Vincent and I were partners for this project, that meant we'd have to talk to each other. Interview each other.

I was already near hyperventilating. No. No, no. I couldn't do that. Not even a little bit. And I was certain Vincent wouldn't want to either.

Mr. Walker continued down the list, but I mentally replayed the sound of Vincent's name, my brain unable to let go.

I couldn't help but think that Vincent's life was entangled with mine, two pieces of string in a messy, twisted knot. I would never be able to look at him without thinking of everything that happened.

Both of our lives, forever altered by the same accident.

*T*he last Friday in November, Greenville had been hit by a snowstorm, one of the biggest on record for that time of year. The temperatures the day before were on the brink of freezing, so rain covered the roads before it all froze into a sheet of ice. Thirteen inches of snow piled onto that, creating the perfect conditions for disaster. Especially since Greenville always under-salted their roads.

That fateful night, a white SUV slammed into a navy sedan on one of the most dangerous curves in the county. It was a blind curve, one where neither driver could've seen the other coming, and on the opposite side of the curve were ditches that swallowed cars whole.

The SUV driver hadn't been wearing a seatbelt and was ejected from the vehicle into the icy night, killed on impact. After ricocheting off the SUV, the navy sedan rolled into the eight-foot ditch, the impact cracking the driver's spine, leaving him with partial paralysis in his lower body. But alive. *Alive.*

Doctors said Dad's death had been quick, painless. Ejected from the car into a tree. Hadn't even had the time to blink. They told us that while Mom was screaming on the hospital floor.

Police said the black ice rendered Dad's brakes useless when he tried to slow down, and there was no stopping him from slamming into the navy sedan, which had been rounding the curve. They told us this while Mom sat practically comatose in the chair beside me, giving no indication that she even heard a word.

Before the accident, I never thought about Vincent Castello. Never. He was a senior, didn't play sports, and from what I could remember, he wasn't very artsy either. Wasn't on any committees. I knew nothing about him.

But now, after the accident, all I could think about was his dad.

"I still can't believe Mr. Walker paired you with Castello," Vesta said in a hushed tone, pulling her PB&J from her packed lunch. She sat on the other side of Bryce, who sat beside me. The lunch tables at Greenville High fit eight people, and ours had always been full. With me, Bryce, Mollie, Vesta, and a few of Bryce's friends, it was a full house. "Like, c'mon, randomly paired? How do you randomly pair the two of you together? Even if it *was* random, he should've had the brain cells to change it."

Castello. Despite how much I agreed with her, I found myself saying, "Don't be mean."

Mollie turned toward me from my other side, her brown eyes wide, kind. Even though she was only a year younger than me, she looked so much *littler*, like she advanced a grade or two. Maybe that was because she was so short, her proportions so small. "I'm sure if you ask Mr. Walker, he'll give you a new partner."

The idea was tempting, so tempting. Mr. Walker knew he'd screwed up. He had looked alarmed when he announced that Vincent and I would be working together. But if I asked for a new partner, I'd be cracking the wall I'd been trying to build. I'd be acknowledging the accident. And I just...couldn't.

"I'm surprised he hasn't dropped out of school yet," Bryce muttered, picking up his carton of milk. "I was half-expecting he wouldn't come back."

"Come back?" I echoed.

Mollie nodded, her long, black hair waving with the movement. "Yeah, he took the entire month of December off too. Probably to be with his dad."

"Or to just skip school." Cameron, one of Bryce's friends, turned to glare at Vincent's table. It was far from ours, nestled along the wall by the windows, almost out of sight. "I heard he's failing nearly all his classes. Even art. Who fails art?"

Vincent's lunch table was only half full, and it didn't look like anyone was talking to each other. He sat with his head bent over something in front of him, and in his hand, a pen moved at a rapid pace.

It was his first day back too. Had people been whispering around him as much as they had around me?

"Hard to pass a class when you're partying all the time," Vesta huffed under her breath.

As I stared down at my panini, I tried to actually

imagine talking to Vincent. We'd been doing these mock interviews for the past semester, so I knew the questions I could ask, but the idea of asking them terrified me. I couldn't imagine getting one syllable out around him, let alone asking him "What's your biggest fear?"

"You look tired," Mollie observed, but her tone wasn't defamatory. It was just quiet, soothing. Two words to describe Mollie in her entirety. "Have you been sleeping well?"

Mollie and I became friends last May when she moved from Addison's private school only a month before the year was over. Kids were already ready for the school year to be over with, especially over the idea of making new friends. Without hesitation, I'd reached out to her, practically pulling her under my wing.

"I'm just not used to waking up so early," I assured her, the lie coming so easily. No one needed to know how little I was actually sleeping.

Vesta laughed loudly at something Bryce said, smacking him on the arm.

Mollie opened her mouth to say something, but Cameron's intrusive voice cut her off.

"You know, Addy, it's good to have you back," he said from across the table, pointing a carrot stick at me. "You're holding up pretty well, too. Which, I'll admit, is kind of surprising. Inspiring, even."

"Cameron," Bryce warned.

"What? I'm *sympathizing*. Having your dad die has got to suck."

The breath I'd been pulling in got stuck in my throat,

several emotions warring for control. I tried to tell myself that Cameron was just your average idiot—a mouth that moved despite his lack of brain cells. He said things like that simply for the shock factor.

"Yeah," I said with a laugh, shaking my head as if I thought he was funny. "It does suck. Thanks for sympathizing."

"I say you should go to Principal Martinez and ask to be exempt from this project. Maybe you can switch out of that class—you shouldn't have to be around Castello."

Mads, another girl at our table, frowned. "I'm sorry, but I'm *so* confused. I get Vincent is seven kinds of weird, but is that why she should switch partners?"

"No, Mads, she should switch partners because his dad is the reason Addy's dad died."

At Cameron's words, my panini suddenly had a bad aftertaste, a sort of stinging flavor that left my mouth dry. *The driver's spine is cracked, leaving one of his legs partially paralyzed.* That was what the doctor had said. I hadn't imagined anyone being so blunt.

I stared at Cameron, unable to feel what my face must've looked like. Was that what everyone thought? That the accident was Vincent's dad's fault?

I'd never heard Bryce's voice as serious as when he spoke. "Dude. Shut up. I mean it."

"His dad didn't kill my dad," I said, but my voice sounded far away. Like a recording, played back at a distance. I gripped my sandwich hard, my fingers leaving indentations in the bread. "There was a lot of snow. A lot of ice. It was an accident."

You wish you could believe that, an insidious voice hissed, and that voice was loud and clear. *But you know you don't.*

Before I had a chance to say anything else, the bell rang. Around me, students began packing up their lunches. Vesta crumpled up her chip bag; Bryce pushed away from his seat to stand. I could still feel Mollie's gaze on me. She seemed to be the only one who could sense something was wrong. I took my time wrapping up my leftover sandwich, ignoring the finger holes I'd gouged into it. When I lifted my gaze, I saw Vincent once more, rising to his feet and tucking the object he'd been bent over—a brown journal—underneath his arm.

"Addy?" Vesta asked. "Are you coming?"

I ripped my gaze from Vincent Castello, shaking all thoughts of him and this day and the accident from my mind. "Coming."

Driving a convertible in the wintertime sucked.

No matter how long I drove, heat on high, the interior never got fully warm. All of the air that did warm up eventually leaked through the canvas top, which was damp after sitting in the school's parking lot all day. Each time the tires kissed a section of ice, the entire back end of the car threatened to spin out, determined to give me a heart attack.

I sat in the driver's seat with winter gloves on, a heated blanket that plugged into the cigarette lighter draped over my lap, and I still shivered like a wet dog.

It sucked. A lot.

Normally this time of year, the convertible would be tucked safely away in the garage with a cloth covering every inch of it. Not even the tires would show. Mom drove the convertible up until the first snowfall, and then Mom and Dad's schedules would shift. Dad would start working more from home and Mom would start driving the SUV—or, if the weather got really bad, he'd drive her wherever she needed to go.

But since the SUV had been totaled in the accident and Mom had the longer drive, she took my old car to work. With my shorter commute on more public roads, I was the one fated to drive this shiny red deathtrap.

For the past hour since school had let out, I'd been just driving around aimlessly. Really, I had nowhere to go. Vesta and Bryce were busy. Mollie's parents always made her finish her homework right after school. I had no one else to keep me company. Driving, though, kept my thoughts at attention. With the snowy roads, I couldn't risk letting my mind wander too far.

I thought I would be more nervous driving in snow, given everything that happened, afraid that being behind the wheel would remind me of Dad's accident nonstop, but I *refused* to even think about it as I drove.

Instead, I sang each song that came on my playlist loudly, my crappy voice distracting me from reality.

At least, until the car slammed into a pothole the size of Kansas, throwing me back in my seat with a hard *thump*.

Thankfully, the sudden jar didn't include a patch of ice or snow, but I hadn't even driven past the pothole for five seconds before the *thud-thud-thudding* began.

A *thud-thud-thudding* that typically meant a flat tire.

No. My fingers twitched as I flipped on my hazards and drove as far into the snow-covered shoulder as I dared. No doubt if I got too close, these ditches would suck the car right in. *Please let it be okay. Please.*

But as I climbed out to stand on the shoulder of the road, staring at my rear passenger tire, I felt my mood deflate. Probably as fast as the stupid tire, which was completely squished flat.

My mind went into overdrive, desperately flipping through options. *It's a flat tire. You can't drive on it, and you don't know how to change a tire. You should call someone. Call Mom. Call Dad—*

A slice of pain ripped through my chest, so sudden and swift that it had me gasping in a frigid breath of winter air. In a situation like this, Dad had always told me to call him. He never bothered showing me how to change a tire; he always said he'd come when I called.

And now, if I called him, he wouldn't pick up. He'd never pick up again.

I tried to shove the crushing feeling down, obliterate the thought, but it kept surfacing. After forcing it down all day, putting on a show for others, now it was impossible. Now there was no one around.

No, I told myself, but the word was almost nonexistent in the raging storm that knocked down my defenses.

As if someone had reached out and punched me, a wrenching sensation had me doubling over. I pulled breath after breath of air into my lungs, but it was never enough. Never left me feeling like I was getting enough oxygen.

I couldn't breathe. The blood in my ears made every-thing too loud. Too loud to hear. Too loud to think. Too loud to think past anything except that I couldn't call Dad. Dad couldn't come change my tire. I had no one.

In snow much like this, merely a month ago.

He grabbed his keys off the counter, stumbling one step as he made his way around it.

I couldn't breathe. The car was icy cold beneath my palms, but I barely felt the chill. I barely felt it when I sank to my knees in a pile of dirty snow. My tights weren't thick enough to provide any sort of barrier, but I couldn't feel the cold. I pressed my forehead to the cool metal, closing my eyes to shield the disfigured, fish-eyed world from view.

Dad stopped at the edge of the couch, but I didn't look at him.

I lost count of how many times I gasped for air, my inhales far exceeding my exhales. Pressure built in my chest until I was sure I was about to die. My lungs were about to burst and I was going to die, gasping for air, on the side of this snow-covered road.

His words rushed together, but only a little. "I'm going to head out to get your mom. Did you want to come with me?"

I couldn't breathe.

My voice was clear, dismissive, and bratty. "No. My show's about to come on."

It was the last thing I'd said to him.

"Tough break."

All at once, my world jerked into focus, the muffled sounds amplifying to a normal volume, the blood pounding in my ears going silent—or at least, quiet enough to hear past—the pressure on my chest lightening to a less life-threatening compression.

When I looked to the voice, not lifting my forehead, I found myself looking into the eyes of Vincent Castello.

He stood not even six feet from me, expression perfectly and utterly blank. No crease between his eyebrows, no frown tugging at his lips. The corduroy jacket he wore had the collar flipped up, the Sherpa lining brushing his neck. Behind him, his truck was parked, his headlights flashing periodically.

My hands on the car began trembling—all of me was trembling so bad that I couldn't even think about speaking. *No, no, not him.*

"Flat tire, huh? That sucks," Vincent said in a low voice. His eyes flicked from me to my car. "Least it's on the passenger's side. Less likely to get clipped by a car while you're changing it."

I stared up at him, just blinking, unable to do anything else. It wasn't his words that punched me in the gut, but his *voice*. I'd never heard it before. Before this year, I'd never had a class with him. He was a senior and I was a junior; our schedules never overlapped. Our lockers were in different sections. Hearing him speak was jarring, as if a part of me hadn't really known that he could. But he was speaking, clear as day.

"You really should get something to crouch on, though." He took a careful step closer, combat boots crunching the slushy grit of the road, and offered a hand. The ring on his middle finger glinted. "Come on, you must be freezing. Whatever you've got on your legs doesn't look thick enough to be kneeling in snow."

I looked at his hand, bronzed despite it being the middle of winter. My body still felt foreign, stiff. *Vincent Castello is offering his hand to help you up*, my brain told me, trying to be pragmatic about the situation despite the hysterics that had controlled me moments before. *Take it and stand.*

I slid my hand into his, and he immediately tightened his grip, drawing me to my feet hard. It felt like I'd been shaken out of my stupor, and now that my body was woken from its numb state, I fully realized how cold I was.

As I looked up into Vincent's eyes, I realized with a bit of a jolt that they were green. Greener than Vesta's. Specks of hazel littered his, tiny little shadows, framed by black lashes.

"I wasn't crying about my tire," I told him in a shaky voice, somehow thinking I needed to make that clarification. My hand was still in his, and I found myself not wanting to let go. I didn't want to feel numb again.

"I know."

His voice was flat. A part of me wondered if he was just saying that to make me feel better.

"Let's pull out your spare tire. You got anything we can kneel on while we change it?" He extracted his hand from mine, and the cool breeze brushed my fingers, chasing away whatever warmth he'd lent me. "You might not mind kneeling in the snow, but I do."

My brain was slow to process his words. *Pull out the spare tire. Need something to kneel on.* Wait, was that a question? "Uh, I have a spare blanket in the backseat. In case of emergencies."

"That'll work." Vincent popped the back end open, the red trunk swinging up to expose the clean space. Dad made sure to keep this thing clean; not even a crumb of dirt was visible. I almost asked Vincent where he thought there'd be a spare tire when he pulled out a panel in the floor, revealing a shiny wheel, the black tread pristine. "You ever change a tire before?"

I shook my head as I pulled open the backseat door and grabbed the wadded blanket.

"It's not that hard." Vincent pulled the tire out of the trunk with ease, leaning it against the car. I folded the blanket in half and laid it over the ground. When Vincent knelt beside me, black jeans flexing, he had the tire jack in his hand. "So you're going to put this underneath the pinch weld."

"The what?"

Vincent reached over and took ahold of my free hand. Before I had a chance to ask him what he was doing, he slipped my hand underneath the bottom of my car.

"You feel that?" He moved my hand until my fingers brushed against a piece of cold metal. "You're going to hook the jack underneath that."

It wasn't that big of a deal, but I couldn't get over the fact that he'd grabbed my hand without thinking twice. He was so calm, so nonchalant, while my insides were a raging tide. How could he talk so easily to me? *Act* so naturally?

From there, Vincent walked me through getting the jack to lift, only a few inches from the ground. He advised me to give the tire a spin to make sure there was enough clearance from the snow. After that, I went to work undoing the bolts that kept the tire to the car.

"You know a lot about cars?" I asked him, straining against the bolts, fighting to free the tire.

"Changing a tire isn't *rocket science*."

I frowned at his tone. It didn't *sound* like he meant to be offensive, but I couldn't tell. "I guess that's one thing I can put down for our interview."

Vincent placed his forearms along his thighs, watching me struggle. "Ah, yes. The interview. What do you think? That we just have bad luck or does Mr. Walker have it out for us?"

"Bad luck," I got out just as the bolt on the tire suddenly loosened, and I lurched forward.

"Great," Vincent said, noting my handiwork. "Now do that again on the other ones."

"I guess I'm not as strong as I thought," I said between clenched teeth, readjusting my grip on the freezing tire iron.

"Your muscles *do* look like they could use some work."

At any other time, I might've fired back a response at that, would've been annoyed or even offended, but I couldn't latch onto those emotions. Not a single one.

Vincent shifted his weight, leaning against the car door. "So, what makes you say bad luck?"

"Out of anyone who could've stopped and helped me, it was *you*."

"Ooh, true." He just watched me, unsmiling. Looking at his mouth had me looking at the lip ring in the left corner. Once my gaze snagged on it, it was hard to look away. Was it cold on his skin? Would it be cold to the touch?

I jerked toward the tire again, shoving the thought away. Even though he couldn't hear what was going on in my head, I felt mortified, face flaming hot.

We worked on pulling the tire off quietly, the only actual conversation being Vincent directing me what to do next with his smooth voice.

Once the new tire was on and I'd tightened the lug nuts as much as I could, I handed Vincent the tire iron. "Can you make sure they're tight enough?" No way did I want my tire popping off mid-drive because my biceps were so puny.

The wrench only moved slightly when Vincent went to tighten the bolts further, and he leaned back onto his heels. "I'm not sure that tire will be able to be fixed—that hole looks pretty big, so it might need a replacement."

A replacement. I wondered if Mom would give me the money I'd need to get it fixed.

"Now you can lower the jack back down," he told me, and proceeded to help me through that step. "Slowly."

After my car was back on four wheels, I pulled the jack out from underneath the pinch weld, unable to fight a small smile. The tire was changed, the new one was on firmly, and I'd done it by myself. Vincent had only stepped in to help me tighten and loosen the bolts.

It felt like a huge victory, even if it was actually a small one.

Vincent and I climbed to our feet, him collecting the

jack and me swiping up the blanket. It was soaked through now, hanging limply from my fingers, which were numb and beet-red, a pins-and-needles-like pain.

"Thanks," I said, grabbing the deflated tire and hauling it into my trunk. Vincent quickly tucked the jack in first. "For helping me. For stopping."

He didn't respond right away, instead squinting against the sunlight that'd poked through the clouds. Though his hair had appeared black before, in the sunlight, I could see it was a deep, rich brown. "This interview thing for psych," he said after a moment, watching a car drive past. "I really need to ace it."

I squeezed my hands together, barely able to feel my fingers. "Meaning?"

"Meaning as much as I'd like to BS the whole thing so we can go our separate ways, I can't risk failing this assignment."

The idea of faking all of the answers hadn't even occurred to me, but it was strange to hear that Vincent had considered it. "We can probably get the interviewing done in a day." The questions weren't *that* complex.

He nodded at that, a clear relief crossing his eyes. "What are you doing tomorrow after school?"

"Nothing."

Vincent started walking backward toward his truck, hooking his hands in his pockets. "Meet me outside the library."

My stomach flipped at his words, for a few reasons. Firstly, because he was telling me what to do—no thanks. Secondly, because they sounded so final. *I can't meet you after school*, I wanted to say. After all that smack-talk about him at lunch today, what would I tell my friends? What would I tell Bryce?

But my mouth never opened, and Vincent was already pulling open his truck door and slipping inside.

My heart was still beating a strange rhythm as I got inside the car. The interior had grown cold while we changed the tire, the air barely warmer than it was outside.

I let out a long breath, watching it fog. What had I just gotten myself into?

three

*O*nce I summoned the confidence to ease back onto the roadway, I drove around for a little while, mostly through residential areas that had been properly plowed. I didn't want to risk missing any more potholes.

When I nudged the convertible into the driveway a little after five, I was surprised to find Mom's car in her usual space in the garage. Knowing Mom, she was probably already in a bubble bath or something, winding down for the night.

My keys rattled as I dropped them on the quartz countertop beside Mom's purse, the air in the kitchen stagnant after being empty all day. The silence was suffocating. I'd ditched my coat and shoes in the entryway, so my bare feet didn't make a sound on the wooden floors, though every other noise became amplified. My breathing. The keys rattling. I looked around the empty room, the hollowness inside me yawning wider.

Things weren't much different before. Mom and Dad

still worked late before. Sometimes I'd invite the girls over or go over to their houses. Rarely was I ever alone.

The changes were most obvious in the quiet moments. Everything in my life had cracked apart, shattered glass on the floor. A part of me wasn't sure what to do—pick up the shards and risk cutting my fingers or just stand still among the broken bits, unable to move.

"Addy?" Mom's voice was faint, a high-pitched soprano that seemed at odds with the darkness that clung to the atmosphere. "Is that you?"

"Yep." It wouldn't be anyone else.

It took Mom less than a second to come into the kitchen. She was still wearing her pink scrubs, though she'd left her shoes at the door. That meant she'd had a good day. Mom usually changed immediately into pajamas if it was a bad day. She worked as a nursing assistant at a senior facility and had returned to work the day we got back from Rickett Falls last week. She'd wasted no time.

Fair hair skimmed her shoulders, knotted and snarled. It had come loose from the bun she normally wore it in. "Where have you been?" she asked.

"I was at Vesta's." My rehearsed answer came out clear. "We're partners on a psychology project. I wasn't sure when you'd be home, so I didn't think to text you."

I could've been honest with her, but I wasn't sure how she'd feel about me being out just wasting gas. Especially in that car. I also had no idea what she'd say if I mentioned Vincent. And maybe more so, I didn't want to bother her by talking about it. Better she think that things were fine.

"Oh." Mom passed a hand over her face as she looked

at me, but her gaze never quite met mine. I couldn't remember the last time she'd looked into my eyes. "Well, I was thinking about having frozen dinners for one more night. I'll stop by the store tomorrow after work."

My stomach turned at the thought of another bland meal from the freezer. "That sounds good."

We stood in the kitchen for a beat longer, both of us pointedly not looking at the other. Mom's gaze fell to her socked feet, and my eyes were latched onto where I'd dropped my keys on the counter. So badly, I wanted to tell her about my first day back at school, but the words just wouldn't come. Maybe even more, I wanted her to *ask*. Ask about my day. Ask me how school was. Ask me how I was feeling.

Mom had taken everything in stride, continuing her life as normal. She'd picked up as many shifts as she could once we got back. She claimed that staying home was only going to make her crazier, and that she needed the busyness of work to keep her occupied.

Well, she'd continued her life *almost* as normal. She hadn't set foot in her bedroom since Dad died. Now she slept in the guest bedroom down the hall.

"I've got homework to go through," I said after a moment, pulling my backpack further up my arm.

I didn't know how, but Mom had tackled her grief head-on and won. I wished she'd teach me her ways, because I was definitely the one getting pushed around by my feelings. My breakdown at the side of the road had confirmed it.

My footsteps on the stairs were quiet, and I kept my

eyes on the floor. Otherwise, I knew I'd see the pictures that hung on the wall. Family portraits—ones I couldn't look at.

Between homework, dinner, and a shower, bedtime would be here before I knew it. This day had flown by, and I'd only been home for five minutes of it.

Exactly what I'd been hoping for.

Before school started Tuesday morning, I grabbed my bullet journal and flipped it open to the to-do section of the weekly spread. *Meet with Mrs. Keller about Snowflake Dance decorations.* It was something that was supposed to be on my list for yesterday, but I couldn't find the courage to face her the first day back. I wanted to fly under the radar as much as I could.

Mrs. Keller oversaw the dance committee, at least when it came to the decorations. She often found additional hands by recruiting people who needed extra credit toward the end of the semester. I'd joined the dance committee when I started high school as a freshman, and slowly made my way to the top of it. At first, it was fun to plan every-thing—I fell in love with nitpicking every aspect. Planning events and dances soon became something I obsessed over, researching things online, watching shows on TV.

I still loved all of it, but the committee served a different purpose for me now: it was a distraction.

Since I'd been out of school since November, I had no idea where we stood on the decoration side of things. Most things could be salvaged from last year, but I wanted to triple check.

That and it took time to triple check, making it easier to avoid a certain someone with dark hair, green eyes, and a lip ring.

I didn't know how I felt about meeting Vincent after school. Well, that was a lie—I was terrified. Whenever I let my thoughts wander to him, I felt I might throw up. Then again, talking to him yesterday while we'd changed my tire hadn't been so bad. I'd been on edge the entire time, but it wasn't horrendous.

I just had to tell myself it was going to be fine.

The art room was at the far end of the school, and Mrs. Keller's door was wide open. She was wiping down the tabletops, her hair pulled back into a strict bun. It always made me smile at how businesslike she looked. As a girl who could appreciate a skirt and tie, I really liked how she dressed.

"Hey, Mrs. Keller."

She immediately looked up at the sound of my voice, and a second later, her face broke into a sympathetic smile. "Addy, hello. It's so good to have you back."

"It's good to be back," I replied honestly, tapping my fingers along my bullet journal. "I wanted to stop by yesterday, but I had so much catching up to do with my other classes. Do you have a list of what we still need for the Snowflake Dance?"

Mrs. Keller straightened, folding her rag in half and heading for her desk. "I made a list yesterday. There's not really that much left to grab."

Clicking my pen, I poised it, ready to write.

"I couldn't find the garlands we had last year—the silver

and white ones?—so we'll need to pick up a few of those. The ones we had last year were about nine feet long, so if you could find, say, five of those, that should be great."

Five 9-foot garlands, I wrote, looping the O's. "Got it."

"Based on the mood boards we developed back in November, were we still wanting to do an archway into the gym?" Mrs. Keller looked up from the screen. "I found a pretty one over in Bayview."

"Is it expensive?" It'd been a long time since I had the chance to check the dance budget.

"We can afford it. If we want it, I can call the store and put it on hold."

These kinds of decisions were so fun to me. I loved envisioning the space, filled with fake snow and sparkles galore. Ultimately, an archway *would* be beautiful—especially if I could get battery-powered twinkle lights to wrap around it. It was what drew me toward the committee in the first place. I wanted to make something beautiful. "Definitely put it on hold."

Mrs. Keller went on to say that she had the paper snowflakes covered as well as the other baubles. Her fifth grade class was going to make paper chains and her freshman fine arts class was going to make a massive banner for the entrance.

Once I finished off the last task on my list—*pick up twine*—I looked up to find Mrs. Keller giving me *the look*. "How have you been doing?" she asked.

"Fine," I said as cheerily as I could, hoping it'd change her expression. "How have *you* been?"

"I know the holidays must've been hard."

My eyes darted desperately to the door. Students were walking around in the hallway, but none came in. "We went to my grandparents', and they kept us company." Mrs. Keller opened her mouth to say something—something else probably supportive and suffocating—but I took a sharp step backward, nearly stumbling over a pulled out chair. "Well, let me know if there are any more things we need. I'll get that archway hopefully within the week."

And then I literally fled the room. I was probably breathing too fast, each inhale loud in my ears, but I couldn't seem to slow it down. I wanted to disappear into the bathroom and never come out. Where was Mollie? Where was Vesta? I needed someone to latch onto—someone to fill my mind with anything but what I was thinking about.

To think about anything other than Dad.

"Addy!"

I turned to find Vesta and Mollie coming toward me, as if conjured by my thoughts. The rising panic that had been threatening to crush me dimmed, just by their presence. "Hey."

"So, we missed celebrating Christmas together," Vesta said, glancing at Mollie. "But we still got you a present."

"We went in on," Mollie interjected, and I realized her hands were behind her back. "Mostly because we knew you'd absolutely freak if you had one of these."

I glanced between them almost nervously now. "I didn't have a chance to get you guys anything."

"Don't even think of it." Vesta waved her hand. "This is

our gift from us. Our way of saying we love you bunches and bunches."

I stepped closer to them, heart starting to beat quicker in anticipation. Mollie withdrew the present from behind her back, exposing a small, wrapped box. "I did the wrapping," she explained, turning the gift over. "Probably why it looks so bad."

"I think it looks perfect," I corrected her, taking it from her grasp. The container was light, and I shook it a little, but nothing rattled. They both watched me with the anticipation plainly on their faces, but I basked in it for a moment, at the excitement in their eyes. I really, really missed them.

As gently as I could, I pried open the wrapping paper, revealing the logo that'd been imprinted on the box. *Gilfman.* "No way," I whispered, staring at the designer box. "You did not."

Both Mollie and Vesta were full-on grinning now. "Won't know until you open it."

I practically tore off the lid.

Ties were my thing. Like, hands-down, if I could only have one accessory my entire life, it would be a tie. I used to try on my dad's ties when I was little, and I guess I just got hooked. My collection was always growing, and this one would be my all-time favorite addition.

The Gilfman tie in my hands was a deep and glorious purple color, and I immediately knew I had no tie like it. There was almost a shimmering quality to it, as if the material was coated in glitter. "This is..." I reached out, tracing a finger along the material. "*Beautiful.*"

Vesta nudged Mollie. "Told you she'd like it."

"I *love* it!" I all but squealed, and several people in the hallway looked over. "Oh my gosh, I've wanted a Gilfman tie my entire life! I can't believe you guys spent so much." They were easily one-hundred dollar ties. Gilfman was an expensive brand.

"You're so worth it," Mollie said, and wrapped her arm around me.

"Absolutely," Vesta said, and did the same. "We've missed you, Addy."

In their embrace, it felt like my insides were about to burst, all the panic from before wiped away. Obliterated. This was exactly what I needed—I just needed my girls.

Throughout the entire day, I was jittery. That was the best it could be described. Even at lunch, Bryce asked me if I'd had one too many cups of coffee this morning. No, it wasn't a caffeine rush. It was the clock ticking closer and closer to three o'clock—closer and closer to when I was meeting Vincent after school.

It sounded insane. Meeting with Vincent Castello was absolute insanity. And it wasn't because he was a senior and I was a junior, and it wasn't because we were complete opposites—it was all because of his dad and my dad.

I was seriously nauseous.

That was probably why I refused to tell anyone about it. Not Vesta, not Mollie, not Bryce. I wanted to get this done and over with as quickly as possible. If they knew, they'd ask questions. *How do you feel about that? Are you okay? Do you want us to go with you?*

They'd give me *the look* and it'd be even more impossible to shove everything from my mind.

I shifted my weight in front of my locker and took a breath in, waiting until my lungs burned to release it.

"Sorry," Mollie whispered through her teeth, her fingers gently scraping through my hair. She was in the process of Dutch braiding my hair back from my face, which I'd requested while we waited for Vesta and Bryce to show. "I didn't mean to pull."

"You didn't," I assured her. I had to crouch so she could reach the top of my head, but otherwise the whole process calmed a bit of my nerves. I kept very still, peering into the depths of my locker. "I wish I could braid as well as you."

"It's because I have three sisters to practice on," Mollie said with a laugh, continuing her ministrations. "And practice and practice. You have perfect hair for it, too. So thick and beautiful."

I smiled a little, even though she couldn't see it. "Someday you'll have to teach me how to do it."

"I definitely will. Turn your head to the other side, could you?"

Hurrying to obey her, I turned my head, my gaze now settling down the senior hallway. Immediately, I saw Vincent by his locker, in the process of loading up his black backpack full of textbooks. He must've had a lot of homework. I watched as he dropped the bag unceremoniously to the ground before withdrawing his jacket.

"Are Bryce and Vesta together?" I asked Mollie.

A lock of my hair, pinched between her fingers, twisted sharply. "Together?"

"Don't they have the same last period class?"

I scanned the hallway, but I couldn't see Vesta's red hair or Bryce's broad shoulders.

Mollie let out a breath. "Oh. I think Vesta had to stop by Mrs. Keller's room after school for some art project. That's probably why she's late."

Mollie hurried her way through the braid, fingers easily weaving in and out. She was finishing tying off the elastic when Bryce and Vesta came around the corner. They were both laughing at something, but Bryce's eyes met mine. "Ah, the braid's looking good, Mollie," he told her as he approached.

Mollie, strangely enough, didn't respond.

"Your hair always looks so pretty when Mollie braids it," Vesta said, reaching out and trailing her fingers along the weave. "I just don't have a face for a braid."

"Yes, you do," I said, but couldn't help it when my gaze once again slid to the figure in the senior hallway.

I watched as Vincent slipped his arms into the sleeves of his corduroy jacket, adjusting the collar so it lay flat against the back of his neck. He curled his hair behind his ear before swiping his bag from the ground and throwing it over his shoulder. Just before he turned, presumably in the direction of the library, his gaze cast lazily down the hallway, falling on me.

Suddenly, I was unable to take in a deep breath.

But then, as though he didn't even see me, he just turned and walked away.

"Guys, I'm *starving*," Vesta went on, crossing her arms over her chest as she looked to Bryce. "Let's go to Mary's Place. I'd *kill* for their grilled cheese."

Mary's Place was one of the only diners in Greenville, and definitely the only good one. For a split second, I imagined going with them to Mary's Place. I imagined ignoring Vincent, who was no doubt already heading to the library. Unless he'd forgotten about our agreement and was leaving instead.

"You guys can go," I said. "I've got some errands I need to run today."

Please don't ask, please don't ask, I silently chanted, and thankfully, my prayer was answered.

"Maybe tomorrow?" Mollie said, holding my stare with wide eyes. "We should go dress shopping for the Snowflake Dance before all the good dresses are gone."

"Ooh, yes!" Vesta clapped her hands. "I'd been putting off getting a dress until we could all go together."

Bryce chuckled, glancing between the three of us. "Which is surprising, since you like to have every outfit planned out."

Vesta stuck her tongue out at him.

I reached up and touched a bump in my braid, feeling strangely out of place next to Bryce and Vesta. Almost like I was a spectator.

Mollie raised her voice to talk over them. "Did you get the whole Vincent Castello situation figured out?"

Hearing his name on her lips caused a flash of panic to bolt through me, as if they already knew what I was planning to do. Bryce and Vesta had turned to listen to my answer with interest. "Oh. Uh. Yeah, actually." The lie fell from my lips before I had a chance to catch it, and more words followed. "Mr. Walker is having me interview someone from a different period class."

"Good," Bryce huffed. "Get as far away from that dude as you can."

I thought about yesterday, how Vincent had gotten out and helped me change my tire. I didn't exactly get *run-away-screaming* vibes.

With an inward sigh, I shut my locker. "I'll see you all tomorrow?" I directed this last half toward Bryce as I threaded my arms through my backpack straps.

"I'll text you," he said with a small half-smile.

I fluffed my coat over my arms as I walked in the direction of the library, the butterflies in my stomach migrating to flutter in my throat. Kids still stood around in the hallways, mingling and grabbing supplies from their lockers. I tried not to meet the eyes of any of them. I didn't need any more *looks* today. And if I avoided eye contact, maybe no one would really remember me walking down the hallway. Maybe no one would notice me meeting Vincent Castello.

The library was tucked in the back part of the school, by the double doors that led out to where the busses were parked. Curling my fingers into fists, I took a step closer to the room, trying as best as I could to peer through the glass window on the door. A few students had already camped out at the library tables, books set open in front of them, beginning their hour of study time. There were no tall, brooding boys lingering about.

"I wasn't sure you'd be coming."

I gasped loudly at the sudden voice behind me, whirling around to find Vincent standing there, one hand in his pocket, the other loosely grasping his backpack strap. My world was off-kilter for several seconds, and I couldn't stop from frantically glancing around, to see if anyone had spotted us together yet. "It affects my grade too, you know."

"Fair enough."

Suddenly, I was nervous all over again, prickly with the weight of his gaze on mine. It was so unnerving, holding his full attention. Because I *did* have it. He was standing in front of me and looking directly at me, waiting for me to speak.

I gestured toward the library doors. "Um, after you?"

Vincent glanced at the students sitting at the tables with disdain. "I wouldn't be caught dead in there. How do you feel about a little road trip?"

A road—*what*? Oh, no, no, no. No way was I getting in a car with him. I tried to imagine it, me hoisting myself into that giant truck of his, settling into the bench seat, trying not to throw up all over the dashboard. Meeting Vincent in a safe, public place was one thing—letting him drive me to who-knows-where was another.

My fear must've shown on my face, because Vincent's frown deepened. "I'm not going to kidnap you." He held his hand out. Was he serious? After a moment, he gestured at me, a little impatiently. "Give me your bag so you can put your coat on."

At first, I stared at his hand, at the ring on his middle finger, wide-eyed. "I just—I'm not sure—"

"I've got a job," he said finally. "My shift starts at four, so I can't sit here and go back and forth about our favorite colors. I figured we could talk about the questions while I'm working."

"Your boss won't mind some high schooler hounding you while you're on the clock?"

Vincent lifted a shoulder. "He won't be there." He gestured for my bag again, his hand still outstretched. "You said so yourself, we can get these questions done in one day. If we do, we'll never have to meet up again."

I had said that, hadn't I? And if Vincent had to go to work, that was still a public space. Besides, would he murder me and risk failing psychology? A part of me doubted it.

The other part, though...

Reluctantly, I passed him my backpack and pulled on my coat. I tried to make my actions as quick as possible, but the way my limbs shook made that difficult. "Thanks."

Those serious green eyes leveled to mine as Vincent returned my backpack. I found myself getting lost in their color. They were just so *deep*. I'd never bought into that old-soul crap, but looking into Vincent's eyes was different from looking into Bryce's. I couldn't quite place my finger on *how* they were different, but their gazes didn't even compare.

With a nudge of his chin, Vincent gestured toward the doors that led outside, to presumably where his truck was parked. "Shall we?"

four

It wasn't snowing today; in fact, it wasn't even that cold out. It had to be above freezing, because the snow on the ground was starting to chunk together. Perfect snowman-making conditions, though I couldn't remember the last time I'd made a snowman.

Vincent drove easily down the snowy roads, one hand loosely gripping the steering wheel. The interior of his truck smelled so good, and for the first few moments, I looked around for an air freshener. But when I didn't find one, I realized it smelled like *him*. Like honey and coffee beans. It was a heady sort of scent, so different from the sharp citrus type of cologne Bryce always wore.

Vincent's truck was spotless—there were no gas station receipts, no old homework worksheets. The only thing on the floor near the toe of my shoe was a leather-bound notebook. I wanted to ask him about it, but that would've required opening my mouth, which I hadn't done since we'd stepped outside of school.

Conversation eluded me—what was I supposed to say

to him? I barely knew him, but such a personal thing had happened to us that made things just...awkward.

I had my arms wrapped around my backpack, feeling like I was moments from freaking out. I cataloged every road we turned onto, memorizing the layout. Just in case.

From the corner of my eye, I saw Vincent look over at me. "We're almost there."

I cleared my throat. "Where is *there*, exactly?"

"Do you go to Hallow often?"

"Sometimes." Hallow was a small town west of Greenville. It was well known for its antique shops and its Halloween event they threw every year. Vesta, Mollie, and I had gone to the Boo-Bash this past year, and it'd been a blast. "Do you work at one of those little shops?"

Vincent flipped on his blinker to turn onto a side street, his brakes squeaking a little as he slowed. "Sort of." He didn't elaborate.

We continued down the road for a little bit before turning into a back-alley lot, one with few cars parked. He slid easily into a space, switching off the engine. "We'll go in through the back entrance."

"Am I allowed to?"

"Who cares if you're allowed to or not?" he asked, popping his door open and letting in a rush of cold air. "Do it anyway."

I was *so* not a rule breaker. Never had been. There was no point in breaking rules, only just to prove that one could.

I unbuckled my seatbelt slowly, unwilling to get out of the truck. A dumpster sat near the middle of the building, trash overflowing from its depths. The back entrances of the building were a little dingy. There weren't any signs above the doors that gave me a clue as to what kind of place we were walking into, which didn't help me in the confidence department.

Vincent rapped his knuckles on the driver's side window. Though his voice was muffled through the glass, I could hear him ask, "Are you coming, or are you going to sit in there and freeze?"

"I'm coming," I muttered, opening my door and hopping out onto the pavement. At the last second, I swiped my backpack up and hooked it over my shoulder. "I brought the interview sheet that Mr. Walker gave us, so it shouldn't take us too long."

He watched me round the front of the truck, slipping his hands into his pockets. "My shift ends at eight, so hopefully it takes at least that long."

I hadn't even thought about how I'd be trapped here—wherever *here* was.

Vincent walked up to a door on the left side of the dumpster, finding a key from his lanyard and sticking it into the lock.

"We're going to have time to just talk?" I clarified once again. "I'm not going to get thrown out for distracting the help?"

"Are you normally this much of a worrier?" he asked in a casual tone, pulling open the door that led to a stainless steel kitchen. There wasn't anyone in the kitchen, but pots and pans were scattered across the countertops, as if someone was going to start cooking soon.

"I'm not a rule breaker. I don't like getting in trouble."

Even if it was some stranger yelling at me, it made me nervous.

Vincent moved over to an area with coat hooks and hung up his corduroy jacket. He looked at me again, as if noting the serious anxiety bubbling up in me. His voice was softer when he said, "You'll be fine, okay?"

Somehow, it was hard for me to fully trust him. I tugged my backpack closer against my shoulder blades.

Vincent headed toward the doorway of the kitchen, and even though the double doors had small windows, I couldn't see where it led; the hallway was too dark. But Vincent pushed open the door with ease, not even glancing back. He just expected me to follow him.

Of course, with a sharp breath in, I did.

And blinked in surprise.

The room that the double doors led into was large and dimly lit, but in a way that made it cozy instead of creepy. The ductwork in the ceiling was exposed, and the brick walls gave the area an industrial edge. Off to the left, there was a wide counter with several people standing in line, but there were booths and tables littered throughout the room. There was also a large wooden stage against the far corner, and someone stood on it now, speaking softly into a microphone.

The smell of coffee beans was strong, and I found myself inhaling deeply.

"Vincent!" a guy standing behind the counter called, and I turned from my gawking to see Vincent throwing a bright teal apron over his head, quickly tying it around his waist. "You're late."

"I'm supposed to start at four," he replied. "It's four-oh-two."

"Still late." The guy's gaze drifted past Vincent to lock on me. He looked like he was in his mid-twenties maybe, hair cropped short, jawline narrow with a speckling of facial hair. He had small and silver gauges in his ears, almost reflective-looking. "And now I can see why."

Vincent glanced back at me before washing his hands at a small sink. "Come over here and sit down, Adeline."

It was rare to hear my full name used. At school, teachers would call out "Addy" for roll call. Not even my mother called me Adeline, not even when she was angry. Dad was the only one who used to say my full name.

Breathe.

Hearing it on Vincent's tongue felt...weird, but I also didn't want to correct him.

There were bar stools up against the far edge of the counter, all of them empty, so I dropped my backpack onto a stool and settled into the one next to it.

"Sorry that he was late," I said to the guy, and when he turned, I could fully read his nametag: *JONATHAN*.

"Not a big deal," Jonathan replied easily, moving to slide a ceramic mug underneath a silver machine. His actions were quick. "It's just the mid-afternoon rush, is all."

Vincent rolled his eyes, but as he looked at the next customer in line, his voice changed dramatically. The serious tone transformed into something light and easygoing, a sound that had me leaning forward. "Hey, welcome to Crushed Beanz. What can I get you?"

Crushed Beanz. I knew Hallow had a coffee shop, but

I'd never seen one this industrial. I turned around to get a better look at the space as another person stepped onto the stage and leaned into the microphone.

"Hey, everyone," the girl said shakily, flapping her paper in front of her. "I wrote this poem last week and wanted to share it tonight, if that's okay."

The people sitting at the tables and booths cheered her on by snapping their fingers.

A poetry reading?

"One of our signature events," Jonathan told me, passing over the mug of coffee to a woman as he guessed my thoughts. "Crushed Beanz has *themed nights.*"

"Themed nights?" I asked, unable to hide the interest from my voice. "What else do you do?"

"There's karaoke on Thursdays," Vincent said, back to the lower tone. He grabbed a to-go coffee cup, and I watched as he pulled out coffee grounds and put them into a metal object, tapping it flat. "Tonight's poetry night."

"And on Fridays and Saturdays we have a live band play," Jonathan added, casting a sidelong look at Vincent. "*Somebody* hogs the stage time."

I waited for Vincent to say more, but only the hum of the espresso machine filled the air.

"*You* perform?"

Vincent sighed. "Don't sound so impressed."

I opened my mouth to object, but the truth was that I *was* impressed. Or the very least surprised. The whole "band" scene did fit him, I had to say—he had that edgy look about him. "Are you the singer?"

"He doesn't wear enough eyeliner to be the singer," Jonathan teased, moving to help the next customer in line.

Vincent didn't immediately answer me, instead handing the cup off to the customer and helping another with their order.

I watched Vincent and Jonathan with interest, noting the way they moved around each other like a choreographed dance. Vincent's hands were skilled as he poured the milk into coffee, turning out impossibly intricate finished products.

Vincent does coffee art, I thought with an inward chuckle. *Mr. Moody does coffee art. Go figure.*

Out of all the scenarios I'd imagined, Vincent Castello as a barista wasn't one of them. A cook at a diner? Sure. An assistant for a law firm? Maybe. But a barista? No freaking way.

Once Jonathan stepped up to ask the last customer in line for their order, so many minutes later, Vincent finally turned to me and answered my question. "I'm the drummer."

"Drummer," I echoed. Yep, it totally suited him. "What's your band called? The Black Tees?"

Jonathan laughed loudly while Vincent scowled. "Untapped Potential."

"I like it," I said honestly, unzipping my backpack to grab my bullet journal. I needed to start taking notes. "How many members do you have?"

"Three. I'm the drummer, Natasha's the guitarist, and Harry's the singer."

I'd gotten my pen out as he was talking about Natasha,

and scrawled quickly to fill in the rest. "How did you three get together?"

When I looked up, I noticed Vincent was arching a dark brow. "You're going to put this in the report?"

I glanced around the coffee shop. "That's why I'm here, right?"

There was something comforting about the atmosphere of Crushed Beanz that made me feel so much more relaxed, my earlier nerves and worries now seeming silly. And maybe it was the fact that Vincent was wearing a teal apron over his dark ensemble, making him seem a little more normal. The lip ring still stood out, as well as his sharp eyes, but there was something less intimidating about him wearing an apron.

Vincent pulled up against the edge of the counter, letting out another sigh, as if this whole interview thing were ridiculous. "Harry and Natasha knew each other before. We put out the ad for a live band, thought it would be good for business, and Harry stopped by. Said they'd prefer to do heavier stuff—they'd been doing acoustic indie stuff up until that point—but didn't have a drummer."

I smiled a little at that. "Insert Vincent Castello."

"I was the missing link," he agreed. "We started playing back in the middle of November, so not that long."

Behind me on the stage, the microphone screamed out feedback, making me wince. Vincent, though, didn't flinch.

"Nice start," I told him. "How did you get into music? How long have you been playing the drums?"

"That was more than one question."

"Can't you multi-task?"

Vincent looked at his hands, as if he was trying to dig deep in his memory. "I guess I've been playing on and off for a few years. Since I was thirteen, maybe? Dad got me a drumkit for Christmas. When Harry was looking for a drummer, I volunteered to audition."

I tried to picture a thirteen-year-old Vincent sitting down at a set of drums for the first time. It made me want to smile, but instead, I wrote it down and referenced the interview sheet Mr. Walker had given us today. "Let's see... What's your favorite memory?"

Vincent's gaze was level on me, but his response never came. The doors to Crushed Beanz chimed as someone walked in, and since I was close enough to the door, I felt the cool air that came with them. I watched as Vincent pulled on his professional face. He didn't smile—Vincent wasn't a smiler, I was learning—but it was close.

He went through the motions of helping the customer while I scanned the next few questions, listening to the whir of the coffee machine cut into the poem being crooned through the microphone. This person was more confident than the rest, and I turned in my seat to watch.

The boy held no paper in front of him; he'd committed the poem to memory. A part of me wondered if he was making it up as he went along. Everyone in the shop was rapt, including me.

"Is that something you'd do?"

When I faced back to the counter, I found Vincent putting a sleeve on a coffee cup and handing it over to a customer. "What?"

"Public speak," Vincent clarified, nodding at the stage. "You strike me as a public speaker."

"I'm really not," I said with a chuckle, running my hands over my planner. All of a sudden, I felt shy, nervous as the attention turned to me. "I feel sick to my stomach whenever I have to stand in front of an audience. I couldn't imagine sharing something personal like a poem."

"Or singing a song."

Just the thought was mortifying. "Never. Ever. Did I mention never ever?"

"Don't let him fool you," Jonathan said, coming up beside Vincent. "He keeps his head down whenever he's performing."

Vincent rolled his eyes. "I play the drums. I *have* to look down."

The barstool creaked as I leaned back, kicking my heels against the base. "You skipped my earlier question."

"Do you want a coffee?" Vincent said, once again deliberately ignoring what I'd said. "We have a good peppermint mocha. Perfect for the season."

Though I wanted to push the issue, I decided to relent. I'd double back on it later. "Sure. Do you have almond milk?"

He snapped his fingers, pushing away from the countertop. His ring clinked against the surface of a teal ceramic mug as he pulled it out.

"I wouldn't be good at this," I said, watching his mechanical movements. He walked over to the collection of syrups and pumped two shots of something into the mug, and then pumped one of another syrup. "I feel like I'd get confused on which syrups to use for which drinks."

"After working for so long, it becomes second nature," Vincent told me, scooping cocoa into the cup and then dispensing a bit of hot water from the machine. "It's not that complicated."

Looks pretty complicated to me, I thought as he grabbed a scoop-looking thing and poured espresso into it. Then he stamped the grounds flat. "How long have you been working here?"

"About three years now. As soon as I turned fifteen, I got a work permit."

I thought about what I'd been doing at fifteen. I definitely hadn't been wanting to get a job—quite the opposite, actually. I'd probably gone shopping almost every weekend, not a care in the world. We'd never been pinched for money—one of the perks of having an investment banker for a father. A weight settled on my chest, thinking about how I'd never needed money, but here Vincent was, working through high school.

Once Vincent finished off the mocha with steamed milk, he sat it front of me. He came close enough that I was once again struck by the vibrancy of his eyes. "Tell me what you think."

He'd filled the cup nearly to the brim, so I carefully lifted it. Part of me was sad to ruin the flower art he'd created with the foam, but I brought it to my lips, fully aware of his gaze on me.

As soon as I took a sip of the mocha, I smiled, the collection of flavors hitting my tongue at once. The almond milk, the cocoa, the peppermint, and... "What else did you put into this?"

"One pump of white chocolate syrup. Does it make it overly sweet with the almond milk? I didn't think of that."

"No, not at all." I took a longer sip to emphasize that fact, the drink immediately warming me up from the inside. I licked my lips. "It's really good."

Vincent looked away, nodding his head ever so slightly. "It's on the house."

Once again, our conversation was cut short by a customer, but it wasn't just one. A steady stream of people started coming through the Crushed Beanz doors, and it seemed like the line never budged. As soon as one was served, another customer would take their place. I didn't mind just sitting and sipping on the mocha—it was tasty, with just the right amount of peppermint. I held the mug between my hands, letting the warmth seep into my palms.

While Vincent filled orders, I pulled out my phone, checking to see if I had any texts. Nothing. The blank screen was one I'd gotten used to over this past month, but I still found myself wishing Vesta or Mollie had sent me an emoji or something. Bryce had said he'd text me, but that conversation was nothing but crickets, too.

Even though I didn't want to explain why I was here, my fingers were itching to tell them, the girls and Bryce. To tell them *something*. Loneliness was keeping me company, and not the good kind.

With that in mind, I set my mug on the countertop, angling it so the Crushed Beanz logo faced away from me, and snapped a quick picture. Upon inspecting the photo, I attached it to a text to Vesta, Mollie, and Bryce separately.

This peppermint mocha is to die for.

I shouldn't have texted them, but it was almost like I couldn't stop myself.

I wasn't sure who'd text back first—if any of them would—but I laid my phone face up on the counter, just so I could see any notifications come in.

Mollie was the first to type back. **Where's that at? Looks delish.**

Me: **Hallow. So cute.**

"So, Adeline," Jonathan said as he slid open the glass pastry case. "Why are you and Vincent playing twenty questions?"

"We have an assignment in psychology where we have to interview each other."

He made a *tsking* sound, pulling out a croissant with a pair of tongs. "Ah, high school. Definitely don't miss it."

The rest of the night continued that way, with quick, stolen moments before another customer came up to order or requested a refill. I waited patiently throughout, scribbling down notes when I could. After a while, I found myself melting into the atmosphere. The industrial vibes, the quiet stream of poetry speakers, and even the noise of the coffee machine—it was like all of those sounds stimulated my mind just enough to keep me present. It was better than spending my time driving around the county, and definitely better than trying to keep my mind occupied at home.

It was nearly impossible to keep my mind occupied at home.

I reread the list I'd compiled about Vincent. *Serious. Drummer in a band. Coffee artist. Great barista.* That coffee was amazing; I'd savored it as long as I could, but there was no stopping the disappointment when I drank my last drop.

However, my list was meager and Vincent's list was nonexistent, which only meant one thing: we'd have to meet again.

I waited for the worry to course through me, but it didn't. Maybe it was because this hadn't been as bad as I'd made it up in my mind.

"I'm going to head out," Vincent declared after he served the last customer in line, just a few minutes after eight. He reached for the straps of his apron before turning to Jonathan. "Do you need anything else?"

Jonathan shook his head. "Nah, I'm good. I think things are starting to quiet down."

The poetry readers had mostly filtered off; it'd been a while since anyone had stepped up to the microphone. The tables and booths were pretty sparse too, with just a few stragglers left with their laptops open or books spread wide.

I shoved my bullet journal into my backpack and swiped up my coat. "It was nice meeting you, Jonathan."

"Hey, you too, Adeline." His smile was genuine, and wide enough to expose teeth.

It was infectious. "You can call me Addy," I told him, just barely stopping myself from saying that I'd prefer it if he did.

By that point, Vincent was already hanging up his

apron, shrugging on his coat. "We definitely didn't get all of the questions," he said as I got closer, flipping the Sherpa collar up against his neck.

"No, we did not. I don't think I got any on the list, even." That made me squint at him. "Do you not have a favorite memory? Is that it?"

A frown twisted Vincent's features, and he shoved through the doors that led to the kitchen, with me following quickly behind. "It's not that I don't," he said, not turning. "It just—I don't want to talk about it with you."

I felt both of my eyebrows shoot up, my good mood cracking a bit. "Wow. No offense taken or anything."

"It's *personal*." His voice was hard as he opened the back door, exposing the cold, dark night. "So I don't want to talk about it."

"Uh, hate to break it to you, but being personal is a part of the assignment. I mean, it was on Mr. Walker's list." And quite honestly, a favorite memory was one of the least invasive of them, in my opinion. "Biggest fear" and "deepest desire" were so much more personal. "Would it help if I shared mine first? My favorite memory was when my mom, my grandma, and I went on a girls' trip to Hawaii for my tenth birthday. We drank out of coconuts and everything."

Vincent looked at me over his shoulder, and if possible, his frown had deepened. "You went to *Hawaii*?"

I huddled deeper in my coat, letting out a silvery puff of breath. "Yeah."

Our footsteps crunched on the snow as we made our way to his truck in silence, awkwardness clinging heavily to the air. *You shouldn't have pressed him*, I scolded myself, angry that I'd thrown away a decent afternoon. *You should've just waited.* For whatever reason, Vincent didn't want to share his favorite memory. I thought it would've been a good memory, but maybe it wasn't—maybe it was his favorite for some weird reason. Maybe it was something he didn't want on some high school report. Whatever the case, I should've dropped it.

I couldn't blame him for not wanting to talk about certain things.

So instead, as I shut the door behind me and settled against the cold seat, I asked, "How'd you start working here?"

Vincent coaxed the truck to life, fiddling with the heat dials. Cold air pumped out first, but hopefully it'd heat up soon. His voice still hadn't lost its rough edge. "My dad owns it."

"Wait, *what*?" My heart jumped inside my chest, my shivering stopping at once. "He...owns it."

"Yeah."

All afternoon, I'd been sitting in the café that Carlo Castello owned—that he'd brought to life. He'd carefully constructed that peaceful atmosphere, he'd organized the theme nights. Mr. Castello had decided to have a live band. It felt like I sat there for several moments, the knowledge and realization sinking in deeper.

Suddenly, my outlook on the afternoon changed, like a steering wheel pulled sharply to the side.

"Dad worked it from the ground up," Vincent went on, not putting the truck into gear. Instead, he looked at the backside of the café. "It used to be his favorite place."

My brain felt disconnected from my body, like I could hear what he was saying but couldn't process it. "Used to be?"

"He—well, he hasn't been here since the accident." Vincent wasn't looking at me as he spoke, voice flat. "He can barely leave the house now."

Every muscle in my body locked up, and I could hear my brain screaming *breathe, breathe* but the air was too cold to draw in. I'd begun shivering again, fingers trembling as I gripped them in my lap.

When I spoke, I didn't recognize my voice. It sounded too flat, too monotone. It sounded a lot like how Vincent spoke. "Can we make a rule?" Vincent didn't respond, so I went on. "We're not allowed to talk about the accident."

Breathe in. Hold it for five seconds. Breathe out. Do it again. And again. Don't think. Don't think.

"Fine by me," Vincent said finally, and looked away.

He put the truck into gear and pulled out of the parking space. Neither one of us spoke the entire way back to Greenville.

five

*E*ver since that night in November, my ceiling and
I had become close friends. I knew every divot on
its surface, every crack, every sliver of a spiderweb in each
corner. Even with the blue tone of night settled over the
space, my eyes quickly adjusted. Nights passed slowly that
way, but it felt like someone had pinned my eyelids back,
and I couldn't rest.

And I found myself not wanting to close them anyway.
Who knew what waited in the shadows of my dreams.

One would think that staying awake all night would let
my thoughts run rampant, but I spent every moment awake
recounting every part in my body. From my toes to the roots
of my hair, I labeled every body part until I had to start
over.

Realistically, I knew at some point I fell asleep during
the night, but the scraps of rest felt just that—scraps, a scattering of moments that I quickly forgot.

Last night had been rougher than normal. I replayed
that final conversation with Vincent over and over, trying to

shove it from my mind once I got too far into it. But it never worked.

My words were easy to recall. *We're not allowed to talk about the accident.*

And I could hear the flat tone of Vincent's response like he was right next to me. *Fine by me.*

Being his partner was a mistake.

"Ooh, what about this one?" Vesta's voice drew me from my thoughts, my hazy, half-asleep thoughts. The slow pop song playing over the dress shop's speakers *so* wasn't helping my sleepiness. I looked up to find her laying a dark green dress against the length of her body. "Is this my color?"

Mollie, who'd had her nose buried in the clothing rack opposite of us, lifted her gaze. "Very pretty, but maybe a bit too short?"

Mollie wasn't wrong. The hemline barely came to Vesta's mid-thigh.

I scrubbed my fists against my eyes, not caring whether it smudged my makeup. The day had been so long already, and it was only half-past four.

During first period, I'd kept my eyes locked to the front, not risking catching Vincent's gaze in the back. And at the end of the day, I'd gathered my things quickly, not lingering in the hallway. Not that I'd expected him to just walk up to me anyway, but I was too afraid to face him, too afraid that being around him would mess with my carefully constructed wall of normalcy.

"I just want something *hot* for the Snowflake Dance,

you know?" Vesta sighed, hanging the dress back on the rack. "Something that's drop-dead."

"You just need something that won't get you thrown out of the gym," I told her with a wink, blindly thumbing through the dresses in my size. I couldn't picture myself in them like I normally could. Last night, I must've gotten fewer scraps of sleep than usual, because I was seriously dragging. "Imagine Principal Martinez's face if you wore that."

"She'd probably pop a blood vessel or two," Vesta said with a laugh, pulling out her cell phone and peering at the screen.

The action made me suddenly aware of my own phone in my purse, so I fished it out in hopes of seeing a text from Bryce. It wasn't the desperate sort of thought that I used to have when he'd texted me, but it was different now—I just wanted conversation. I wanted the distraction of texting someone back and forth, waiting for their response. My mind was craving it, hoping he'd sent *something*.

Despite his "I'll text you later" comment yesterday, he never did—he didn't even respond to my coffee pic. But that didn't really mean anything, right? Vesta hadn't replied either.

Apparently, it wasn't "later" yet.

"You think Bryce isn't feeling it anymore?" I asked while scrolling up to see the last time he'd texted, the night after the accident. ***I'm so sorry, Addy. Here if you want to talk.*** I took a deep breath and shoved my phone away.

When I looked up, I saw Mollie staring at Vesta, and

Vesta fiddling with a hanger. "Well..." she started hesi-
tantly, but then cut herself off. "You never know how boys'
minds work."

I narrowed my eyes at her. "You know something."

"No!" Her head flung up, red hair tossing. When she
spoke, her voice was an octave too high. "I don't. But I'm
sorry he's acting weird."

I studied my best friend for a long moment, trying to
gauge whether she was lying. If she was, *why?* To spare my
feelings? Bryce moving on would be crappy—making it the
worst junior year on the planet—but it wasn't like we were
even together.

"Speaking of boys," Vesta said quickly, flapping her
hands over the rack. "Did you hear Mollie's got a
boyfriend?"

It wasn't just me who'd gasped; Mollie's jaw dropped as
well. "What are you talking about?" she demanded, almost
sounding angry. "I don't have a boyfriend."

"So you're not dating *Jackson Mannerfield?*"

I was immediately wide awake. Jackson Mannerfield? I
thought I heard her wrong at first. Quite honestly, my brain
couldn't process the idea. They were total and complete
opposites. She was shy, reserved, while Jackson was the
class clown with a big personality. Mollie was a sophomore
and he was a senior. He was captain of the basketball team,
never tied down to one girl for too long. Heck, Vesta had
said that he and his on-again, off-again girlfriend had just
broken up—for the tenth time.

It wasn't hard for me to understand why he might be

into Mollie—the amazing girl that she was—but he was *so* not what I'd envisioned for her. Not in the slightest.

"We're *not* dating!" Mollie rushed to object, her face flushing a deep red. "Where did you even hear that from?"

"The girls on the volleyball team talk," Vesta said with a shrug. "They said he'd asked you out."

"He did." She was still blushing, but she didn't look happy about it. Instead, she pressed her palms against her face. "But I told him that my dad doesn't let me date—which is true."

I blinked, trying to imagine how *that* went down. "And what did Jackson say to that?"

"He just laughed, like I'd told him some inside joke or something."

I could see a guy like Jackson laughing at the idea of not being able to date—he'd had girlfriends ever since the third grade.

"I'm just saying, if a guy like Jackson asked me out, I wouldn't be making excuses to say *no*." Vesta moved over to the little cluster of white dresses. "I'd be trying to figure out how I could say *heck yes*."

Mollie's expression darkened, and so did her voice. "That's because you don't care about letting down people important to you."

"Whoa!" I felt my eyebrows jump as I glanced between them. But though I was surprised, Vesta was the one with a red face now, locked in a stare-down with Mollie. "Uh, where did *that* come from?" They were completely fine the day before when they gave me the tie—what had changed in the past twenty-four hours?

I waited for one of them to fill me in on the tension brewing in the air, but Mollie just let out a huge huff and snatched up a dress. "I'm going to go try this on," she grumbled, stomping off toward the dressing room without another word.

"What was that about?" I asked Vesta, feeling completely lost. Mollie *never* got angry—I hadn't even been sure she was capable of anger.

"No clue." Vesta grabbed two white dresses, dodging my gaze. "I'm going to try these on too."

And then I was left alone at the dress rack, watching her walk away, listening to the faint music coming through the overhead speakers. Clearly I was missing something, and the prospect of being purposefully left out on a friendship secret was disorienting. Something had happened, but they wouldn't tell me what. *Why?* Our friend group wasn't usually like that—we never kept secrets from each other.

I turned back to the dresses, feeling much more awake than I'd been when we started our search. Whatever was going on, I'd find out sooner or later.

Once I got home from the shopping trip, I took all of my bags up to my room, immediately hanging the dress I'd gotten up in the closet. I didn't think about it much when I'd picked it out—I hadn't even tried it on. Upon looking at the navy sequins, I decided it would do.

Which was surprising. Normally I was more into shopping for event dresses. I'd been a neurotic freak over picking out my homecoming dress, determined to go all the way out to a handmade boutique in Bayview so no one had the same dress as me. Being the chair of the dance committee meant that I needed to look fantastic, if not the best at the entire dance.

This time, I'd just picked one out on a whim, barely glancing at the color.

Moments like that had me wondering if going back to "normal me" was even achievable anymore.

I'd convinced the girls to stop by the art store while we were at the mall, which wasn't hard since when they emerged from the dressing rooms, neither of them did a whole lot of talking. And they absolutely didn't talk to each other. I'd managed to get all the garlands, twine, and varying shades of blue acrylic paint that Mrs. Keller wanted, but they were out of faux snow.

I made a note in my bullet journal that when I went to Bayview to pick up the arch, I'd look for snow as well.

In my journal, which I laid out flat against my bed, I flipped to the notes section where I'd filled out info about Vincent. The list stirred unease in the pit of my stomach. I'd left the page free of doodles, zero life added to the paper. It looked horrible in contrast to my other spreads.

Even if I were to add any details, what would they be? Not pencils—Vincent didn't strike me as the scholarly type —but maybe something to do with music. Cute music notes, maybe drumsticks? Maybe little coffee cups?

I shook the idea from my head before I got up and grabbed my markers. Besides, I didn't know what was going to happen. I wasn't sure if I wanted to continue the project with him—or if I even could. Was it even possible to pretend that Vincent Castello was *not* Vincent Castello? That he wasn't related to Mr. Castello, that he wasn't attached to the worst day of my life?

My bed creaked as I shifted on it, drawing in a shaking breath. Junior year was an important year for grades; I couldn't let this project slip through the cracks. But still, what was I going to do? The prospect of continuing made me nervous, and so did the idea of quitting. I'd have to choose, though. One or the other.

By Friday at lunch, Mollie and Vesta still hadn't really spoken to each other, at least not that I'd seen. Bryce even whispered a quick "What's going on with them?" to me as we walked down the hall, but I'd merely shrugged in response; two days later and I still had no clue.

"So, Mrs. Keller wants to get those old columns out of the basement for the Snowflake Dance," I said halfway through lunch, tracing the note I'd made in my journal with the clicking part of my pen. "Bryce, do you think you could get a couple of your friends and help haul them out? Maybe the Friday before?"

"Should be able to," he said while he chewed his bread-stick, not caring that his mouth was full. "Cameron, you strong enough?"

The boy scoffed. "*Please.* Do you have to ask?"

Perfect. Flipping my pen around, I checked off *hauling help.* "Do you think you could borrow your dad's truck?" I asked Bryce. "There's this arch Mrs. K wants me to pick up from Bayview, but I don't think it'll fit in the convertible." Heck, my backpack barely fit in the convertible.

He made a smacking sound with his mouth. "That I can't do. Dad doesn't let me drive it in winter, and no way he'd let me go all the way to Bayview."

Okay, that sucked. Maybe Mrs. Keller would have to figure out a different way to get the arch. In all honesty, *she* should've been the one getting it—she probably could've been reimbursed for gas mileage or something. Well, probably not.

That's what makes you chair of the committee, a stupid voice whispered in the back of my head, and that stupid voice was right. If only that stupid voice had a truck.

I looked up from my planner to find Vincent striding across the length of the cafeteria, journal tucked under his arm, heading for the double doors that led into the hallway. A stroke of inspiration struck me, but was quickly dulled by apprehension. Vincent had a truck, but it wasn't like I could just send him off on that errand for me. Did I really want to be stuck with Vincent in his truck for two hours? Would he even agree to help?

I was back to that debate: continue the interview or ask Mr. Walker for a new partner. If I were alone, I might've started listing out the pros and cons in my journal.

The hard part's already out of the way, I told myself, watching as Vincent ducked out of the lunchroom. He didn't even sign out with the cafeteria monitor. *You already told him not to talk about the accident. It'll never come up again.*

"I've got to talk to Mrs. Keller," I announced to the

table, scrambling to repack my lunch and snatching up my journal. "I'll see you later."

Mollie watched as I pushed to my feet, but she didn't say anything. Vesta didn't give any sort of farewell either. I guessed their silent treatment had spread to me.

After signing out with the cafeteria monitor—what was I going to do, run around and vandalize the school?—I hurried out into the hallway, looking in both directions for a certain tall, broody boy. Both wings were empty, not a soul in sight.

Vincent literally walked out of the cafeteria a minute ago—how had he gotten so far? I decided to head in the direction of the senior lockers, keeping my fingers crossed that I'd discover him there.

I passed a few signs advertising the Snowflake Dance, and even the *Welcome Back, Greenville!* sign that the faculty hadn't taken down from the first day back from break.

It was impossible to believe I'd already been back for a full school week. December had felt like the month that'd never end, but here I was, back in classes. Sure, my sleep schedule was still off, and my friends were short-circuiting, but I was surviving.

As I rounded the corner, I saw him. Standing so far down the hall, unnoticed, gave me a moment to watch him. Vincent Castello had one hand braced on the green locker door, the other in its depths, searching for something. His black hair was tied back out of his face by a hair elastic, in a way that normally I would've found unattractive, but some-how, it looked right on him.

My spine straightened with a jolt. *Ew, stop being such a stalker. Just...go.*

So I went. One foot in front of the other, propelling me toward him. I had to clear my throat to summon my voice; it had run and hid, scared. "Hey."

"Hey," he returned, and though I'd been hoping he'd keep going, he said nothing further.

Great. So I'd be the one carrying the conversation. "We should talk about the project."

His hand stilled, his eyes locking on his bag. "What about it?"

"Well, I mean, we should talk about when we should meet next, yeah?" I reached up and brushed my fingertips along my tie, the smooth fabric comforting. "We've still got a lot to cover."

"No offense, but it's hard to be...open with *you*."

I blinked at the bluntness of his statement, taken so aback for a long moment that no words formed. Instinctively, I knew exactly what he meant. It wasn't hard to be open with me, Addy Arden, but to be open with me, the girl who shared a similar life experience with him. One might've thought that'd make it *easier* to be open, but in this case, I thought it was more difficult.

"Honestly," I found myself saying, "the feeling's mutual."

Vincent finally met my gaze. Understanding rested within his green eyes.

"I think it would help if you got to ask the questions this time," I told him, hugging my journal close to my chest. "I was putting you on the spot at Crushed Beanz, and it should be an equal kind of thing."

He reached up and ran a hand across his mouth and then hooked that hand around the back of his neck. "How about we share what we want to share? We'll look over the questions and answer whichever ones we want instead of asking. That way we're not..." He trailed off.

"Forced to share something we don't want to?" I finished for him, smiling a little. "I like the sound of that. Are you working tonight? I can swing by." And maybe coerce him into making me another one of those coffees.

The bell overhead rang, startling me enough to take a step back from him. "The band's actually playing tonight," he said as students began filing out of their classrooms, and he slammed his locker door shut. "But tomorrow, I work in the morning. Seven to noon. Stop by then."

And with that, Vincent started off down the hallway. I'd forgotten about his band. Untapped Potential was playing tonight. As Vincent's form mixed in with the crowd before being swallowed whole and disappearing entirely, I made the decision then and there: I'd be swinging by Crushed Beanz tonight after all.

Six

The last time I'd gone out on a Friday night, it'd been mid-November. I couldn't even remember what I'd done at this point, but I *missed* it. I missed getting out of the house, hanging with friends. And even though I'd be going to Crushed Beanz alone, I was so relieved to be doing something. It was another step in the right direction.

I'd never been to any sort of concert before, except maybe those high school band concerts that happened twice a year. Although I wouldn't necessarily call a three-member band playing in a café a concert. What would that be called in the musical world? A gig? Whatever it was, I hadn't been to one before. What was I supposed to wear?

Vincent had said they were into "heavier stuff," so did that mean my normal skirt and tie combo would stick out like a sore thumb?

As I stepped into Crushed Beanz with a navy skirt and matching tie covered up by my red pea coat, I realized the answer was yes. Yes, I would stick out.

The lights were dimmed super low in the café, creating

a moody sort of atmosphere that fit the idea of a live band perfectly. But even through the dimness, I could see that everyone was dressed in dark colors or jeans—no A-line skirts in sight.

Crushed Beanz was *packed*. I'd thought it was busy on poetry night, but this was much different. Someone must've pushed the tables from the center of room to a different spot, because no one was sitting down. There were so many people that I couldn't quite see the stage, and the space felt hot from all the bodies inside.

Just as the door slipped shut behind me, the band started a song, kicking off with a wave of drumbeats. From where I stood frozen by the door, I couldn't see Vincent, but I found myself smiling, picturing him on the stage. When the singer—Harry—started the lyrics, the crowd began to cheer.

The idea was a little funny, in a way. A group of people cheering on a small band in a coffee shop.

"Addy!" a voice called over the noise, and I turned to find Jonathan leaning against the coffee counter, waving me over. He'd folded his apron over his waist instead of wearing it around his neck, and dusted his palms across it. "Hate to break it to you, but if you wanted to be in the front row, you needed to get here about a half hour earlier. Those people won't let you anywhere near the band now."

"I definitely don't want to take an elbow to the eye." I started unbuttoning my coat as I got closer, glancing toward where the stage was. "Isn't this a fire hazard?" I asked him, only half teasing.

"We're not even at capacity. Imagine about forty more

people in the lounge, and *then* there'd be some fines."
Jonathan gestured to the array of coffee machines. "Pick
your poison. I bet I can make you a better coffee than
Vincent can."

I slid onto a stool, shaking my head. "I don't know, that
peppermint mocha was pretty good."

"Hey, I taught the kid everything he knows." Jonathan
snatched up a coffee mug, starting the process. Determina-
tion was clear on his face. "We'll see whose is better."

"Can you add extra shot of espresso to it?" I asked on
impulse.

"You looking to pull an all-nighter?"

Feigning nonchalance wasn't that hard. "I've got a big
assignment due on Monday."

That did the trick. He started measuring out the
espresso without another word. While Jonathan busied
himself making the drink, I turned in the direction of the
music, trying to catch a glimpse of the stage.

Harry's voice was low and smooth, the kind that could
give goosebumps. Hypnotic. "*Cut me up and cut me fine,
all I know is that I'll have one hell of a time.*" The girl's
voice cut in, a sweet complement to his tenor. I wondered
what their acoustic stuff sounded like—something like a
lullaby, surely.

"Okay, moment of truth." Jonathan set the mug down
in front of me. He'd filled it exactly as Vincent had—to the
brim—but instead of a flower, Jonathan had poured stars
across the surface, a mini set of constellations. "Whose
peppermint mocha is better?"

With steady hands, I lifted the cup to my mouth, taking

a long sip of the hot drink. The peppermint hit my tongue instantly, as well as the strength of the espresso. The cocoa was there, but it was missing something...

I met Jonathan's gaze. "There's no white chocolate."

"White chocolate?" Jonathan frowned. "We don't put that in the peppermint mochas."

"Vincent did." I took another sip, pretending to debate a bit more. "Yours is a bit more bitter."

"You asked for more espresso!"

The way his eyes widened made me nearly laugh aloud. "It's good, truly. Not as sweet, but that's okay."

All of the anticipation deflated from his gaze, and he fell back on the opposite counter. "I can't believe he put white chocolate into yours. He's not much of a freestyler."

This time, I did laugh out loud, imagining Vincent freestyling with *coffee syrups*.

"Okay, Jon—hit me with a refill," a new voice said, and from the lounge came a girl. She held an empty teal coffee cup, Crushed Beanz's signature color, rolling it back and forth between her palms. Her outfit drew my attention immediately—it was a tattered black dress, but it looked purposefully tattered, with torn lace and exposed stitching. Her black hair hung perfectly straight to her elbows, and her eyes were rimmed with dark shadow. She was so pretty, looking like something from an indie pop magazine. "Half shot this time, 'kay?"

Jonathan frowned at this, but took her cup and flipped the lid off. "I miss being a teenager. Drinking this much coffee this time of night would murder me."

"You're *twenty-five*," the girl scoffed. "Hardly old man

material." Her smoky eyes glanced my way, posture perking up. "Oh, hey. Sorry if I interrupted."

"You didn't," I assured her, at the same time Jonathan said, "This is Vincent's friend, Addy. Addy, this is Stella."

She started grinning as soon as he said Vincent's name, her eyes widening. "You're friends with the drummer, huh?"

"Well, *friend* is a strong word—"

Stella waved her hand, never losing the excited look. "But you're here for him. That makes you more than acquaintances."

"They have a project for school," Jonathan supplied before I could, and he passed over her refilled cup. "Some sort of creepy interview thing. Talk about invasion of privacy."

"No, I think that's fun. Helps build friendships." Stella came a bit closer, leaning her elbow on the countertop. "I *so* love your tie, Addy. It's such a look."

I glanced down at it. "Business casual's my thing, I guess."

"I have a friend who's really into business casual too—it so suits you." Stella looked like she was going to say more, but the song rose to a higher note, the beat picking up, and a male singing voice was suddenly clear as a bell, as lilting as a professional.

"And for all it's worth, I think I'm falling apart."

A dreamy expression passed over her face, and if people could've actually had hearts in their eyes, Stella definitely would have. It was like the male voice sung straight to her soul. "It was so nice to meet you, Addy," she said before heading back out to the crowd, not glancing back.

Jonathan couldn't hold back his laugh. "Don't be offended—I'm surprised she even said goodbye."

"She must really like the music."

He gave me a knowing smile. "No, she really likes a certain singer."

"She likes Harry?"

"I'm assuming. But then again, all girls like guys in bands, don't they?"

I snorted at that. "Not me. I'm more of a jock type." I thought about Bryce, quarterback of the football team, frequent dodger of my texts. Whatever had been going on between us, it was safe to say that it'd just fallen by the wayside. A burst of disappointment welled in my chest, but it wasn't as severe as I'd been expecting.

I pulled out my cell, checking a social media app while Jonathan helped another customer who'd walked up. As soon as my screen loaded, Bryce's latest photo update filled my view. The photo was of a group of five people posing in front of two crudely made snowmen. Bryce was presumably the one taking the photo because he wasn't in it, but someone else caught my eye. I had to do a double take when I realized who it was.

Her red hair was unmistakable even though the image was grainy and dark. *Vesta.*

She had her arm around a girl from her grade—Eloise, I thought her name was—and was leaning into one of the snowmen's sides. Vesta's smile was wide, goofy, eyes looking straight at the camera.

It wasn't like she couldn't hang with Bryce and his friends, more so that it was *strange* she was. I'd always assumed that Vesta's only connection to Bryce was through me, but clearly that wasn't the case.

Bryce had posted the photo thirty minutes ago. The icky feeling intensified.

Not knowing whatever secrecy thing was going on between Mollie and Vesta was one thing, but in a selfish way, it stung to know they were having fun without me. Mollie never talked to me about Jackson, Vesta and Bryce had been hanging out—it felt like I'd come back into a whole other world.

It was stupid of me to assume I could just pick right up where things had left off. But still, I'd hoped.

The stars in my coffee were muddled now, but I stared at them, the warmth of the drink doing nothing to thaw my chilled insides.

"So, you want the dirty details on Vincent for your project?" Jonathan asked as he laid his elbows on the countertop, leaning on the surface. "I can give you the inside scoop."

My movements were numb as I drew my bullet journal from my purse. "Duh. Make it as scandalous as possible."

"Well, Vincent *hates* oranges, for one. We had this orange-flavored drink and he practically gagged each time he had to make it." Jonathan tapped his chin. "Carries that journal around with him everywhere. I think it's a secret diary, honestly."

I stopped writing. "This is what you call dirty details?"

"Hey! I'm getting to the good stuff. Uh, let's see. Well,

his dad always talks about how the kid liked to jump off stuff when he was little. I guess he liked to jump off their shed and into their pond."

"That's normal kid stuff, isn't it?"

"Well, according to Mr. Castello, the pond was only four feet deep. I guess Vincent sprained his ankle really bad."

I felt my eyes widen. "Where's his mom?" I asked, because I knew that I could ask Jonathan. Vincent might never tell me, but Jonathan would. "Is she still in the picture?"

Jonathan shook his head. "She left."

"*Left.*" The idea was so foreign to me that I couldn't believe it at first. I knew parents walked out all the time, but I'd never met someone who'd had a parent leave. Never. "Recently?"

"Oh, nah. It was when he was little, I think. Maybe nine?"

I tried to picture little Vincent, nine years old, confused about what was going on. Had he known what it meant? Had he thought his mom would come back?

I sat back on the barstool, setting my pen down and wishing I'd never asked. That seemed like something Vincent definitely wouldn't have wanted me to know.

"Vincent has a hard time opening up to others," Jonathan went on, this time looking out at the gathering of people. "But once you get that kid to smile, you know you're in his top ten."

Jonathan had to push up from the counter when a

customer walked up, and chatted with them cheerfully. In stark contrast, I felt heavy, weighted to the stool.

It was just Vincent and his father, had been for years at this point. That thought carried the most pressure. What would've happened if it was Mr. Castello who'd passed away in that accident? What if he'd been hurt worse? Vincent would've been all alone.

Better me be alone than him.

The thought startled me, as did the stinging behind my eyes.

I shoved my bullet journal back into my purse and grabbed my coat, because right away, I knew I couldn't stay there. Couldn't sit there and wait for him to finish playing. I couldn't face him.

"Whoa, you heading out?" Jonathan asked, and quickly swiped a to-go cup. "Here, take the rest of your mocha with you."

"On second thought, I don't need all that caffeine," I told him, hastily shoving my arms through my sleeves. "Can you *not* tell Vincent that I was here?"

"Sure thing," Jonathan said slowly, appearing confused, but he didn't question it. "See you later."

I finished buttoning up my coat and headed for the door; the heat of the café was stifling now. Each breath I drew in was choking, too hot.

Just before I pulled open the door, I glanced toward the band, listening to the final beats of the song. The crowd parted just a little bit as they swayed, finally giving me a glimpse of the stage.

The singer came into view first—Harry. He was hard to miss with his shock of wavy red hair, so long that it brushed his shoulders. A black tattoo embraced the skin of his throat, almost in the shape of a hand. He was cute in a rocker kind of way, and I could see why anyone would've had a thing for him.

But then my gaze slid past him to Vincent, and that thought slipped out of my mind.

His expression was focused, eyes on the kit in front of him. Even from where I stood, I could see that the hair near his temples was damp. Vincent moved swiftly to hit the final beats of the song, second nature.

He drew the drumstick down one final time as the song ended, the crowd's clapping drowning out Harry's final note. Then someone filled the open space, severing that quick connection, and Vincent disappeared. I could still see him in my mind's eye, drumsticks in hand, expression as focused as it'd been when he made coffees.

Dedicated. That was a good word to describe Vincent. I barely knew much about him, but instinctually, I knew that.

I ducked my head as I shoved the door open, the biting cold instantly hitting my cheeks. Despite finally getting the chance to go out on a Friday night, I found myself wishing I'd just stayed home.

Seven

I used to look forward to Saturday mornings. Dad would make his signature coffee milkshakes for him and me while Mom would make breakfast, and we'd all eat together as a family. Family dinners were rare in this house—Mom always worked odd shifts and Dad was never home for lunch—but Saturday morning breakfasts were a staple.

Now, Saturday mornings consisted of me in my house robe, sipping a glass of orange juice at an empty table.

Mom hadn't emerged from her bedroom yet, so I'd made my own breakfast. The waffle in front of me was slightly soggy; I hadn't let it cook long enough in the toaster. Mom had forgotten to buy maple syrup, so it was plain and boring and sad.

Like my life.

I grimaced at my waffle. *That was angsty.*

For the first time since everything had happened, I found myself testing my tolerance, like walking up to a lake and dipping a toe in to see how cold it was.

I unpacked that mental super-glued, stapled, taped up box I'd sat on a shelf and let myself remember Dad. His milkshakes were always perfectly made. Half coffee, half ice cream. I'd tried making them one morning in December in Rickett Falls, before anyone would wake up and see me do it, but couldn't get the ratios right. Too bitter, too watery.

In this moment, with the quiet chatter in my ears blaring loud, I remembered all the times he added a shot of alcohol to his.

I drew in a long, slow breath, letting my lungs fill to the brim, before slowly releasing it. The breath wiped the feeling away, put it back in the box. No more thinking about it.

A sudden knock at the front door had me nearly spilling my orange juice. Who would be knocking at nine in the morning on a Saturday?

As I passed by the window in the kitchen, I could see that the snow was starting to come down pretty heavily, gray clouds thicker than they'd been yesterday. Despite the beauty of the scene, my stomach tied in knots. The idea of driving the convertible to Hallow in freshly dumped snow made me nervous. But Vincent was expecting me, which knotted my stomach even more.

Wrapping my robe tighter, I stopped in front of the door, hoping I looked at least slightly presentable. As I pulled it open, worry over my appearance fled to the back of my brain.

Vesta and Bryce stood on the front porch, bundled in their winter gear. Vesta liked to wear white in the winter to blend in with the snow and to make her shock of red hair pop further, so her white coat was buttoned to her throat. Bryce, standing ever so slightly behind her, wore a dark gray jacket and held a paper bag.

Half of me wondered what was in the bag. The other half wondered what they were doing here. Together.

"We come bearing gifts!" Vesta exclaimed with a megawatt smile, voice much too loud for a Saturday morning. "Show her, Bryce."

Unceremoniously, Bryce offered the paper bag to me. "It was Vesta's idea. She texted me at the crack of dawn."

"Don't listen to him. It was almost seven-thirty."

The bag crinkled as I peeked inside, and the scent of strawberry and sugar glaze hit my nose at once. Despite the strangeness of them showing up here, a small smile crept across my face. "A jelly donut?"

"Strawberry. Your favorite, of course," Vesta explained, taking a step closer to the door. "Can we come in? You don't have to share, but we'd love to keep you company."

I clammed up. I'd planned on finishing my waffle and heading upstairs to get ready to head to Crushed Beanz. "The—well, the house is a disaster. I'd be embarrassed for you to see it."

The rejection flew from my mouth before I even had time to think about it. It would've made sense, inviting them in. I would've had someone to talk to. But there was something about this scene—something about the two of them standing together on my front porch—that left me feeling unsettled. Left me thinking about how the two of them had hung out last night together, too. Left me wishing they'd never stopped by in the first place.

Bryce glanced behind me, no doubt noting the clean section of the house displayed through the open doorway. Thankfully, though, he didn't comment on it. "We *did* kind of barge in without warning, Vesta."

"We're her best friends. We're allowed to barge." Vesta took another step closer, but this time it was only to wrap her arms around me. Her words were quiet in my ear, almost desperate-sounding. "Call me if you want to do anything, okay?" She lowered her voice even more. "I'm sorry for everything with Mollie. I know that put you in an awkward place."

"I just wish I knew what was going on," I said, pulling back to look at her face. "What made you two argue in the first place?"

"I don't even want to talk about it. Water under the bridge. I texted her last night, and I think we're on the same page." Despite the light way she spoke, her gaze was a stormy green, troubled and worried. "I just want you to be okay. I'm always here if you want to talk."

I still wished she'd tell me what was going on, but I was more relieved that they'd figured whatever out. "We'll do something soon, okay? How about a sleepover this week?"

Mid-week sleepovers weren't uncommon for us. In fact, they were almost a necessity. Mollie wasn't allowed to stay overnight, since her parents were super strict, but she'd always stay as late as possible.

Vesta nodded quickly. "Please. How about Wednesday?"

Throughout our conversation, Bryce lingered on the

porch, just listening. "Sounds great," I told Vesta, wrapping my arms around myself.

"I'll meet you at the car," Bryce told Vesta as she brushed past him, hovering along the rail of the porch. Once she was far enough away, Bryce lowered his head to peer directly into my eyes. The blue was shining, brilliant in the morning light. "I know we haven't gotten the chance to really talk."

Oh, he wanted to talk *now*, while I was still in my PJs and Vesta was sitting in his car? "We've both been busy." I couldn't help but think of his snowman picture.

"Well, maybe we can get together one day and get lunch. Catch up."

Before, my insides would've been doing a happy dance at his offer. I would've immediately texted the girls, planning what I'd wear. But now that excitement wasn't there. I just shifted the paper bag in my grip, hoping my smile seemed genuine. "Yeah. Sometime next week?"

Bryce nodded, turning and stepping off the deck without a final farewell.

I shuffled the bag under my arm and shut the front door, leaning against it with a sigh. A few seconds later, I realized that Bryce hadn't kissed me goodbye. We'd rarely kissed since we started talking—only on very special occasions—but Bryce used to always give me a peck on my cheek in goodbye. He hadn't done it this time, hadn't done it since I'd come back to school. When was the last time he did that?

It probably wasn't a good sign that I couldn't remember.

"Addy?" Mom asked as she emerged from the guest

bedroom down the hallway, rubbing at her eyes. "Who was that?"

"Bryce," I said, leaving Vesta out at the last second. "He brought a jelly donut. Want to split it?"

I wanted her to say yes so badly. I wanted her to smile, follow me into the kitchen, sit down and break it in half with me. I wanted to be more than two housemates. We'd never been *that* close before—I'd been such an independent kid—but right now, I just longed for mother-daughter time.

But Mom didn't feel the same. "I'm actually going to shower and head to the grocery store. If you need anything, text me, okay?"

She didn't wait for me to say anything in response before she disappeared back into the guest bedroom, leaving me in the foyer by myself.

Dad would've split this with me, I found myself thinking, flinching at the idea the second it registered. Anxiety poured through me, like feeling I was seconds away from throwing up. That nothing in my body could settle. On the brink of exploding.

No. That box was closed. I'd glued it shut again. I'd put it on the shelf. No more memories.

Testing the waters, peeking into those memories, was off-limits. There was a reason it was forbidden in the first place.

By the time I managed to get to Crushed Beanz, it was half past eleven o'clock. The roads weren't that terrible, but with all that snow last night, I'd been extra cautious and drove slow, much to the annoyance of everyone driving behind me. I knew I was coming in toward the end of Vincent's shift, so I wasn't sure where that left us if he had something else to do afterward.

When I walked into the café, though, there were already a few people sitting at the counter, sipping their cups of coffee and munching on whatever sweet treats they'd picked from the pastry section. I hesitated in the doorway, and while I debated what to do, Vincent came out of the back room with his teal apron on, carrying a tray. His eyes immediately found mine.

"Welcome to Crushed Beanz," a feminine voice greeted, and I glanced over to find a girl behind the counter, her light hair woven up into two buns on her head. I hadn't noticed her at first, but she had on a teal apron as well. She gave me a bright grin before turning to finish making a to-go order, assuming I'd step in line.

I didn't realize how much I'd been expecting to see Jonathan until I didn't see him. The safe and familiar dynamic of the coffeehouse now felt off.

Instead of stepping into the line, I found a booth near a window out in the lounge area, laying my coat over the edge of the table and pulling out my journal. My weekend boxes weren't as thick as my weekday boxes—before, I tried to give myself a break from my lengthy lists on the weekend —but I'd managed to cram several bullet points into today's box. *Go to Crushed Beanz. Chat with Vincent about questions. Text Mollie to check in. Finish my English homework.*

With a purple pen, I checked off the first one, drawing a little bubble around the second one just for fun. Even from where I sat, the coffee machine was loud as it whirred to life, but in a comforting way. That plus the soft music playing over the speakers filled the white noise in my brain.

It stayed busy enough that Vincent never came over. I had my back to the counter, so I couldn't catch his eye unless I turned around. For a little while, I doodled, listening to the door chime again and again as customers came and went.

When my page became full enough that any more doodles would look too cluttered, I pulled out my phone, deciding to check off something else on my list.

Me: *Hey, girl. Happy Saturday! Are you doing anything fun today?*

It didn't take long for Mollie to type back a response, my phone vibrating in my hand.

Mollie: *Babysitting my sisters. If I don't text back, they've stolen my phone and probably buried me in the backyard. Send reinforcements.*

Me: *Don't worry, I don't think they'd be strong enough to break ground. It is frozen, you know. And I'm just hanging out today. I ran to that café again. Who knew working in a coffee shop was relaxing?*

Mollie: *College kids everywhere, actually. ;) Also man, I could use a coffee—can you send me some virtual caffeine?*

Me: *Sent!*

I set my phone down with a soft breath, shifting in the

seat. Condensation settled thickly on the window, drops of water dripping down the pane. I reached out and traced my finger along the glass, making a little heart.

"Hey."

I looked up to find Vincent without his apron on. He settled into the booth beside me, placing his own jacket and journal on the table.

To my surprise, he set a to-go cup down in front of me before he leaned back in his seat. "Fancy seeing you here."

"I was in the neighborhood," I said, trying to channel his nonchalance, but not quite nailing the tone. I picked up the coffee cup, bringing it to my nose. "In the mood for some free peppermint mochas, too."

"Well, I am the reason you had to drive all the way out to Hallow. I figured it's repayment for the gas."

Taking the drink from him, warmth spread through me, almost like I'd already taken a sip. He brought me a drink— did this mean we were making strides toward friendship? Mentally, I shook the thought off. No, not friends. This was all simply transactional; coffee in exchange for gas, answer in exchange for answer.

I took an experimental sip. So freaking good. "Much tastier than gas."

It'd been a joke, but he didn't laugh. His gaze was steady as he watched me take another sip. Every time he looked at me like that, it made me squirm. It felt like he was trying to read my mind or see into my soul.

"What do you write in your journal?" I asked, nodding toward it.

His eyebrows lowered ever so slightly. "What do you write in yours?"

Ah, right, was that me crossing that "no asking each other questions" line we'd drawn? "It's more of a to-do list and habit tracker than a diary," I told him, flipping through the pages so he could see. I wasn't embarrassed to show him. "I theme each week and keep my drawings consistent. It's a fun little outlet. See, like here"—I traced my fingertips over where I'd written *arch* and *faux snow*—"these are the last few things I need to pick up for the dance."

"So you're creative," he said, examining each page as I flipped through.

"Not really. Not much outside of this. I do this more for the planning element. I...I like planning things out."

Vincent thought about it. "Planning gives you a sense of control."

I couldn't help but frown. "Are you analyzing my answers?"

"It's for psychology. Aren't we supposed to?"

"I think you're supposed to do that *privately*." Hearing him psychoanalyze my answers made me feel uncomfortable, like I was a bug under a microscope. At least when I'd asked Vincent questions, I was more interested in hearing his answers than scrutinizing them. "Like, in the report. Not to my face."

"Ah." He nodded, but it was slow, almost sarcastic. "Got it."

I gave him as serious of a stare as I could. "What do you write in your journal?" Sure, we'd agreed on a no-questions rule, but I'd answered his. He could answer mine.

Vincent surprised me by grabbing his journal and dropping it in front of me. "See for yourself."

Testing the waters, I pried open the first page, waiting for him to react, but he didn't. Heck, he didn't even look concerned. Was he playing me? Was it just a homework sort of journal?

As I scanned the page, I figured out why he didn't care. "Is this written in gibberish? Did you invent your own language to hide your private thoughts?"

"What, you don't journal your private thoughts in a different language?"

I blinked at the words on the page, but they didn't magically translate themselves. "Are you serious? Is this, like, a made-up language?" I didn't know whether to be impressed by the dedication or freaked out.

One hand ghosted over his hair, curling a few strands over his ear. "It's Italian."

"Like, coherent Italian?"

"You mean *fluent*? Yes."

I flipped to another page, the language continuing. "How do you know to write in Italian?"

He tapped his fingers on the surface of the table. "My mom taught me. My parents are both Italian, but she was born in Italy."

As soon as he brought her up, everything that Jonathan said came flooding back in perfect clarity. "That's really cool. I wish I could speak a different language."

"I can't really *speak* it that well. Just write it."

I traced my fingertips over the looping cursive of Vincent's writing, feeling the inflection of his pen in the pages. The way the lines were formed almost looked like poetry, a beautiful sort of sentence structure that had me unable to look away. Vincent's scripty scrawl was almost better than mine, though I'd never admit it. "Are these songs you're working on?"

"Maybe."

It was very clever to write a journal of private thoughts and songs in a different language. The ultimate layer of secrecy. I wished I knew even just a tiny amount of Italian, enough to decode one phrase. "So what does this say?" I asked, pointing to one of the lines.

"It says 'none of your business.'"

I opened my mouth, ready to snap back, when I looked up and saw that there was amusement in his eyes. Though it didn't touch his mouth, it glimmered in his gaze.

We looked at each other for a long moment before I took another drink of my mocha. "I'm an only child," I told him.

Vincent tipped his head against the booth. "I have a little brother. He's seven."

I jolted in surprise. I hadn't known that. "What's his name?"

"Frankie. Or, well, it's Franklin, but he pretends he's named Frankie instead."

I fought back a smile. "Franklin does sound like a mature name for a seven-year-old."

"Apparently it's a family name. His dad's named Franklin too." Vincent shrugged, leaning back. I caught on immediately—Vincent's dad's name was Carlo, not Franklin. "He's a good kid, though. He's practicing his Italian, too, I guess."

"When did you see him last?"

"Oh, I've never met him in person. We just write letters back and forth."

I slowly slid his journal back to him, forcing myself not to ask more questions about that relationship. Curiosity was killing me. I couldn't imagine what it would be like to have a sibling but never meet them, to only communicate through letters. If I were Frankie, I knew I would've been excited to have a pen pal. If I were Vincent, I wasn't sure how I'd feel. Excited, maybe, but it would be a potent reminder of a mother who'd left me.

Vincent's lips pulled into a soft frown, the expression darkening his eyes. "You feel sorry for me."

"I don't," I said honestly, wondering if he believed me. "I'm just trying to picture myself in your shoes is all."

"Aren't you supposed to save the analyzing for the report?" he replied ironically. His eyes fell to the hearts I'd traced, lingering there for a long moment. "My birthday's February fourteenth."

"Mine's October twentieth." I gestured to his notebook. "You're not writing any of this down."

"Your birthday's October twentieth, you don't have any siblings, and you like planning." Vincent raised an eyebrow. "Am I missing anything so far?"

His moods were so hard to get a grasp on. Our earlier interaction at Crushed Beanz had felt different. This didn't necessarily feel hostile, but it definitely didn't leave me feeling warm and fuzzy inside. A part of me wanted to throw my hands up and walk out. If he didn't want to do this, fine.

But another part of me, a strange part of me, wanted to know more. Like the idea of walking away now was just impossible to imagine.

"I wanted to be a wedding planner when I grew up," I said, tapping my journal. "Or any kind of event planner, but I'd like weddings. Yeah, they'd be stressful, but I think they'd be beautiful too."

"*Wanted*? You don't want to do it anymore?"

"Well, I guess I still do. As I grew up, I started to realize I'm not sure I've got enough of a backbone for it." From what that I'd heard and seen on TV, wedding planners had to be firm, take charge of everything. It sounded fun in theory, but there was more to it than just lists. "My parents never thought I had the right personality for it."

Vincent, though, didn't seem to doubt me. "It sounds like it'd be the perfect job for you. You don't strike me as the kind of girl to back down from a challenge."

Which is why I'm here talking to you. "We'll see, I guess. I still have a year to figure everything out before figuring out a major and all that." I knew Vincent was a senior, though, and that he *didn't* have a year to figure everything out. Had he started putting in college applications yet? What kind of work did he want to do?

"I plan on helping my dad out with this place for as long he needs me," Vincent said, practically reading my mind. "He hasn't been able to keep up with it since...well. So I'm here almost every day picking up shifts and crunching numbers. He looks them over, of course, but I'm trying to learn how to do them myself."

"Is that what you want to do? Run this place?"

Vincent seemed just as surprised by the question as I felt asking it. "I don't know."

And that was it. No explaining. Nothing more.

Neither one of us was quick to offer up another fact about ourselves. I tried to remember the list of questions on Mr. Walker's sheet, but I'd accidentally left it at home, and my brain was blanking. Still, I felt like I'd gotten a lot of good facts about Vincent, about his family life.

I looked down at my bullet journal, at where I'd written my Snowflake Dance list, and I leaned forward until my chest touched the edge of the table. "So, I actually have a favor to ask, and you can totally say no."

Vincent didn't answer, but just stared me down. It made me more nervous.

"I've got something I need to pick up over in Bayview, but it won't fit in my car. But it *would* fit in your truck bed."

"You want to borrow my truck?" Disbelief was thick in his voice.

"Uh, more like, can you be my chauffeur? I'd pay you for gas, of course," I rushed to say. "And even pay for lunch, since I know it'll be a drive. I don't know why Mrs. Keller had to pick out an arch so far away—"

Vincent cut me off. "Mrs. Keller?"

"It's for the Snowflake Dance." The confusion hadn't disappeared from his gaze, so I added, "It's the winter dance the school throws each year."

"I know what it is. I'm just trying to figure out why you

volunteered to be the one to go all the way to Bayview to pick it up."

"I'm the head of the committee. It makes sense that the task falls to me." Even though I was super bummed that it had. "You can totally say no. I can see if I can get it delivered or something, or just ask Mrs. Keller to pick it up. I just thought—well, I thought I'd check."

As my question lingered in the air, I regretted having asked. Something about asking him for a favor made my cheeks burn.

Before Vincent could answer, a sharp trill filled the air. I knew it wasn't my phone—none of my ringtones sounded like that. But he reached over and passed his fingers through his jacket, pulling out a phone in a hard, black case. Once he glanced at the caller ID, his expression seemed to harden. "Would you excuse me for a second?"

I was startled by how formal the question was. He quickly slid from the booth and the front door chimed moments later. Through the window, I saw him outside, placing the phone to his ear.

I forced myself to turn back around, not wanting to spy. Instead, I flipped to my notes section on Vincent and filled out all of the new facts I'd learned about him, including his little brother, Frankie.

It was strange getting to know Vincent's personal life. For so long, he'd just been some guy in a grade above me. I'd listened to the gossip and just assumed he was a partier, reckless, but nothing he'd shown me or told me hinted at that. In fact, I couldn't imagine Vincent at a party at all. I couldn't imagine him dancing to the music, red cup in hand, flirting with girls. The image just didn't compute at all.

The door to the coffeehouse chimed again, and Vincent reappeared at the table. His face was a mask of anger and frustration—his eyebrows were drawn together, lips forming a livid line. He scrambled to get his jacket on, hands shaking as he stabbed them through the sleeves.

"Is everything okay?" I asked, looking closely at his expression for the tiniest of cracks.

"If you still need a ride Tuesday, we can go then. That's the next day I have off."

Of course he didn't answer my question, but I didn't quite care about his response, not when he looked so upset. "Vincent—"

But he didn't stay long enough to listen. After snatching his journal up from the table, he turned on his heel and headed for the doors by the counter, shoving through them without pausing to say goodbye to the barista. I stared at the doors for a long moment, watching them swing back and forth from the force, but Vincent never reappeared.

eight

*I*t was rare that I had dreams, but if I did, if I fell asleep long enough to have them, they were always nightmares.

The feelings of the dreams lasted longer than the memory of them. Most of the time, I'd wake up with no recollection of *what* I'd dreamt, only with the haunting way they made me feel. Like I wasn't alone. Like I wasn't safe. Like impending doom was inching its way closer and closer to my life for a second round.

This time, though, I remembered my dream in full.

I'd been walking through the hospital as if in slow-motion, the walls around me fuzzy and faded, like my brain couldn't recall the details perfectly. A man led me through the hallways, dressed in black with a word etched on the back of his jacket. POLICE.

In my dream, I had no idea what was about to happen.

We'd turned a corner, and Mom was there, just standing in the middle of the hallway. Her pink scrubs matched the ones she wore to work. Her hair had been pulled out of its bun and hung in brown tatters around her face, tangled and gnarled. Tears were tracking down her cheeks, mascara running in black rivers against her fair skin.

I'd stopped in the middle of the hallway, just staring at her, trying to understand why she'd be so sad.

It wasn't until she looked at me that I remembered. *Dad.* I was here for my dad. The police officer had picked me up from the house. He'd brought me here. And Mom— Mom was looking at me with a gaze so wild and so hysterical, as if she'd been moments from breaking down before she saw me. I thought I'd be her saving grace, something that'd keep her strong, but I was the opposite.

As soon as she saw me, she started to scream.

And I jerked awake as her sob of pain echoed into the real world, mixing with the blaring noise of my cell phone alarm. I kicked at my covers, the weight of them feeling crushing, suffocating, like they were trying to trap me to the bed and trap me to the memory. *Breathe*, I tried telling myself, but it was as if there wasn't enough oxygen in my room. *Just get the blankets off. Get them off.*

In an effort to scramble upward, I cracked the back of my head on my headboard, the pain strong enough to shake the disorientation. The room suddenly spun back into focus, and I could hear beyond the ragged pace of my breathing or the rapid beat of my heart.

For several moments, I just sat there, trembling, listening to the beeping of my phone. I couldn't bring myself to reach over and turn it off; I was trying too hard to stuff the residual panic down. It didn't seem fair that I could dream a memory with such perfect clarity, especially since it was a moment I'd been fighting tooth and nail to forget.

All of a sudden, my bedroom door swung open, and Mom stood on the other side in her scrubs, her hair still wet from her shower. "Addy?" she asked, obviously taken aback by me sitting up in bed. "I thought you were sleeping through your alarm."

"No, I'm awake," I said, but I didn't sound awake; I sounded half-dead. Maybe it was because trying to force those emotions down took so much focus, or maybe it was because I could still hear Mom's scream in the back of my mind. I reached over and turned off the alarm, granting us blissful silence. "I was just thinking."

"How you can think with that noise is beyond me," Mom muttered to herself, and grabbed the door handle. "I'm going to blow-dry my hair and head to work. It doesn't look like they plowed the roads that well on our street, so be careful going to school, okay?"

I reached up and scrubbed my fingers along my scalp, fingers catching on the knots and tangles from a night of tossing and turning. "Okay."

Mom hesitated in the doorway like she wanted to say more, but ultimately turned on her heel and pulled the door shut behind her, leaving me alone in the dark bedroom.

The dream wouldn't have been so bad if it weren't so

realistic. So much an echo of what had actually happened. Mom, crumbling to the floor of the hospital, screaming as if she had no idea what else to do.

And me, helpless, kneeling with my arms around her as if my sheer will would keep her from falling apart. In real life, it never worked. I was glad I never made it that far in my dream.

Pushing to my feet seemed like a chore, but it was one I had to do. I had to begin week two of being back to school, face the day. I didn't want to dive under my covers, anyway —I didn't want to risk dreaming again.

The air was cold as I drew my blankets all the way off, the floorboards colder as I placed my feet on the ground, but I already felt numb.

When I peeked through my bedroom curtains, I found a layer of beautiful, fresh white powder coating everything. After checking my phone for any texts, I sighed. Was a snow day too much to ask for?

But all through the morning, I couldn't shake that feeling of dread. I just needed to get to school. I just needed to be around people who'd force me to concentrate on the moment at hand, because even though I tried to concentrate on brushing my teeth, on pulling on my tights, on tightening my tie, I still caught my mind wandering. Still caught myself remembering Mom's scream.

I wondered if it would ever be a sound I could ever truly forget.

I'd timed my arrival perfectly, because I managed to snag a close-ish parking spot before the flood of student drivers pulled in. The roads weren't terrible, but I'd definitely gone slow enough that leaving early had been a good idea. I cut the engine, and almost instantly, cold started creeping in.

The sky was beautiful as the sun started to rise over the horizon, with a mixture of deep reds that melted into orange. Winter in Greenville was usually gray and dull, and even though snow clouds might move in later and cover it, there was no eclipsing the sunrise now.

Too busy lost in the sky, I didn't notice when I stepped on a patch of ice. My ballet flat lost purchase and my feet totally went out from underneath me. I slammed down on the pavement, landing on my butt, all of the air expelling from me with a sharp gasp.

For a long moment, I just sat there in shock, teeth vibrating.

This is just not my day.

"Jeez, are you okay?" A hand slipped against my back while another found its grip underneath my forearm, both in tandem guiding me to my feet.

"I'll let you know when I can feel my butt again," I answered shakily, looking up to where Jackson Mannerfield stood over at me. *Way* over me. He was almost freakishly tall. He could easily go on to play professional basketball with his height, and from what I've heard from Bryce, agents had their eyes on him. "That was so embarrassing."

Even worse was that Jackson had been the one to scrape me off the ground. "Nah, I think only I saw," he said cheerfully, watching as I dusted myself off.

I thought about Vesta teasing Mollie about him. I could see what she meant, of course. If a guy as pretty as Jackson paid attention to me, I was sure I'd be making up excuses to go on a date with him too. But looks weren't everything.

"Beautiful sunrise, huh?" Jackson said as he walked beside me, hooking his thumbs through his backpack straps. "I miss summer."

I glanced at him from the corner of my eye, trying to figure out why he hadn't walked ahead already. "I think the snow is pretty."

Jackson shrugged at that, still walking alongside me as we got closer to the school. "Can I ask you a question?"

"No, I'm not doing your homework."

"Ah, you're *funny*," he said in a voice that sounded like he believed the opposite, but he still gave a genuine smile. "Does Mollie really have a no-dating rule?"

I felt an immediate surge of protectiveness, so strong that it made me feel almost angry. "She's not like everyone else you hang around with. Mollie's a good person."

Jackson looked amused. "What's that supposed to mean?"

"I thought it was clear. Play any games with her, and you'll regret it." Not sure how I'd make him regret it, but I could figure out something.

"What makes you think I want to play games?" he asked, still with that annoying, self-satisfied smile. "I'm just asking if she was telling the truth or trying to let me down gently."

By that point, we'd made it to the building's entrance,

but I turned and faced him. "The fact that you have to ask just makes it clear that you don't know her. So do her a favor and find someone else for a rebound."

With that, I hauled the door open and walked inside, not bothering to prop it open for him. I gritted my teeth, anxious he might try to catch up with me, but this time, he wisely let me pull ahead.

I'd meant what I'd said to Jackson—Mollie was a good person and deserved better than a guy who changed girlfriends every other month. She deserved someone who loved her and cherished her, and if I had to go Mama Bear to protect her, I would.

He might've actually liked her, maybe thought she was cute and funny, which she totally was. But guys like Jackson tended to like things because they couldn't have them—once they got them, *poof*. They bailed.

I didn't linger at my locker. As soon as I got my coat off and gathered my things, I headed to psychology. Only two people were already in the room, and Mr. Walker wasn't one of them, which was strange. He never left his classroom unsupervised.

It took a little bit of time for Vesta to slide into her usual seat in front of me, leaning her elbow on my desk. "I think the world hates me," she announced. "When I went to my locker, Larissa was asking Jordan—the sophomore Jordan—to the Snowflake Dance. She got a coffee and a sign that read, '*I would like it a latte if you were my date.*'"

"Aw, that's cute." When I pictured it, I couldn't help but smile. "Why would the world hate you?"

"They were doing it in front of *my locker*. It's just wrong."

Talking about the Snowflake Dance made me think about Bryce. I'd become more and more sure of the fact that he wasn't going to ask me. He supposedly still wanted to meet up and talk, but I couldn't imagine he was going to talk about the Snowflake Dance, given how awkward our interactions had been lately. We'd been talking so little lately as it was.

"You've got a grumpy look on your face," Vesta said. "Is your singleness getting to you too?"

"I just don't feel good," I grumbled, scraping my fingers through my hair. "And I fell in the parking lot, so that didn't help my mood."

A woman walked through the door, carrying a piece of paper. "Hello everyone," she greeted, even though the bell hadn't rung yet. "I'm Ms. Sharp, and I'll be your substitute for the day. Your teacher left this note that we'll be working on your group assignments with your partner today."

No. *No.*

This was it. This was the doom that had been barreling toward me.

Vesta raised an eyebrow at me. "So you're going to work alone, huh? Want to join Kyle and I's group for the day?"

I'd told Vesta I switched partners. I'd told her I wasn't working with Vincent anymore. Vincent wasn't in the room yet—maybe I'd get lucky and he'd be out sick this morning.

I could've come clean with Vesta now, told her the truth. But then I thought about her showing up on my doorstep with Bryce, and her in the photo that Bryce had posted, thought about the secret fight between her and Mollie.

All of that combined made me not want to be honest with her made me almost sick at the thought.

And if I told her about Vincent, Vesta would no doubt say *something* about the accident. I couldn't think about that today. Not after that nightmare.

Maybe Vincent won't show. I clung to the thought like a life raft. *One minute before the bell rings.*

Ten seconds before the school officially day started, I was proven wrong.

Vincent sauntered through the door with his textbook casually tucked under his arm, his dark hair pushed back out of his face. He didn't glance my way as he headed toward his seat, and I definitely didn't linger on him long.

Instead, I gathered my things with shaking hands and rose to my feet. "Where are you going?" Vesta asked as the bell rang, eyes following me. "Addy?"

I walked up to the substitute teacher, forcing my expression to sag, grimacing as if in pain. My heart was pounding, because even though my brain knew there was no other option, lying to an adult made me want to throw up. "I'm not feeling well," I told her in a soft voice, hoping it sounded believable. "Can I go to the office?"

"Of course," she said, sympathy melting into her gaze. "Try getting something from a vending machine—sometimes nibbling on food can help."

"I'll try that," I assured her, struggling to keep my sick façade up even as relief swept through me. I'd dodged a bullet this time, but what if Mr. Walker was gone again tomorrow and the same sub was here? What if he pulled another "work with your partner" day?

Even with my free pass to go to the office for this period, the relief was short-lived. Once that dissipated, that dread returned in full force. No matter what I did the rest of the day, I couldn't shake it.

nine

*M*ollie tapped her pencil against her kitchen table in a steady rhythm. "Why do they make us learn math?"

"So we can use it in real life," I answered without looking up from my own math worksheet. "It does come in handy sometimes."

It wasn't often that I went to Mollie's house, mostly because it was always loud. With three sisters, there was always something going on, and someone was almost always shouting. After school today, I welcomed the noise, the chattering of her two younger siblings as they watched cartoons in the next room over, even though I was trying to concentrate on my homework.

Mollie's steady tapping stopped. "Did you do anything fun this weekend?"

"I went to that coffeehouse on Saturday," I said, still not looking up. "Worked through my journal for a bit. Then I ran a few errands. Nothing too crazy." Expertly leaving out the part about the live band at said coffeehouse. "How about you?"

Mollie chewed on her lower lip. "I actually went to a basketball game on Friday."

"Greenville's?" I hadn't even realized there was a basketball game, but it made sense that the season was starting. "Did you go with Vesta?"

"No, we're still kind of on the outs."

On the outs? Vesta told me that it was all water under the bridge, that she'd texted Mollie and worked everything out. Had she lied?

Mollie set her pencil down and instead started tapping her fingers against the table. "Has she talked to you about anything at all?"

Now I looked up, analyzing her expression. "If you mean has she talked to me about your fight, no. I'm still in the dark, by the way. Are *you* going to fill me in?"

"Oh my gosh, would you turn that off?" Mollie's younger sister, Bree, said from the living room. "*Wonder Tunes* is for babies."

"Is not!" her littlest sister, Nicole, fired back. Four girls under one roof with a three-year age difference between each. As an only child, I couldn't even comprehend it. "If it's for babies, why does your foot always tap when the theme song comes on?"

"You guys, enough!" Mollie turned in her chair, glaring at them through the archway. "You're both babies, so shut it."

Bree rolled her eyes. "Nice comeback."

"I can send you to your room if you want. Since, you know, I *am* in charge until Dad gets home."

Neither Bree nor Nicole had anything to say to that. Nicole punched the buttons on the remote control, increasing the volume of her TV show, effectively ending the conversation.

As Mollie turned back in her seat, I looked at her expectantly, waiting for her to answer my question. But she remained silent, her chest slowly rising and falling.

Whatever. Let her and Vesta fight. I couldn't help fix anything when I didn't know what exactly was broken.

The silence between us was so prolonged, filled with singing cartoons in the background, that when Mollie spoke again, it startled me. "Do you still like Bryce?"

So many times, I'd turned to Vesta and Mollie when Bryce and I had first started talking, asking them for tips or things to say. They'd coached me through it, just as excited as I'd been that Bryce Calhoun was paying attention to me.

When had that excitement disappeared—for all of us?

"I think we missed our chance," I told her, surprised by how much I believed my words. "I think we would've made a great couple back in the fall, but things are different now."

"Why are things different?"

"Why do you think?" I let out a long sigh, plunging ahead before she tried clarifying. "We're getting lunch sometime this week, so maybe I'm just overthinking it."

Mollie pursed her lips. "I think you deserve someone better."

Now I set my pencil down, frowning. "What's that

supposed to mean? Better than Bryce?" Even though my voice was defensive, I found myself deflating a bit, her words tumbling over and over in my mind. Was she really wrong?

The front door creaked open, followed by a jingle of keys. "Mollie?" a deep voice called into the house. "Whose car is out front?"

An idea came to me as soon as I heard his voice. "That's mine, Mr. Brooks!" I called to him, scattering my homework around me and swiped my pencil back up. "I thought I'd come work on homework with Mollie after school."

Mr. Brooks was a big man, broad shouldered and tall. He took up the entire doorframe as he stepped into it, loosening his tie in the process. Worry lines wrinkled his forehead, making him look perpetually angry. But he wasn't an angry guy. Mr. Brooks was sweet—strict, but sweet. When I'd met him last summer, I remembered wishing my dad was more like him.

I cleared my throat, forcing my eyes to focus on the equation in front of me. "So far, I'm halfway done. Mollie, you're breezing through your worksheet, aren't you?"

She looked at me suspiciously, as if she knew I was putting on a show but couldn't figure out why. "Yeah."

"Well, make sure you're doing it right," Mr. Brooks told her, stepping through the dining room to get to the kitchen. "Bree, turn that TV down. You know what I said about the volume being over halfway."

I could hear Bree say, "Give it to me, Nikki."

And Nicole's sharp response of, "It's *my* turn for the remote."

"Mr. Brooks, I've got a question for you," I started, waiting for him to turn around before continuing. "Before you say no, remember who you're saying no to."

He gave me a tired smile. "Addy Arden, the girl who keeps Mollie on the straight and narrow?"

"Exactly." *Because Mollie has* such *a hard time staying out of trouble.* "You know our friend Vesta, right?"

That smile of his disappeared. "The girl who tries to pull Mollie *off* the straight and narrow?"

"Dad," Mollie sighed. "She doesn't do that."

Even her dad was having issues with Vesta. My hope for what I was about to ask lessened. "Well, I'm going to her house on Wednesday and we're going to have a little girls' night. I was hoping Mollie could come."

The lines on his forehead deepened. "You mean, like, a sleepover? On a school night?"

"We get into bed by ten o'clock," I assured him, keeping my confidence in place even though his frown was a little intimidating. More like majorly intimidating. "We get to school on time. We keep the junk food to a minimum." Okay, maybe the last one was a lie, but he didn't need to know that.

"I'm sorry, Addy, but Mollie isn't allowed out on school nights," he answered, and turned toward the fridge.

Last card I've got to play. "I know, I was just hoping maybe this time you could make an exception." I tried to mimic the expression I'd given the substitute teacher this morning, but perhaps a little less ill. "I just haven't gotten to be with everyone since...since everything happened, and things have been so hard, you know?"

Though I was channeling those fake emotions to fool Mr. Brooks, I found a very real pressure start to build behind my eyes, an ache forming in my throat. I'd tiptoed too close to the edge again, got too close to the sadness I tried so hard to avoid.

But it worked. The lines returned to their normal resting state, Mr. Brooks's eyes softening. I could practically see the gears working in his mind. *Yes, Addy Arden has had a rough go of things lately. She hasn't been over as much, but it's understandable as to why. What am I supposed to tell her, no?*

"You can promise me in bed by ten?" he asked, tipping his hand. "You wouldn't lie to me?"

Even before he'd finished his sentence, a wide grin split across my face. "Yes, of course. Mr. Brooks, you're the best dad in the world, you know that?"

The words tasted horrible on my tongue, like someone had taken a piece of sandpaper and scrubbed at my taste buds. Curling my fingers, I forced my mind to clear, forced the emotions back into the box. The taste, though, remained.

"Get your homework finished or else I might change my mind," he said warningly, but I caught him smiling just a little as he turned away. "When you pack your things, Mollie, make sure you have your inhaler."

Mollie didn't look as excited as I'd been expecting. "I always do, Dad."

"You've got plans on Wednesday," I informed her as her dad ventured further into the house, triumphant.

"Addy—"

"No excuses," I declared with a shake of my head, tapping my pencil against my worksheet. "I suggest you figure out whatever's going on between you and Vesta before Wednesday, or we're going to have one awkward sleepover."

She sighed heavily, falling back into her seat. "Has anyone ever told you how devious you are?"

I couldn't help but grin. "If the shoe fits."

The next day, Mr. Walker was thankfully back at school, and didn't allow class time for the partner project. But this time, Vincent wasn't there. After the starting bell rang, a part of me expected him to just show up tardy—maybe he'd woken up late—but he never appeared.

Which was unfortunate, since we were supposed to go to Bayview today.

I wondered if he'd forgotten. Or maybe he was sick and couldn't find a way to let me know. I wished I would've asked for his number so I could text him, but then again, I couldn't imagine the actual act of texting him. Vincent didn't strike me as a texter. He wasn't sitting at his usual lunch table, nor did he stop by his locker after school.

I kind of sounded like a stalker, keeping an eye out for him, but we *did* have plans.

Ha. Vincent Castello and I had plans. So bizarre. Even more bizarre that it was becoming a normal thing—us hanging out together. Mega weird.

"Hey," Bryce said as he came up to where I stood at my

open locker, his wave of citrus cologne hitting my nose. He must've just put some on. "I finally get you alone."

He leaned against the locker beside mine, looking a little out of place. I couldn't remember the last time I'd seen Bryce one-on-one, without anyone else around. Had it really been since the fall?

"What are you doing tomorrow?" he asked. "I can't hang out today, but maybe we can get dinner?"

"Mollie, Vesta, and I are having a girl's night." I'd already booked the nail appointments—one of our favorite ways to pamper ourselves. "What about Thursday?"

"I've got a tutoring session." He watched me pack my math book into my backpack. "You're having your sleep-over, huh? That's cool."

I cast him a sidelong smile, tucking my hair behind my ear. "Sorry, but no boys allowed."

When he looked at me like that, with his baby blue eyes wide and open and unsure, it was easy to see what had drawn me in to him in the first place. He was just so cute. So kind. Mom had immediately fallen in love with him when he came to study at the house once. Even Dad had liked him, and dads weren't supposed to like any prospective boyfriends, right?

"What do girls even talk about for that long?" Bryce asked. "Do you just gossip?"

"Oh, yeah. I've missed out on an entire month—I've got to catch up on all the Greenville scandals."

I wasn't sure whether Bryce knew anything more about Vesta and Mollie's fight, if I was supposed to call it that. I couldn't figure out why he *would* know, but I also didn't want to talk about them with him. Gossiping about that felt like a violation of girl code.

"Did you end up finding dresses for the dance?" he asked.

He was asking about the dance? Did that mean he was about to ask me to be his date for it? My heart started beating a bit faster at the idea. "Uh, yeah."

"What colors did you guys end up going with?"

Was he asking so he could match me? "Mollie's is gold, Vesta's is white—of course." It was her signature color. "And mine's a navy blue."

Bryce took in the information with a nod, straightening from the locker and leaning in close. "Listen, I—"

"Hey, you two," Vesta greeted as she walked up, zipping her coat. She was looking down and must not have noticed the moment between Bryce and me. "I saw Mollie heading for the bus."

"Did you talk to her?" I couldn't keep the hope from my voice; maybe things could go back to normal in time for the sleepover.

But Vesta frowned a little. "No, I just saw her walking. It would *suck* to not have your license, wouldn't it?"

"She'll pass the test someday," I said with total faith, drawing my coat from my locker. I'd told Vesta this morning that Mollie was joining our girls' night tomorrow, and she seemed excited about it. It left me wondering if things were okay on Vesta's end, but not on Mollie's. Sure seemed that way. "Hopefully the roads aren't bad. I've got to drive all the way out to Bayview."

Well, maybe. I figured maybe once I got home, I could

see if Vincent's number was listed one of those online phonebooks, or I could try to dig up one of our physical ones. A long shot—our phonebook was probably outdated anyway—but it was worth a try.

"By yourself?" Vesta asked. "I can tag along, if you want. Keep you company. I don't have anything to do but homework, and who cares about that?"

My fingers fumbled with the buttons. I hadn't realized she'd offer to come with me. Quickly, I searched my brain for an excuse. "I'm okay going alone. I like to...think." *Ha, yeah right.*

"That's a long way to drive by yourself," Bryce said, his voice tinged with worry.

"I'll be fine," I assured them, and slammed my locker shut. "I'm a good driver."

As we walked outside, I saw it immediately. All the air in my lungs came out in one *whoosh.* Vincent's black truck was pulled up in the space behind my convertible, looking like a hulking monster beside it.

I must have been the only one to notice because Vesta and Bryce kept chatting without missing a beat. I could barely hear what they were saying. There was no way I was climbing into Vincent's truck with them there.

Through the windshield, I could see Vincent had his head down, tousled dark hair hanging in his eyes. He hadn't seen me yet. "Crap," I said suddenly, stopping in my tracks. "I forgot my textbook."

Bryce shook his head. "Your algebra one? I saw you put it into your bag."

"No, my—uh—history book. We've got a quiz tomorrow and I really should study."

The benefit of both of them being in a different grade than me was that they had no idea I was lying. Instead, they both shrugged. "Well, text me when you get back into town, okay?" Vesta said, reaching out and giving me a hug. "Let me know you're safe and sound."

I promised her I would before turning on my heel and quickly heading back into the building. It felt cowardly, running and hiding, but I had no choice. My body had already decided, already started carrying me back inside and away from potential confrontation.

To at least be a little bit truthful, I walked all the way back to my locker and pulled out my history textbook, shoving it into my backpack. The unnecessary weight was annoying, but compared to the guilt of lying, it didn't seem so bad.

Still, I lingered by the doors for a moment, afraid that Vesta and Bryce wouldn't be out of the parking lot yet.

"Addy?"

I turned around to find Mr. Walker watching me, coat on and satchel over his shoulder. He looked so short in the doorway, maybe only a few inches taller than me. "Hey, Mr. Walker."

I half expected him to keep walking, but he hesitated, obviously trying to decide if he wanted to say whatever was on his mind. "Have you started your peer interview yet?"

Oh, that's it. "With Vincent, you mean?"

His expression tightened a bit. "Yes, with Vincent. Pairing you up wasn't intentional, but—I'll be honest—I've been waiting for you to come and ask for an alternative assignment."

Knowing even Mr. Walker had a prejudice against Vincent made me feel oddly annoyed. Or maybe he was just nervous for me, wanting to look out for each of us. "We've already started interviewing each other."

"And how's that going?"

In the grand scheme of things, we really hadn't discussed much. We hadn't talked about Vincent's favorite memory—and I wasn't sure if we'd get to that one—hadn't touched on biggest fears, biggest dreams, and plenty of other things. "We're getting there. He's got a job, so it's been hard to work around that."

"Well, I'm proud of you for sticking it out. Especially given the situation between your families."

The situation between your families. The way he said it sounded so clinical, as if we had a family feud rather than—

"Thanks. Have a nice night, Mr. Walker," I told him with a sharp inhale, turning and shoving through the doors without a second thought. Even if Bryce and Vesta hadn't left the parking lot yet, I didn't care. I just couldn't stand talking to him anymore.

Fortunately, Vesta's tan car was gone, and so was Bryce's.

Vincent, however, was staring straight through the windshield at me.

Anticipation stirred within me, and I found myself walking faster, each step propelling me closer and closer to him.

ten

"Took you long enough," Vincent said as soon as I pulled the passenger's side door open. He folded up his journal, tucking the pen into the loop on the side. "Why'd you have to go back inside?"

So he *had* seen that. "I forgot my textbook."

"Ah, so it had nothing to do with you not wanting your friends to see you getting into my truck?"

Vincent's voice was level as he spoke, and even his expression was neutral when I looked up in surprise. "Of course not," I said, but the words sounded phony. I was good at lying to everyone but Vincent? Not fair. "I didn't realize you'd be out here waiting for me."

"I told you we'd go to Bayview on my day off."

"Yeah, but you didn't mention that you'd pick me up after skipping school," I pointed out.

Vincent put the truck into reverse, expertly slipping out of the parking space. "I had errands to run."

"Uh, I'm not sure you're allowed to run errands during school hours."

He didn't seem too bothered by the prospect of getting in trouble. He merely shrugged, switching the subject. "Did you know that Jackson likes your small friend?"

"Small?"

"'Short' sounded rude."

That got a surprised laugh out of me. "It's not. She *is* short. But Jackson...he just thinks she'd be a good challenge." I could practically read his mind: he only wanted her because she'd told him that she wasn't allowed to date. "Off-limits" didn't exist with that kid.

"I don't know," Vincent said, slowly braking at a stop sign. His tires protested a little bit, a shuddering effect that I could feel with a jump in my pulse, but Vincent seemed to barely notice as he eased up on the pressure. "From what he's said to me, he really seems into her. I guess they talked at a party and really clicked."

My brain snagged on one thing first: Vincent and Jackson talked? Why? Were they friends? They seemed so drastically different. And then the rest of his words sunk in. "A party?" I frowned and looked at him head-on. "*Mollie* went to a party?"

"Jeremy's New Year's Eve party. At least I think that's the party Jackson mentioned. I can't really remember." Vincent risked a glance from the road to me. His black hair was tucked behind his ear, giving me a clear view of his features. "Why? Does Mollie not usually go to parties?"

"Never." I slumped back in my seat, feeling more confused than before. Just when I felt like I was understanding my friends again, something new popped up. Mollie at a *party*? Mollie had a curfew of nine-thirty on weekends. How on earth did she get permission to go to a party? Especially a New Year's Eve party. My brain couldn't even grasp the image of her sneaking out.

I couldn't think about that now. There was no point in dwelling on the unknown when I couldn't ask Mollie about it. That'd have to wait. Bayview was a long drive, and right then and there, I made the resolution that there would be no awkward silences.

Instead, I'd make this trip productive. I reached down into my backpack and withdrew my bullet journal. "I love horror movies," I told Vincent, the words sounding a bit random. "But no one watches them with me. My friends love comedies and romance—yuck. Horror? Right up my alley."

He took the subject change in stride. "What's your favorite horror movie?"

"Ugh, don't ask me that," I groaned, slipping lower on the bench seat. "Because it's impossible to choose. You'd have to ask me about different tiers—wet-my-pants scary, cheesy scary, or cinematically scary."

Vincent made a noise, and if I hadn't known any better, I would've said it sounded like a chuckle. "Give me all of them."

"Hmm. Have you ever seen the movie *Darkness Within*? That was scary. I couldn't sleep for a week." I tapped my finger along my chin as Vincent waited to turn onto the main road. "*Mirror Man* had some really good cinematography. I never thought much about that aspect of scary movies before, but it plays an important role, you know?"

"Oh, *absolutely*."

He was definitely mocking me, but I wasn't letting that steer me off course. "For cheesy scary movies, *Evil Killer Babies* is my favorite."

Vincent looked over at me, skeptical. "You're making that up."

"You've never seen it?" I started to grin, trying to imagine Vincent sitting down and watching even five minutes of it. "Oh, you have to. It's the worst movie ever, but it's *brilliant*. I die laughing every time."

"I thought you said you didn't like comedies." He finally pulled out onto the main road, which would take us out of town.

"I don't, but this is a movie trying to be seriously scary— which makes it hilarious. You need to watch it sometime. It might become *your* favorite cheesy horror movie."

He shook his head, but said, "Do you own it?"

"Uh, of course! I could bring it over sometime and we could watch it."

The words were out of my mouth before I even registered what I'd said. I'd just invited myself over to Vincent's house to watch a movie. When I looked up to see Vincent's expression, my insides twisted almost painfully. His brows were raised; he was clearly taken aback by my proposal. Probably trying to think of a polite way to say no.

"Or," I rushed to say, stumbling over my words, "I can just loan to it you. That's probably easiest. Unless you don't really want to watch it, which is okay too."

Vincent didn't say anything, which in that moment was *so* aggravating. I wished I knew why he gave such selective responses, why sometimes he'd just pretend he didn't hear something. Was it because he felt uncomfortable? Because he didn't know how to respond? I had no clue.

But then he said, "It'd be rude to deprive you of watching your favorite movie, wouldn't it be?"

I started to smile when I realized what road he'd turned onto. Ice water dumped over my skin, freezing me to the seat, freezing my eyes out the windshield in front of us.

Growing up in this area, living here my whole life, helped me recognize roads in an instant. We'd just turned onto Ridge Road. I'd never liked Ridge Road, hating the big ditches it had on either side, hating the winding, sudden curves.

With all of the snow, it was hard to really see where the edge of the pavement stopped too, especially when everything drifted...

"Please," I whispered, voice barely a sound. Barely louder than the frantic beat of my heart, than the blood rushing in my ears. Pressure built in my chest, making it feel tight, about to explode. "Stop the truck."

"Stop? Why?"

He hadn't started braking, but I felt him let up off the gas. "Stop the car," I repeated, or at least I thought I did.

Vincent processed my request—my plea—a second too late. He'd crested the hill that had obscured the sharpest turn in Fenton County from view. I recognized it in an instant.

I hadn't seen the scene of Dad's accident in person, but in my mind's eye, it was perfectly clear.

Navy sedan barely visible from the giant ditch.

White SUV crashed into a tree.

Broken glass scattered across the snow.

Hole in the windshield.

He was killed on impact—a monotone voice. *Didn't feel a thing.*

My hand scrabbled for the door handle, tugging against the locked door frantically enough for Vincent to react. "Wait! What are you—Adeline!"

I managed to unlock the door and throw it open, even though the truck was still moving. Barely. Vincent had started braking at the first signs of my panic, but he hadn't come to a complete stop. Not yet.

In some corner of my brain, I knew jumping wasn't the best idea. Not when we were still moving, not when there were ditches, but I was so disconnected from that part of my mind that the thought zoomed past, as if we were still going fifty miles per hour.

Giving myself no time to breathe, I jumped out of the truck.

eleven

I thought I'd land on my feet, which, looking back, was a ridiculous thought.

I lost balance as soon as I hit the ground, a combination of my momentum and the ice patches underneath the soles of my shoes screwing me over. I was lucky I hadn't fallen into the eight-foot ditch, missing it by mere inches as my hands fought for purchase in the snow. Clumps laced with stones sliced at my fingers, and I could hear Vincent's truck tires squeal in protest as he slammed on the brakes.

The sound reminded me of Mom's scream.

As I came to a stop on my side, I had one thought: *what the heck is wrong with me?*

The world stopped spinning as I pushed to my hands and knees. Snow covered me, pressed against my bare palms, but I could barely feel the sting of the cold. The fall had knocked the wind out of me, and each gasp of icy air burned my lungs.

Distantly, I knew I was shaking like a wet dog left out in the cold, shaking like a leaf in strong winds, shaking like a girl who'd faced a ghost of the past. The images of the cars were still burned into my imagination, still bloody, still broken.

I heard a door slam, then Vincent's loud, shaky shout. "Are you insane? You're freaking insane! You just *jumped* from a moving vehicle!"

His shadow fell over me as he came close, and even though I looked up at him, I couldn't really see him. The fish-eyed lens layered over my vision made things blurry, wavy. Even my voice didn't sound right. "It wasn't moving that fast."

"It was still *moving*." Vincent's gaze caught on something at ground level, a sharp breath pulling in through his teeth. "Adeline, your *hands*."

My palms were still flat in the snow, but when I looked down, I saw that there was red smeared in the white. I'd torn my tights, too, and the bare skin of my knees pressed into the ground. My coat seemed to be okay—dirty, but not torn. All at once, the sharpness of the pain broke through my awareness, my hands throbbing with the ache.

When I lifted my palms to inspect them, my stomach rolled. Long, jagged edges cut across my skin, dirt sticking to the wounds, melted ice mixing with blood.

"Ow," I said belatedly.

Vincent knelt beside me in the snow, his jeans immediately dampening. "You think?" Gently, he reached over and held my wrist lightly, angling it so the blood wouldn't trickle onto my coat sleeve. His touch was soft, as if my wrist were made of glass. "Jeez, why would you jump from the truck, Adeline?"

"I don't go on that...curve. This is the road—" I cut myself off, finally able to draw in a breath that seemed to stick. "I don't go down this road." He would know what this road was. He would know.

"How do you get to school if you don't go down this road?"

This was one of the busiest roads in the town, especially during rush hour. It was a direct route from commercial Greenville to the residential side, but it wasn't the only road.

"I take Brewer."

"Brewer," Vincent echoed. "You add an extra five minutes to your commute just to avoid this road?"

I pulled my hand from his, wincing from the pain. "Yeah."

I prepared for him to make fun of me. Call me a drama queen. As time stretched further, I realized he wasn't going to. Vincent just regarded me silently, both of us kneeling in the snow, the chill finally starting to raise goose bumps on my exposed skin.

After a moment, Vincent cleared his throat. "Come on, let's get you back to the truck. I've got a first-aid kit in the glove box."

Much like Jackson had yesterday, Vincent helped me to my feet, and I relied on his strength to pull me up. I was still shaking all over, but not from the cold. The tremors were coming from my core—I couldn't suppress them. My legs wavered from the pressure, and I realized for the first time how much my knees hurt from landing on them. I moved to take a step and immediately one of my legs buckled.

Vincent stepped closer, grip tightening. "Are you okay?"

No, I was going to die from embarrassment. For a moment, I leaned against Vincent, trying to steady myself. I inhaled deeply, his scent filling my nose. He smelled like honey and coffee, comforting and warm.

"I don't even know why I did that," I murmured, looking down at my torn hands. "I just jumped. I didn't even think."

"Fear does that. Fight or flight," he said, helping me back to where he'd stopped the truck.

Fight or flight. I'd definitely tried to take flight. "You'd think the idea of jumping out of a moving vehicle would be worse."

"Sometimes all you think about when you're scared is getting away."

I still felt that way. We were too close to the curve—if I moved my head, I would be looking at it. I would be picturing crunched cars and broken glass. *Push it down,* I told myself, trying to control my breathing.

"Too bad I didn't stick the landing," I said as Vincent pulled open the passenger's side door and helped me inside. Unsurprisingly, my joke fell flat.

Once again, Vincent made that chuckling sound, but his expression was hard to read. He popped open the glove box and pulled out a small red first-aid kit, opening it up and immediately finding the gauze.

"What's your biggest fear?" I asked him, knowing that I was breaking our rule.

To my surprise, Vincent answered this one, but didn't look at me while he did. Instead, he focused on extracting a small antiseptic wipe. "Losing my dad."

There was something in the way he spoke that felt so *real*. He wasn't saying that to inadvertently hurt me—he was being honest. "Because it's just you two."

"I can't imagine life without him, without the café. It's unthinkable." Vincent looked up at me through his lashes, the green shuttered with black. "Your turn."

Something in my stomach tightened at the way he looked at me. So badly I wanted to lie and say "clowns" or "spiders," but I knew the truth. "This road."

That intensity didn't leave Vincent's gaze until he looked back down to my hand. He dabbed the wipe across my skin, trying to be as gentle as possible. A lock of dark hair fell across his forehead, and as he pushed it away with a ringed hand, I was struck, rather randomly, with how *attractive* he was.

It was a stray thought, like "oh, the sky is gloomy today"—"oh, Vincent Castello is good-looking." He wasn't cute in a way that would normally catch my attention, what with the long hair, lip piercing, and ripped jeans, but there was something about his eyes. The seriousness there, the way he watched me. It made everything in my body *aware*, tingling all over.

I looked at him for a long moment. He had secrets in him, so many. I wanted to know them all. I wanted to pry his head apart and peek inside, see everything that made him tick. That was the whole point of the project, but it was more than my grade propelling me now. It was so, so weird how invested I was in getting Vincent to spill his life story. I didn't even understand it myself.

Vincent crumpled up the wipe and moved to the gauze next. "I'd use a normal bandage, but I must not have restocked them last time."

"That's okay," I replied, but my voice was way too high to sound normal. Vincent looked up again, probably afraid I was going into shock or something, as another idle thought ran across my brain: *He's even prettier than Bryce.*

"Did you hit your head?" he asked.

"What? Why?" Had I said the Bryce thing out loud? Oh my gosh.

Vincent continued wrapping my hand. "Just trying to figure out if we should stop by an ER or something."

I shook the strange thoughts from my mind. "I'm okay. I think my hands and knees took the brunt of it." My skin poked through the tatters in my tights, but thankfully, the scrapes weren't deep enough to break skin. The fabric, though, was beyond saving.

Once Vincent finished wrapping the gauze around my palms, he said, "Next time, let's wait for the truck to actually stop, yeah?"

I traced the gauze with a finger. "Yeah."

Vincent lingered for a moment before taking a step back to shut my door. I looked at the tears in my leggings. There was no way I'd want to wear these in public. Without thinking further, I reached under my skirt for the band of the tights, wiggling them down past my knees.

So when Vincent rounded the corner to the other side and opened his door, he saw me in the process of taking off my tights. He faltered for a second, averting his eyes, before getting out, "Uh, are you—what are you doing?"

"They're ripped," I said in a *duh* tone, careful not to put too much pressure on my injured palms. At least his reaction took my mind off the road in front of us. Took my mind off my aching hands. "Relax, it's not like I'm taking my skirt off."

"Yeah, but you're literally *undressing*." His voice sounded so distressed that I nearly had to laugh.

With one final tug, I pulled my tights completely off, sliding my feet back into my flats. "Actually, I *undressed*. Past tense. You can look now."

When he glanced back into the cab, his gaze immediately fell to my bare legs. The cold air slipped against them, causing me to shudder.

When Vincent finally climbed into the truck, I could've sworn his cheeks were red. "I'll turn around and we can go down Brewer, okay?"

I sagged a little in the seat, relief making me dizzy. After shoving my tights into my backpack, I shot him a look full of gratitude, refusing to look out the windshield. "Thank you."

Mrs. Keller should've warned me that the arch was ginormous. It looked like it was made out of a white wicker and lattice-like material, with blue vines laced through it. I had zero idea how I was supposed to be getting it anywhere. It definitely wouldn't have fit in my car.

"This'll be a breeze," Vincent had said once he got a look at it. "I've got straps in the back that'll hold it down."

"It'll fit?" I hadn't been so sure. Maybe on its side...

But Vincent had no doubts. He and one of the store employees worked on getting it out to the back of his truck while I gathered the fake snow. I hadn't been sure how much to get, so I just got three big bags worth, hoping it'd be enough.

I hadn't thought about the car ride home with it, though. Vincent's truck didn't have a backseat, so I had to hug a bag on my lap and let the other two rest in the space between us. The plastic of the bag made my hair feel staticky.

My hands no longer stung, but every once in a while, they'd throb. If I shifted my fingers enough or curled my hand around the faux snow, they'd hurt. Hopefully I'd be able to hide the injury from Mom. That would get difficult to explain.

By the time we pulled back into the school's parking lot, it was a little after seven, the sun completely disappeared from the sky. "I'm sorry that you wasted your day off on this," I told him, feeling guilty.

"I didn't mind. If I did, I wouldn't have agreed to it." The statement was so simple that I found myself just nodding. Vincent stopped the truck in the space beside the convertible, shifting the gear into park. "I can come early tomorrow to drop the arch off."

"You're seriously a lifesaver. It'll look great at the dance."

Vincent's face glowed with the dashboard lights, but in the darkness, it was impossible to see the color of his eyes. "I can't imagine having to be in charge of dances. It sounds like a nightmare."

That made me smile. I couldn't quite imagine Vincent Castello in charge of a dance either. "I can't imagine you *attending* one."

"No kidding."

Around the bags of snow, I lifted my palms, bandages facing him. "Thanks for this."

"Can I ask you something?"

I wanted to tease him and say "actually, that's against the rules" but he'd said it so seriously that it made my heart skip a beat. "Sure."

"Have you ever talked to someone about everything?"

Something tight and prickly swept through me, and the longer I looked at him, the stronger it became. All of the thoughts I'd been keeping pinned back rallied at the encouragement of Vincent's question, ready to break free and overwhelm me. "We said we wouldn't talk about the accident."

"I don't mean the accident," he said evenly. "I mean losing your dad."

He had on that stupid blank expression and it made me want to hit him. Hit him so hard that my stupid palms would bleed again. That spiky sensation flared into anger, ready and hot. "That's not any of your business," I all but snapped, pushing against the seatbelt latch. "You don't know anything about it."

"I don't," he agreed, but spoke quicker now, as if trying to get the words out before I left. "I just know if I were your position—"

"But you're not," I cut him off sharply, shoving my door open. I'd been so hasty that I almost clipped the side of my convertible, catching the truck's door at the last second. "Save the psychoanalysis for the report."

"Adeline." Vincent's hand came down on the bag of fake snow that sat between us, refusing to let go. "If you have panic attacks so often, you should—"

"I don't have panic attacks."

He raised an eyebrow. "Oh, yeah? What do you call jumping from a vehicle? Or how you reacted to your flat tire?"

Of course Vincent got to witness both of these instances, but he didn't get it. He didn't know the truth. Those weren't panic attacks. He'd said so himself, today was fight or flight. As for my tire, that was grief trying to spill out. And I couldn't let it. A momentary lapse, but not a panic attack.

"You know, I think I've got enough for my report." My voice shook as I spoke, and I tugged the snow from his grip, forcing all three bags into my arms and climbing out of the truck. I couldn't listen to him talk like this. "Hopefully you've got enough for yours." And I shoved the passenger's side door shut behind me.

I almost expected him to roll the window down, not letting the conversation end on that note, but he didn't. He also didn't pull out of the parking space. He just sat in the idling truck, no doubt waiting for me to look over, but I sure wasn't going to. I should've listened to my gut instinct before. Pairing with Vincent Castello had been a mistake.

After shoving the bags of snow into the backseat, I jammed my key in the ignition, barely having enough time to buckle my seatbelt before I pulled out of the space, leaving Vincent and his stupid opinions behind.

twelve

$\mathcal{I}$'d been ready to get Wednesday over with as soon as possible.

In first hour, I locked eyes with Vincent the moment I entered the room. He was never in his seat before me, so my gaze had automatically snagged on his sitting figure. His expression was blank, tapping his pencil on the top of his desk. His inky hair swept cleanly over his forehead, partially hanging into his widened eyes. Even from here, I could see where the light reflected off the metal of his lip ring, drawing my gaze to his mouth. Both corners were turned down in a frown.

Yeah, well, that made two of us. I'd torn my gaze away before I glared at him, my jaw aching from how tightly I was clenching it.

And then, in second hour history, Mrs. Hoff surprised the class with a pop quiz, and I was *so* not prepared for it. Talk about irony.

When I saw Mrs. Keller between classes, she told me that Vincent had dropped off the arch this morning, and it suddenly made sense why he'd been in class early. "He brought it in before school," Mrs. Keller said. "That thing is *heavy*, but I think it's going to look nice. Don't you?"

I smiled and nodded, but I didn't want to confess to her that this was the first time I had no vision for the dance.

But the icing on the crappy cake was when I walked to lunch.

Just as I stepped into the cafeteria, my eyes sought out my usual table, noticing every seat was filled but one. Mine. It was the space between Mollie and Bryce, empty and awaiting me, but that wasn't what had me pausing in my tracks.

It was the fact that, underneath the table, I could see Bryce reaching to trace an outline on Vesta's bare arm. I couldn't see her face, or Bryce's, but it didn't matter. Especially not when Vesta moved her fingers away from her bag of chips to circle Bryce's hand, holding it there for a long moment.

One second ticked into two, and then three, and then four.

They weren't technically holding hands, but it was pretty darn close. Too close.

I quickly backed out of the cafeteria, slumping against the cool concrete wall, just breathing, brain connecting so many pieces.

Vesta hanging out with Bryce. Showing up on my doorstep with him. Almost every time I'd seen Bryce, Vesta was there.

No. Vesta would never do that to you. You weren't seeing what you thought you were seeing.

I took the ugly feeling and shoved it down, deep down, to a place where it would take a while to crawl back out from. Trapping the thoughts. I was getting good at that, pushing things away. It was almost scary.

With a deep breath in, an even deeper breath out, I walked back into the cafeteria. Bryce had pulled back his hand at this point, and Vesta turned to smile at me as I sat down. The emotion slammed against the bars of its cage, but at least it was contained. Unpacking my lunch bag, I smiled back, even though it pinched.

For the entire period, I didn't think about Bryce and Vesta, and I definitely didn't think about Vincent. I didn't once glance in his direction. Instead, I munched on my panini, pretending I didn't have a care in the world.

When had putting on a mask gotten so easy?

Before our appointment at the nail salon, the girls and I stopped at Mary's Place for dinner. Vesta invited Bryce, and I forced myself to believe it was just because he was a part of our friend group. She knew I liked him and wanted him around more.

Do *you like him?* my mind whispered, and it was just another thought I pushed away.

"I still can't believe you slipped in your driveway," Vesta said, gesturing with her fork toward my hand. "I'm glad it wasn't a concussion or anything worse, though."

Mollie was busy cutting through her double chocolate chip pancakes with the side of her fork. She and Vesta sat in the booth across from Bryce and me, and Bryce's shoulder was pressed against mine.

"No kidding," I scoffed, tracing the bandage on my hand. I'd found adhesive bandages in our medicine cabinet, so I got to ditch the bulky gauze. It'd been easy enough to hide it from Mom—I'd only saw her briefly at night, when I came to get a glass of water from the fridge, and I was able to hide my hands in the pocket of my sweatshirt.

"I thought Dad would end up changing his mind about tonight, but he ended up giving me the okay." Mollie didn't lift her gaze from her pancakes. "As long as we stick to our bedtime, it should be good."

Bryce snorted. "You guys have a *bedtime*?"

"Of course," Vesta answered breezily. "It's a school night—I don't know about you, but *I* need my beauty sleep."

I'd started to roll my eyes when Bryce said in a teasing voice, "I don't know about *that*."

The mood shifted immediately. Mollie's eyes met mine for the first time since we'd sat down, her stare oddly intense. At surface level, Bryce's words didn't sound like anything. But the longer his response hung in the air, and the longer no one spoke, the tenser the booth became.

Maybe it was because I could still clearly see the picture of Vesta on Bryce's feed, but I couldn't help but wonder if he was purposefully being flirty. *No*, my brain said at once. *He's sitting beside* you. *He likes* you.

"Can I steal a fry?" I asked Bryce, deciding to ignore what he'd said entirely. I didn't even wait for his approval before grabbing one, swiping it through his pile of ketchup.

"What, your salad isn't filling enough?" Bryce lifted his arm and laid it across the back of the booth, angling his body toward mine. "Did you end up running your errands yesterday?"

I settled deeper beside him, his clean, minty smell coating my senses at once. "Yep. Got the arch for the dance and delivered to Mrs. Keller this morning."

"Whose truck did you use?" Vesta asked.

Oh, *crap*. Why hadn't I thought that through? Crap, crap, crap. "Uh, a friend of mine drove me over there. Her name's...Stella."

I held my breath, waiting for them to pry, but Bryce just nodded. "Well, hopefully it was worth it for the drive."

"I still have to find a date for the dance," Vesta announced, stabbing her fork into her fruit dish. "I mean, even Mollie's got a date—"

At that, Mollie's head whipped up, her cheeks immediately darkening. "*Vesta*."

"Keeping secrets from me?" I tried to keep my voice neutral, but jealousy coursed through me. It seemed like a line crossed, one best friend kept out of the loop. "Who asked you?"

Bryce picked up another fry. "Jackson Mannerfield."

Uh, *Bryce* knew and I didn't? And also, *what*?

If at all possible, Mollie looked redder. "He didn't ask me to the dance. He just asked me out again...on Monday."

"Monday!" Two whole days ago? And she was *just* getting around to telling me? After I'd given him that speech about leaving Mollie alone, he just went and messed with her again? *Seriously?* "Okay, I take back my earlier statement. Tell me *everything*."

"Okay, okay," Bryce said, lifting his palms into the air. "I'm going to go to the bathroom and avoid the girl talk. I'll be back."

Mollie watched nervously as Bryce pushed to his feet, and his warmth faded from my side almost immediately. She still had a few bites of her pancake left, but only pushed them around her plate, soaking up the chocolate sauce. "He caught me before school, when I was on my way to first period, and asked me out."

"That is *so* not what I heard," Vesta was quick to butt in. "I heard that he pulled you into an empty classroom so you two could be alone. He asked her if she'd seen the new superhero movie out, and she said no, and he said—"

"He just asked if I'd go with him to see a movie," Mollie said with a frown. "And that maybe we could go sometime after school together. I can't believe the gossip mill is *that* detailed."

I blinked several times, but the words still didn't make much sense. "And you said..."

"That I'm not allowed to date."

Vesta let out a dramatic groan. "Which I can't *believe!*"

"I'm *not* allowed to date," Mollie repeated, with a note of defensiveness in her voice. "And come on, I know why he's doing it. He's messing with me. I mean, why else would the captain of the basketball team even look twice at *me?*"

It broke my heart that Mollie shared my suspicion, and I nudged Mollie's leg underneath the table. "He sees how amazing you are, of course." The words were for Mollie's sake, because no matter how hard I wished they were true, I still couldn't shake the idea that Jackson had ulterior motives.

"Or he sees me as some type of challenge, in which case, no thanks."

"When are you allowed to date, Mollie?" Vesta asked, voice taking on an edge that didn't sound teasing. "Maybe if you give him a date when he can actually ask you out instead of playing hard to get, he might stick around."

I shot her a look, one torn between incredulity and annoyance. "Maybe she doesn't *want* him to ask her out again."

"She does. Don't you, Mollie? Just because Mollie's not allowed to date doesn't mean she doesn't want to."

"Can we stop?" Mollie asked with a timid voice. "Can we stop arguing? Bryce is going to be back any second and I *really* don't want to talk about this around him."

I couldn't let go of my frustration that easily. With everything that had happened today, I was reaching my boiling point. All of my annoyance with Vincent made it that much harder to calm down. Why was everything so unbelievably annoying as of late? Things between us had never been this tense.

I turned to Mollie. "Why don't you talk to me about any of this?" I demanded, my frustration now targeted at her. "Heck, even *Bryce* knew. Why aren't you telling me any of it?"

"It's not important," she protested, a worried crease between her brows. "With everything you're going through, I just don't want to—"

"Wait, everything *I'm* going through?" So many emotions barreled through me that I had zero idea what was showing up in my expression. "So that's why you two are censoring everything—that's why you wouldn't tell me why you were fighting. Because you don't want to...what? *Burden* me? Seriously?"

Neither one of them spoke, but they both looked properly chastised.

It was funny. When my friends mentioned the accident or my dad like that, my brain just kind of emptied. Everything sinking down the drain. There was nothing but an accelerated heartbeat, all of the air vanishing at once.

Fight or flight.

"Tell me right now," I said. "I don't want to be in the dark of our friendship. Why were you two fighting?"

Mollie turned in her seat to face Vesta, eyebrows up and expectant. I stared the two of them down, waiting for one to crack first, to spill the beans, to tell the truth. Vesta gave me a sad expression, like I was supposed to take pity and let her off the hook, but no way. I was done being left out.

Except time ticked on, and still, no one confessed.

"I'm not feeling up to a girls' night tonight," I told them, grabbing my coat from where I'd shoved it against the wall. "Let me know when you two want to be honest."

As soon as I said that, I regretted it. How could I demand honesty if I wasn't giving it in return?

"Addy—" Mollie started, but I shook my head, not wanting to listen.

I shoved out of the booth just as Bryce was returning

from the bathroom. "Whoa, where are you going?" he asked, and then looked at all of us. "Girl talk over?"

"Yep." I hastily stuck my arms in my jacket, pulling my car keys from my pocket and heading for the door. "Girl talk over."

S tupid Vesta.

       Stupid Mollie.

Stupid Bryce.

Stupid Vincent.

Stupid psychology project.

Organizing my thoughts about Vincent Castello was next to impossible when I kept being reminded of our last conversation. Who was he to tell me that I needed professional help? With all of the stuff I'd heard about his home life and about him being a partier, *he* was the one who needed help. Not me.

And no, therapy wasn't a bad thing, but I was *fine*. More than fine. I was organizing the Snowflake Dance, I was acing all of my classes, and I was...

Fighting with my best friends.

Fine.

My house was quiet as I wrote, my penmanship growing angrier and more scattered the longer I attempted to write this stupid paper.

Vincent Castello thinks highly of his opinion and has no regrets for willingly giving it. Though one might wonder if there's a sensitive guy behind that wall of his, there isn't. Trust me.

I wondered if Mr. Walker would get a kick out of that. In all honesty, probably not. He'd probably give me a F if I turned this in. So I flipped a page in my notebook, trying again.

Vincent Castello has parts about him that make one wonder if there's something deeper, and underneath the layers, there is more. More to the uncaring, mindless jerk who doesn't care what people feel. He makes coffee art—how cute.

Not for the first time, my thoughts were louder than the silence in the house, but this time, I refused to push them down. I relished this frustration. Anger was safe.

As soon as I finished this paper, I'd never have to think of him again. I'd never look in that back corner of the classroom, never show up at Crushed Beanz. Even though that coffee was delicious, and I'd probably be missing a piece of my soul if I never tried it again.

No. I didn't care. After everything, I didn't care.

I heard the hum of the garage door begin to roll up as Mom finally got home around six-thirty. I quickly debated whether I wanted to pack up my things and retreat to my bedroom before she came inside, but I fought the urge, forcing my pen to scribble across the page faster. The ink smudged a bit as my hand passed over what I'd written, but I didn't care.

If I talked to Mom about fighting with Vesta and

Mollie, I had no idea what she'd say. I liked to think she'd side with me, but a part of me wondered if she'd say something like, "Everyone's entitled to their secrets." And they were. Heaven knew I had plenty of my own.

But it was different. There I was, demanding the truth from my two best friends. I knew *something* was going on. They just wouldn't tell me what. It wasn't as if they were coming to me, asking me if I had been hanging out with Vincent. If they'd asked, I would've told them the truth.

Mom took her time shuffling into the entryway, making a show of slumping her shoulders. "Hi, Addy," she said as she unzipped her coat. "Working on homework?"

"Yep."

"What subject?"

"Psychology."

She made a little humming noise but didn't inquire further. In my mind, I tried to tally up all the times I'd seen her in the past few days. Sunday, she'd been home, claiming the TV. She wasn't really watching it, though. Her eyes had been too unfocused for that. Monday morning, she came into my room when I'd awoken fresh from my nightmare. Tuesday, I saw her sitting on the couch, but our conversation lasted only a few minutes until I'd headed up to my room for the night.

After hanging up her coat and purse, Mom ventured into the kitchen, grabbing a glass from the cabinet. "Aren't you supposed to be at Vesta's tonight?"

Briefly, I wondered what Vesta and Mollie would be doing right now. Did they go to the nail salon without me? Were they watching a movie? Or did Mollie just go home?

I pushed that from my mind, refusing to care. "Why? You don't want me here?"

The snapping words were out before I'd even thought twice about them. I kept my eyes on my paper, my pencil writing frantic nothings now. I couldn't concentrate enough on words to make them flow the way they were supposed to.

Mom's voice was filled to the brim with shock and something that sounded like defense. "Why would you say that? I'm just surprised to find you home, that's all."

All the fire that came with being angry at Vesta, Mollie, and Vincent came to the surface, hot and burning. "Oh, that's right, *you* just don't want to *be* home."

She came close enough to the counter to lay her hand flat on my bullet journal, forcing me to glance upward to find heat in her gaze. It was strange seeing so much emotion in her eyes; for the past few weeks, it looked like she'd been stripped of her emotions. Even in Rickett Falls, she'd acted on autopilot. I didn't even think she'd cried while we were there. Then again, neither had I.

"You think I don't notice you're gone all day too?" she asked, and at first, her voice was quiet. "What about Tuesday?"

"I had to get something for the Snowflake Dance," I retorted, rolling my eyes. "That's practically homework."

"And Friday night? More homework? And Saturday morning?" Mom hadn't moved her hand, and the pages wrinkled slightly beneath her fingers. "I have work. One of my coworkers is in the late stages of her pregnancy, and I'm picking up a few hours in her shift. That's why I'm away all the time. I'm not out with my friends."

Me either, I wanted to tell her, thinking about all the times I'd just driven aimlessly, mindlessly, singing to music I didn't care about just so I could keep my mind busy.

"Do you know how hard it is to be the sole source of income?" she demanded, and every part of me locked up, wondering how far she'd take this line of conversation. "How stressful? In a house this big, it's *scary*."

My chest buzzed with a prickly emotion. *Scary* was the fire in her eyes. *Scary* was the box of emotions shaking in my mind, quaking, threatening to break free. "Then sell the house."

"Sell the house!" she echoed, withdrawing her hand and throwing it into the air. "Sell the memories, too? Sell everything we've ever known? Don't you think we've had enough change?"

I thought about how selling the house would make things easier on me. I wouldn't have to keep my head down as I walked through the house. Perhaps the silence of a new one wouldn't feel as deafening. Mom wouldn't be sleeping in the guest bedroom anymore.

"I'm going up to my room," I told her instead of answering, gathering my things.

"Yes, go and lock yourself in your room," she called after me, the second I had my back turned. "That's the same thing as being out with your friends, you know!"

"Why don't you go lock yourself in yours and try it out?" I fired back, glancing over my shoulder to see her face as I added, "Oops. You don't go in there anymore, do you?"

Mom's face slackened, that fire in her gaze vanishing. It was as if I'd socked her in the stomach, because once the heat was gone, pain filled its place. *Too low*, I thought frantically. *Too low of a blow. Apologize, apologize.*

But I couldn't. It was as if someone had taped my mouth shut, super-glued it, stapled it, because there was no parting my lips. I stomped up to my room, eyes down the entire time, and locked the door behind me.

My breathing was ragged, gasping. And the pressure— there was so much *everywhere*, in my chest, in my eyes, in my throat. *You will not cry*, I told myself as sternly as I could, channeling all of my frustration toward that order. *You will. Not. Cry.*

If I cried now, for the first time since...there'd be no damming it back up.

I moved over to my window and shoved the pane open, letting the icy air hit me like a wave. I pictured crystals of frost sticking to my throat, expanding until there was no breathing around them. Breath after breath, desperate for the relief.

I didn't know how long I stood there. Long enough for my nose to go numb, long enough for my lips to feel like ice. Long enough for goose bumps to thread over my skin, like little fingers pressing on every inch of me. Long enough for any tears that may have been in my eyes to freeze, forbidden to fall.

Getting into a fight with my best friends meant that if I went to the lunch table, I'd be admitting defeat. Waving a white flag. I'd be saying, "Yeah, you're keeping secrets from me, but I'm cool with it."

And I wasn't.

So instead, I ate my lunch in the library. It was quiet during lunch hour, and with the librarian in her office, there was no one to yell at me for eating my paninis between the history books and the nonfiction aisle. I'd told her I'd be studying, and she'd been kind enough to let the cafeteria monitor know.

While I chewed, my phone vibrated. Even before I looked, I knew who'd be texting.

Mollie: *Are you coming to lunch?*

I didn't respond. Instead, I set my phone on the table and opened my bag of chips. After a minute passed, another text dinged through.

Mollie: *Addy, I'm sorry, okay? Where are you? I'll come sit with you.*

She'd come sit with me. If she was still fighting with Vesta, she was most likely feeling uncomfortable there without me. She wouldn't come tell me the truth.

I silenced my phone and flipped it over so I couldn't see the screen, but I still stared at it, torn between texting back something snarky and telling her where I was.

One hand and a leather-bound journal slammed onto the table's surface, eliciting a startled gasp from me. "Well, *there* you are. Had trouble finding you."

I looked up to find Vincent staring down at me in my newfound lunchtime habitat. "I'm hiding from the rest of the world," I informed him, tone cool. "And you, actually."

His dark hair was loose around his face today, not styled back. The black t-shirt had so much writing on it that I couldn't quite tell what it said. In one swift movement, Vincent slid into the library seat across from me, crossing his arms on top of the table. "You might need a new hiding place."

"How'd you find me anyway?"

"Cafeteria monitor. Told her I needed to find you for a homework question." Vincent leveled his gaze to mine. "We haven't finished our psych project."

"Uh, yes we have. Or *I* have." To punctuate this, I flipped my bullet journal open to the page I'd been scribbling on last night and tossed it in front of him. "See?"

Vincent scanned the page, eyebrows drawing together. "*A bland, emotionless robot who does more staring than speaking?*"

"When's the last time you had an expression on your face other than an upside-down smile?"

That upside-down smile deepened. "A little harsh, don't you think?"

"Please," I scoffed, turning back to my sandwich. A piece of cheese oozed from the side of the crust, and I swiped it with my finger. "We all know you're going to write something equally harsh about me. You've probably got it written down in your little Italian journal. *Addy, with her skirts and ties, puts on a lying mask to conceal the fact that she has panic attacks. Especially around cars. Coincidence? Unlikely. The girl needs help.*"

Vincent narrowed his eyes at me, his long lashes nearly

shielding their color. "I didn't say what I did to be offensive, Adeline, and you know it."

"Why'd you say it, then?" I folded my arms over my chest. "Were you *concerned*? I'm flattered."

"I know what grief does to people."

"I'm not grieving," I told him without thinking.

We just watched each other, my words hanging in the air. The words alone proved how *not fine* I was. What kind of girl didn't grieve her dad's death? No doubt that question was thrumming through Vincent's mind right now, but his expression was empty. Emotionless. As usual.

Until it fissured. Like a ripple in water, a new expression took its place, one that had lit something behind his eyes. "When I was nine, my mom took me to an amusement park. Just her and me. We spent the entire day riding every ride that we could—I was a short kid, so there weren't many—playing every game, trying every food from the stands. She bought me a t-shirt and a hat, gorged me on cotton candy and funnel cakes."

I held the panini in my hands but didn't raise it to my mouth for a bite. I could only stare.

He blinked once, twice. "That's my favorite memory."

A thick silence fell between us. A weird sensation darted through me the longer it dragged on, the longer neither one of us spoke. But as my mind whirred around Vincent's admission, I saw it for what it was: a white flag.

"Why?" I demanded. "Why is it your favorite memory?"

He didn't answer right away, instead glancing down at

his fingers. "She left us the next day. I woke up, and she was gone."

I slammed the sandwich back down. "*What?* That's when she left? She—she gave you the best day of your life and then just *left?*"

"It was some sort of final goodbye, I guess. But she accomplished what she wanted. It'd been the best day of my life."

Rage flooded through me. This kind of anger almost felt murderous. "Do you have the return address from the letters Frankie sent you? I think I need to make a road trip and rip your mom's head off. Actually, what's her name? She doesn't deserve the title of mother."

The entire world stopped in an instant. Because in response to my murderous rage, Vincent *grinned.* Though perhaps a touch bitter, the smile stretched across his face, his lip ring shifting with the movement. The smile even had teeth. All at once, the anger and resentment disappeared— gone, evaporated, replaced by the sheer surprise at seeing Vincent's smile.

"I've come to terms with it," he said, leaning his head on his upturned fist. "If she's happier with some guy named Franklin, living in the middle of nowhere and trying for round two, so be it. As long as she never abandons Frankie like she ditched me."

His forgiveness was mind-boggling. I seriously couldn't wrap my head around it. "Has she ever written you?"

"Once. That was the first letter. She told me about Frankie, told me that he's happy to know he's got a brother out there in the great unknown. She didn't tell me why she left, didn't apologize. She said she missed me, though, and wished she could see me again. When I sent a letter back, it wasn't to her—I addressed it to Frankie."

I let out a breath, picking back up my sandwich. "Good." She didn't deserve a letter from him. "I'll still egg her house if you give me her address."

The smile he gave me was dimmer now, no teeth, but it was there. Suddenly, something Jonathan had said came back to me. *Once you get that kid to smile, you know you're in his top ten.*

I would've chalked it up to Jonathan overreacting, but given how I'd hung out with Vincent several times and this was the first I'd seen him smile, it made sense.

"I thought you weren't allowed to eat in here." Vincent glanced around at the high rafters of the library.

"Oh, you're not," I said, popping a chip into my mouth to punctuate my statement. "I'm becoming a rule breaker, didn't you know?"

He rolled his eyes at my sarcasm, and without waiting for an invitation, he reached for the bag and helped himself to a handful. "So, why are you in here? For real."

I reached up and adjusted the fit of my tie, because even though I wore it deliberately loose, it felt constricting. "I'm mad at my friends."

"Ooh, do tell."

"They're just...keeping secrets. And not telling me things because they're afraid they'd be a burden." I let out a strangled sigh. "And Mollie—she hasn't told me anything about Jackson. Heck, *Bryce* knew more about the two of them than me."

"*I* know more about the two of them than you," Vincent pointed out, which only helped my case. "But sometimes it's hard to talk about that kind of thing. Do you and Mollie normally talk about crushes?"

Honestly, we never had. Sure, we'd talked about Bryce, but the topic of her love life had never surfaced. She'd always said she couldn't date—I'd never thought to ask her whether she wanted to. Vesta's response yesterday at Mary's Place came back to me. "She's the one who never offers information."

"Hey, just trying to help you figure it out. Everyone has their reasons for keeping secrets. Whether it's because they feel guilty or because they're not ready to talk about something yet. I know what that's like."

His words bounced off my brain, making more sense than they should've. *I know what that's like too,* I longed to say, but instead took another bite of my panini, making sure it was too big to speak around.

"Are you going to come to Crushed Beanz tomorrow?" he asked me.

"Why would I?"

He let out a low breath, one that sounded like a laugh. "Was the music that bad last week?"

I felt my eyes widen, my heart stuttering a beat. "Did Jonathan tell you I was there last Friday?"

"I saw you head out the door like the place was on fire. It was a little humbling if I'm honest."

I debated throwing a chip at him. "I had...things to do." *Like trying not to break down.* "But you guys were good.

Really good." If I concentrated hard enough, I could almost feel the drumbeats vibrating in my chest.

"We could go to Crushed Beanz after school again," he said after a long pause, his gaze heavy on me. "I know your report's all nice and fancy, but I'm not sure I have enough for mine."

Truth be told, I didn't quite have enough, either. There was nothing I'd rather do than spend the day at Crushed Beanz and then listen to Untapped Potential play.

"I've been thinking about reworking a paragraph or two," I said, and then offered the bag of chips to him, a little white flag of my own.

Vincent's eyes softened, like he was about to smile, but not quite. "Then tomorrow it is."

fourteen

One of the worst things about fighting with my best friends was the crushing need to know what they were doing, but not being able to ask. Mollie never really kept up on social media, but even Vesta's page was silent. No status updates, no photos. Bryce's was the same.

I couldn't even social media stalk them to pass the time, to fume over what they were doing without me. Rude.

So instead, I drove.

I liked driving around Addison, a city about fifteen minutes outside of Greenville. I liked weaving through the fancy neighborhoods. Everyone out here was either a lawyer or a doctor or some fancy politician, and I liked looking at the grand houses, trying to picture what kinds of families lived inside. The lawns were all manicured, snow scraped expertly off the black-topped driveways. Luxury cars were almost always secured inside an attached garage, out of sight and out of reach from even the idea of rust.

A part of me wondered what it'd be like to grow up here, surrounded by money. The fanciest thing we owned was this convertible, and its resale value depreciated every single time I backed it out of the garage. But what would it be like to have pictures on the walls worth more than a down payment on a house? What would it be like to drive somewhere and have valet, to have someone come in and clean your house for you, to go to lavish galas?

Mollie used to live in Addison up until last May, before her dad got a new job and downsized. Taking them out of their private school, moving them to Greenville a "quaint lifestyle." In some ways, Greenville was quaint. The houses were smaller, the stores were a bit more Mom and Pop than chain franchises. There was a better sense of community in Greenville, so I understood why Mr. Brooks would want to move here, closer to this school.

If I lived in a beautiful house like the ones I drove past, I'd hate to have to move. I'd hate to have to leave this neighborhood, especially since they salted their roads like pros. Greenville needed to take notes.

I pulled the convertible into the closest gas station, sidling up beside a pump. On the other side of the pump, a girl in a pretty floral-printed suit stood in front of a shiny black SUV, her trench coat unbuttoned. Her dark hair was cut in a pixie, eyes shielded by sleek glasses. I wondered how much of her outfit was designer. She looked like a movie star.

She caught me spying, flashing me a smile full of teeth. "I love that coat. Is that Gilfman?"

I glanced down at the red and white plaid coat I had on, nodding. I'd never been a girl who paid attention to name brands, but I did know that. While I slid the fuel nozzle into the car, I said, "I think it's from a few years ago."

Which probably wasn't the best thing to say, because didn't rich people believe that last season clothes were the equivalent of garbage? Or maybe that was only how they were portrayed in movies.

"I dig it. Gilfman's pieces are some of my favorites. Have you checked out their silk ties?" She nodded her chin at me, and I realized she could probably see the collar of my tie poking out through my coat.

I thought about the tie Mollie and Vesta gave me, still sitting on my desk. "I've seen one."

The girl turned from where gas was pumping into her own car to pop open the rear door, rummaging around for a moment. "This is one of their latest. Look how gorgeous, yeah? The ripples in the colors are to die for."

The stranger passed the silk tie over to me, and I couldn't help but agree with her. The print was busy, busier than most people would prefer, but the mix of pastel blues and greens gave the tie a design that mimicked watercolor. I slid my thumb over the neck, imagining what it'd be like to wear it, to fit it around my collar. "This *is* pretty."

"Keep it."

I looked up to find the girl giving me that same smile, one that was almost intimidating. When I opened my mouth to protest—I seriously had to be holding a one-hundred-and-fifty dollar tie in my hand—she cut me off. "I rarely wear neckties. I'm more of a bowtie girl myself." She gestured to the bow tied neatly at her collar.

"I've never met another girl who wears ties," I admitted, still admiring the cloth in my hand. "Not a girl my age."

And she *was* my age. Or, at the very least, looked close. With her sunglasses on, it was hard to tell. "Same here. That's why I want you to keep it."

The gas station door dinged as it swung open, and a girl in a pastel pink coat came trotting out. "Margot, they didn't have those gummy worms you wanted, so I got bears instead. And got weird looks for it, by the way. I think usually little kids buy gummy bears."

As the girl in the pink coat got closer, I realized there was something about her that stuck out to me. Something familiar. Her hair was dark brown and curly—not as curly as Vesta's, but wavier. She'd braided half of it back out of her face, weaving it so the strands looked like a crown.

When her gaze slid to mine, though, her eyes widened. It struck me then who she looked like—she almost reminded me of Stella from Crushed Beanz, just the total opposite. Wavy brown hair instead of straight black, pink clothes instead of maroons and grays, no makeup instead of the heavy eyeliner.

But there was something about her eyes and the way she looked at me. Wait. *Was* that Stella?

"Gummy bears?" The girl at the pump—Margot—sighed, turning around to face her friend. "Those *are* for children. Worms, however, are more refined."

The girl had stopped staring, practically tearing the passenger door open and sliding inside without another word. At the same time, my gas pump clicked off, and I reached for the nozzle with one hand, still clutching the silk tie in the other.

"Are you sure about the tie?" I asked Margot, even though I was feeling several kinds of confused. I'd struck the lottery of ties and there were no strings attached?

"Of course. Us tie girls have to stick together," she said with a sideways smirk, and slid into the black car. With how tinted the windows were, she disappeared the second she closed the door. Only a handful of seconds passed before she pulled out of the lot, tires squealing in protest of a fast acceleration.

I looked down at the silk Gilfman tie, at the watercolor pattern that would look so cute with my teal skirt. That was the weirdest encounter I'd ever had.

I thought about the girl in the pink coat. She couldn't have been Stella, I decided. Stella had been so bubbly and friendly at Crushed Beanz; no doubt this girl would've said something if they were the same person. Were they related, maybe?

I slid the tie into my coat pocket. I needed to stop by Addison more often.

When Friday rolled around and I still hadn't made up with Vesta and Mollie, a part of me wondered, a bit frantically, how long this would stretch out. What if they never budged? What if they never told me what was going on? Vincent was right—everyone was entitled to their secrets. But was their secret worth losing our friendship over? Was I the kind of friend who would force it out of them?

The situation with Mom wasn't any better. We hadn't spoken to each other at all yesterday—I'd heard her rummaging downstairs, but I hadn't gone down to investigate. When I finally got thirsty enough to venture to the kitchen, she'd already locked herself in the guest room for the night.

At lunch, I'd been surprised to find Vincent already sitting in the library when I walked in, leaning his chair back onto two legs. He'd had his journal in front of him, tapping his pencil lazily against it. His green eyes had slid to mine. "Took you long enough."

Despite worrying about what I should do with my friends, I found I didn't mind this new lunchtime routine at all.

I couldn't quite pinpoint what had changed between Vincent and me, but something had. Maybe it was the fact that he started to smile around me—something so innocent and yet so abnormal for him. But when he smiled, he seemed so much more *human*. Easier to relate to. Easier to relax around.

And it *was* easier to be in his presence. Maybe it was because those uncomfortable conversations were out of the way. But as we talked through lunch, I'd felt more relaxed than ever.

"When are we going to watch *Evil Killer Babies*?" I asked as Vincent pulled out of the school's parking lot, fixing him with an expectant stare. I'd done a good job of keeping my head down as we climbed into the truck, still too afraid anyone would see. Sure, I was more relaxed than ever, but that didn't mean I wanted to face everything just yet. "You've already accepted the offer, can't back out now."

"The title could've been much more creative," he said with a little sideways frown. "It's quite unimpressive."

"Judgey. Once you start watching the movie, I'm sure it'll be a fast favorite." I settled in my seat, watching as he turned left onto Brewer. "Hallow's the other way, dude."

He snorted. "I have to stop home real quick, if that's okay."

Wait. *Home?* Like...where his dad would be? My voice was clipped with panic I tried to shove down. "Why?"

"I just need to check something. It'll take a minute. Hopefully less." He cast a glance in my direction before settling back on the road. "Hey, what's the deal with the ties? I don't think I've ever seen a girl wear so many ties."

I wasn't sure if he was deliberately trying to change the subject or not, but my brain refused to slip off that path for a long moment. *A minute. Hopefully less. You'll just sit in the car.* "What's the deal with you always wearing black?"

"I like my outsides to match my insides."

Whether or not he'd intended it, I felt my lips twitch. *Unacceptable.* "It makes me feel professional. The only way I accessorize is with ties." And I liked it that way.

"Professional," he echoed. "Like, wedding planner level of professional?"

That smile I'd been shoving down broke free. "You remember that, huh?"

"I've never known anyone who wanted to be a wedding planner. Kind of hard to forget." Vincent reached over and turned up the heat, angling one of the vents in my direction. Warmth fluttered across my face, shifting my hair against my skin. I reached up and pushed it behind my ear, catching Vincent's gaze as I did so. He looked back at the road. "How are your hands healing?"

I glanced down at my palms. I'd been able to take the bandages off this morning, the skin starting to heal over. "Good, I think. They don't really hurt anymore."

Vincent nodded slowly but didn't say anything.

After taking the back way to the residential area—relief poured through me that he hadn't taken Ridge Road— Vincent started to slow down. His eyes trained on a specific house, and when I looked over at him, I saw that his features tensed.

"Of course," he muttered under his breath, turning the wheel sharply and angling into a driveway. He cursed once, low under his breath.

Vincent put the car in park, face pinched into an angry mask. The only time I'd seen him angry was last Saturday at Crushed Beanz, but that'd only been for a moment. The emotion was stark and fierce on his face now. "Stay here," he told me, voice tight. "I'll be right back."

"Are you okay?" I asked, but he was already hopping from the cab, the door slamming behind him. That seemed to be a question he didn't like answering.

Vincent hurried up the wooden ramp that led to his porch, the wood light and new-looking. With a tightening sensation in my throat, I realized it probably *was* new. Maybe a month old.

As I sat in the car, I realized it was strange that Mr. Castello was home from the hospital so soon. With his injuries, I would've thought he'd be in the hospital for months, but he must've made great improvements.

Vincent had left the truck on, so warm air still pumped from the vents, making me a little too hot in my coat. I rolled down my window, letting some of the heated air out.

I sat in the quiet for only a moment before I heard it—muffled shouting coming from the house. A breath caught in my throat. I couldn't tell if it was Vincent or a different voice, but concern swamped through me, so much that I couldn't push it all down.

Popping the door open as gently as I could, I hurried out into the snow. Curiosity propelled me forward, but also something pinched behind my ribs. Vesta would've told me I was being nosy. Mollie would've told me to stay in the car. I *should've* stayed in the car, but I was already walking up the ramp, reaching for the front door handle.

Before I could push it open too far, a voice rose. "You can't keep sending away the nurses, Dad! They're the ones who make sure you don't fall during the day—"

"I know what they're for!" a deep voice thundered back, loud enough to cause me to flinch over the threshold. It sounded as if they stood on the other side of the door. "I don't need them."

"Yeah, *okay*. And how long have you been on the kitchen floor, surrounded by broken glass, huh?"

I drew in a sharp breath, an image filling my mind. The pinching in my chest intensified tenfold, aching worse than my palms. This was personal, an argument that wasn't meant for bystanders, but there was no unhearing it.

As soon as I opened the door and peered inside, I came

face to face with a photo of Mr. Castello—or I assumed it
was him. It hung on the far wall. He had his arms up in the
air, but what drew my attention was the white piece of
paper that was at his stomach, black numbers written on it.
He was wearing exercise shorts and a blue tank top, his hair
pushed back by a sweatband.

My brain hadn't really processed what the photo
meant until I looked over at the next one, and the photo
was almost identical, except Mr. Castello's hair was
shorter and he wore different colored clothes. Vincent
was in this one, but not dressed in the same athletic
attire.

Around Mr. Castello's neck in this photo hung a silver
medallion.

Mr. Castello is a runner, I thought to myself dimly,
peering at the pictures a bit closer, noticing other runners
in the background. No. Mr. Castello *was* a runner. Judging
by the wide, elated smile on his face, it was clear that he
loved it. The medal proved he was good at it. And Vincent
was there, cheering him on.

Mr. Castello was a runner.

And now he was paralyzed.

My skin was hot, hot, too hot, too tight, but I couldn't
tear my gaze from the photographs, glancing back and
forth, praying that they'd change. I wouldn't be staring at
Mr. Castello fresh from a race. No, I'd see him celebrating
because he'd won a chess match. Painted a pretty picture.
Finished building a model boat. Not him finishing a run,
not posing doing something he loved that he could never do
again.

Your dad did this, a voice whispered. *And you didn't stop him.*

The entire time I stared at the photos, the shouting continued, rising to a crescendo. *"Let go of me!"* Mr. Castello yelled, so loud that it nearly shook my eardrums.

"I'm not going to leave you on the floor!"

"Just leave me *be!*" Mr. Castello's voice cracked on the last word, the anger breaking into a pain so profound that it was impossible to think past. When he spoke again, his voice was considerably smaller. "Just leave me be."

If Vincent responded, I didn't hear it. Couldn't hear anything over the loud voices in my head. The box on my mental shelf tipped on its side, smashing to the ground. Any second and it'd all come dripping out—

Vincent came storming around the corner, and even though I expected him to come to a halt when he saw me, he just barreled past, right out the door.

I didn't even think to grab the door behind me; my body was shaking, as if my soul were about to burst from my skin. *Mr. Castello was a runner, he was a runner, and you took that away from him. It's your fault, your fault, your fault.*

Vincent stopped in front of his truck, splaying his hands flat on the hood. "Why?" he demanded, but I wasn't sure if he was speaking to me. "Why can't he just *let me help him*? Why can't he just listen? For once in his life, just *listen*. He knows he can't do this on his own—he *knows* that. Lying in a bed of broken glass should prove that!" Vincent tore a hand through his hair, as if the action would soothe the anger inside him. "But he sends away every single one of the nurses. Every time one gets assigned, he sends them away—like Saturday. He can't be alone, and he doesn't *get* it. It's hard for him, but it's—for me, I'm just —*why?*"

I knew I should've said something encouraging, but the box—it'd opened enough to eclipse every other thought.

I'd never escape the truth. And I shouldn't. It was all my fault.

Dad jingled the car keys in his hand, trying to draw my attention away from the TV. "I'm going to head out to get your mom. Did you want to come with me?"

"No. My show's about to come on," I said, frustrated and stubborn and bratty. He shouldn't have been going, but I was too angry to stop him. And no way did I want to get into a car with him. Maybe he'd get pulled over by the police. Maybe that'd put him on the right track.

I'd kept my gaze glued to the screen until he walked past me and into the kitchen, through the kitchen into the garage. And when the door shut, I felt all of the air rush from my lungs. I hadn't realized I'd been holding my breath.

I'd let him leave, and he never came back. He would never come back.

I'd let him leave, and it killed him. It almost killed Mr. Castello, too. It was my fault. All my fault.

Dad's expression when I said no, that I didn't want to go with him—I'd never let myself think of it again, but now I couldn't *unsee* it. Couldn't get the disappointment out of my head. There was no breathing around it, no pretending the truth didn't exist anymore.

My dad...my dad was dead.

Because of me.

"I'm sorry," he said after a moment, voice so low it was barely audible. "I shouldn't have said that all in front of you, I just—" Vincent turned around then and paused when he looked at me, concern flooding his features. "What's wrong?" he asked, but his voice was so quiet, as if he'd whispered. Maybe he had.

I drew in a ragged breath. "It's my fault," I said, or at least I thought I said it. I couldn't quite hear my words. There was a humming in my ears that drowned out everything, everything but the in and out gasping of my breathing. "It's all my fault."

His gaze was filled with something serious as he traced my face. "What's your fault?"

"It's my fault your dad can't run anymore." *It's all my fault, all my fault, all my fault.*

"Adeline, why—why would it be *your* fault?" Vincent demanded, almost sternly, trying to lower his head so I'd meet his eyes. "Don't say that."

"It was," I insisted, the pressure in my throat growing tighter and tighter until my words sounded nearly hysterical. "My dad had to go pick up my mom from work." Mom hadn't wanted to drive in the blizzard, but since she still had to make it in for her shift, Dad had offered to drop her off and pick her up. Dropping her off was the easy part. Dad never drank anything before noon. "I knew he'd been drinking, and I didn't stop him."

The words came pouring from me, even though the pain in my chest was enough to make me feel like I was about to be sick. The only reason I wasn't hurling right now had to be the cold air, freezing my throat.

I was breathing faster now, too fast. "He asked me to go with him. I was so mad at him. Why would he drink if he knew that he had to pick up Mom? But I knew—I *knew*—I should've driven and gotten her instead. I knew I should've but I—I just—"

"*Did you want to come with me?*"

"*No.*"

I could still hear the garage door shutting behind him, the sound of a chapter ending, a coffin closing—because he would never come back.

When I looked up at Vincent, his face was blurry, the tears in my eyes making it impossible to see straight. I couldn't see his expression, couldn't make out the frown that was no doubt on his lips. "It's all my fault he's gone."

And then whatever grip I had on this moment of time slipped between my fingers, and there was no holding back the dam of emotions any longer.

fifteen

I didn't fall to my knees screaming like Mom had when she'd realized Dad was truly gone. I didn't beg and plead and bargain to any higher power that would listen. No, it was too late for begging. Too late for forgiveness.

I'd never be able to hug him again. Never be able to ride in the car with him again. Never be able to apologize for all of the bratty comments I'd made. I'd never be able to have milkshakes with him on Saturday mornings. Never be able to split a jelly donut with him. Never have the chance to make things right between us.

That pain sliced through me and cut me open, leaving my insides raw and bleeding. The infection ran deep, straight to my soul, and there was no clearing it out.

My dad is dead. He's dead, and he's never coming back.

Sob after body-wracking sob worked through me, fracturing through my bones and marrow, but I couldn't fall into the snow. I wanted to—my knees were threatening to give out—but something was holding me upright, holding me tightly so that I couldn't fall completely apart.

But there was no keeping me together. No keeping the tears at bay any longer. Forcing them down for so long left me rotted on the inside. The box of everything spilled over, all the memories and the guilt and the crushing grief consuming me at once, threatening to swallow me whole.

I was numb to everything except the tightness surrounding my body, like a tether keeping me to this world.

When I caught a whiff of a honey scent, when I felt the bind around me shift ever so slightly, I realized it was Vincent holding me up. His arms were the vise around me, holding me so tightly to his chest that I could barely breathe. My own hands were clutching the soft fabric of his shirt, exposed from his unzipped jacket. I didn't know what would happen if I let go, but I just knew it'd be a bad idea.

Distantly, embarrassment scratched at me, because he was seeing me break into thousands of tiny, irreparable pieces. But along with that embarrassment was relief—I didn't have to go through this alone.

I had no idea how long I clung to him, how long I sobbed into his shirt, gasping things that didn't make sense. I could feel one of Vincent's hands in my hair, smoothing its way down in a comforting gesture. He said nothing. He just held me, and hummed.

It was a song I didn't know, a lullaby I'd never heard, but its peacefulness coaxed its way into my bloodstream, calming the fire inside me. One moment at a time. The pain was still there, a jagged hole torn in my chest, making it near impossible to breathe around.

Breathe, my brain told me, but not in the old way I'd been used to. Not in the way that buried things deep, but in a way that brought water to the fire, pairing it with Vincent's song. *Breathe.*

Clawing my way back from the edge felt impossible, but slowly, my sobs filtered into shaking gasps and shivering sniffles.

Still, I clung to Vincent. Clung to him shaking, afraid to pull away.

"It's not your fault," he murmured after a long moment, voice low enough that I could feel the rumble in his chest. It sounded like a lullaby itself. "It was an *accident*, Adeline. An accident. It would've happened if your dad had been drinking or not."

"He was going too fast." I swallowed hard, hating how broken I sounded. My eyes felt swollen and my throat ached. "He wasn't wearing his seatbelt."

"Did you know that my dad was going too fast too?" Vincent asked, keeping me pressed to him. It was like he knew I didn't want to move away. "Took the corner too sharply. He swung into your dad's lane to correct, and couldn't veer out of it in time. Did you know that?"

I blinked, the world finally, finally coming back into focus. It still blurred around the edges, but I could see Vincent's front door wide open, see our footsteps in the snow. "Don't lie," I whispered. *Don't lie just to calm me down.*

"I wouldn't lie, Adeline. Not about this." The hand in my hair fell to smooth down my spine, and even through my coat, I shivered from the touch. "It wasn't safe for you to be out in that weather—it wasn't safe for *anyone* to be out in it. Don't take the weight of his actions on yourself, okay?" And then, gentler, barely even a word, he repeated, "Okay?"

I pulled away from him, feeling like one half of a magnet tearing apart from the other. Nearly impossible, but I did it. I knew what my face must've looked like. Puffy. Swollen. Red. Tear tracks staining my cheeks, probably peppered with mascara. "I should've stopped him."

Vincent drew his hands back so he could use them to frame my face, tilting my head back so I could peer straight into his eyes. "What would've happened if you had? If you'd gone with him? You could've been in that accident. You could've swerved off the road and nosedived into those ditches."

I hated that he was doing this, trying to shift the blame from me, because deep down, I knew it was mine to own. The guilt was like a brand. For the accident. For not being more loving. For not hugging Dad one last time. I'd checked out of our conversations long before the accident, when his drinking had gotten worse. It'd been a long time since we'd last had a good conversation, and now we never would again.

The tears pooled once more, threatening to spill over as I whispered, "My dad's dead."

There was so much pain in Vincent's green gaze that I nearly choked out a sob. He slid the pad of his thumb along my cheek, wiping away a tear that slipped free. "I know." He leaned closer, so close that I almost thought he'd touch his forehead to mine. "And I'm so sorry."

Vincent's eyes were hypnotic, and the longer I stared into them, the more my resolve crumbled. They helped me feel grounded in the moment, in reality. There was no surrendering the grief and guilt in its entirety, but the slightest amount faded away, the relief like a punch to the stomach. Vincent's hands held me together, wiped away the icy tears that burned down my cheeks.

The moment I'd feared since November had finally come to pass—facing the guilt and pain and grief and moving forward. It was impossible to think about, impossible to comprehend, but with Vincent's gaze on mine, the impossible felt ever so slightly achievable.

He leaned closer, just a fraction of an inch closer, but suddenly he was *everywhere*. His honey scent, bombarding my senses, the green of his eyes, all I could see. The mood changed in an instant, because I was only aware of his mouth and that lip ring and how good it felt to be in his arms, held so tight.

"Are you going to be late for work?" I whispered, sniffling, still holding onto his wrist. It was so warm.

"Arriving late and not getting fired is a perk of being the owner's son," he said with a small, wary smile. Like he was afraid to talk too loudly, afraid to smile too widely.

I found myself staring at his mouth, speaking before I really thought about it. "I like it when you smile."

His lips twitched upward. "I'll try to do it more often."

Vincent waited for me to pull away first, and after a few

more moments of breathing, feeling his pulse beneath my fingers, I did. The warmth from his body disappeared, and I was suddenly on my own, untethered. He eyed me, as if waiting for me to begin crying again.

"I'm okay," I assured him, reaching up and pressing my palms to my cheeks. My tear tracks were cold, but my skin was warm. "I've just never...I didn't let myself think about it."

"Ever?"

"Ever." Now that the numbness was wearing off, the cold of the air had started to hit me, and snow was soaking through my flats. "Sorry you had to witness that."

His green eyes were vibrant as they sought out mine. "I'm not."

The words made me feel even more grounded, made me unable to look away. "Are you...are you ready to go?"

"Do you want to go back home?" he asked. "I totally get it if you'd rather go home."

Home sounded like the last place I wanted to be. I didn't want to face another round of tears and darkness, with no one to help pull me out of it. Though I'd faced the grief and guilt and still struggled to wade through the agony of it, I wasn't sure I was ready to face seventeen years of memories, and the knowledge that there'd be no more new ones.

"I want to go with you," I told him in a decisive tone, heading toward the passenger door. "If you still want me to."

"You don't even have to ask," he answered immediately, moving to his own side.

The words were meant to be reassuring, surely, but they caused some different part of me to shift. Not pain in my chest—a flutter of something else.

Just before I turned to climb into the truck, I remembered the front door. But when I looked, I saw Mr. Castello over the threshold.

I'd never seen Vincent's dad before the photographs, and in a strange way, the two of them looked dissimilar. Vincent's hair was black, a slight wave to his locks, but Mr. Castello's hair was a very light brown, threaded with peppery gray. It was also curly, cropped short to his head. Their facial features were different too; Mr. Castello's jaw was narrow, whereas Vincent's was wide. From here, though, I couldn't tell what color Mr. Castello's eyes were.

I wondered if he'd heard all of that, wondered if he knew who I was.

His expression was sad as our eyes met through the windshield. Mr. Castello only watched me for a brief moment longer before shutting the front door, closing off our connection.

"You ready?" Vincent asked, eyes on me.

The concern hadn't left his expression, nor had the wariness, but I did my best to give him a reassuring smile. "Ready."

It was a little after six o'clock when Harry walked into Crushed Beanz. At first, I hadn't noticed his presence. The door chimed again and again while I was there and I'd gotten used to not looking up, doodling in my bullet journal. I'd planned ahead and packed a few markers this time so I could start outlining next week's spread. It was going to be snowflakes, in honor of the Snowflake Dance.

But when the chair beside me scraped out, I startled, turning to look at the lead singer of Untapped Potential.

His red hair was pushed back behind his ears. Though it was winter, he wore a flimsy jacket, no hat, no gloves. His nose was red, hinting at how cold it must've been outside.

A brilliant smile broke across Harry's face. "Man, you *are* pretty."

Despite everything that had happened mere hours ago, I felt amusement trickling in. Harry's grin was wide and infectious. "You sound surprised."

"Well, see, I asked Vincent if you were pretty and he hesitated. I thought he was lying when he said you were."

"You *hesitated*?" I asked Vincent, almost offended, but then I registered the last part of what Harry said. *He said you were.*

Vincent, who'd been helping a customer, scowled at his bandmate. "I didn't hesitate."

He didn't hesitate.

Harry rested his elbow on the top of the countertop, leaning his head into an upturned hand. He gave me his full gaze, the blue in his eyes piercing. His hair looked even redder under these lights, and a faint sheen of freckles dotted his nose. His face gave the illusion of boyishness, a guy with the enthusiasm of a child. However, taking in all of him—his ripped black jeans, holey sweater, rings all along his fingers— was a different story. Especially with the tattoo on his neck.

I'd been right the other night; the tattoo *was* a hand, or a loose outline of one. Three lines crafted the image, almost like a sketch of fingers, curling around his throat.

"So, your name is Adeline, huh?" he asked, his voice gentle now. Conversational, as if we were already close friends.

"Uh, just Addy," I corrected, wishing another customer would walk in and prove to be a distraction. His undivided attention was a little disarming, but not in a bad way. "I go by Addy."

"Vincent called you Adeline."

"Vincent doesn't know what a nickname is."

Harry's grin broadened. "I like her. Let's keep her."

Vincent set down a mug of steaming water in front of Harry. I'd drank my mocha a while ago and decided that I wasn't allowed to have a refill. For the first time in a long time, I wondered what sleep would look like tonight, hoping it would be good.

Harry barely gave his mug a glance. "You know, normally I have to stare into Vincent's dull eyes, but now I get to stare into yours. It's my lucky day."

All at once, understanding dawned, and I couldn't fight a smile. "You're trying to flirt with me." The realization was almost a shock; it'd been a while since someone had openly flirted with me.

Harry's smile widened, exposing a dimple in his cheek. "Am I that obvious?"

"Harry here is a notorious flirt," Vincent said with a sigh, leaning against the counter opposite of us. The line had finally disappeared, if only for a moment. "Flirts with any girl with a pulse."

"Not true," Harry protested, turning his puppy-dog gaze back to mine. "Only the real pretty ones."

I snorted. "That was shallow, you know that, right?"

"No, that was a *compliment*." Harry batted those ridiculously long lashes, and in that moment I could totally see what Stella saw in him. He *was* cute. So totally not my type, but still cute. "Ooh, I know. You've got a boyfriend."

"Harry, leave her alone," Vincent told his friend, in a tone that sounded a bit less than friendly.

Harry gazed at me over the rim of his mug, still daring me to answer. Now that I knew he was flirting, I almost wanted to laugh aloud. It was easy to tell that this wasn't serious flirting. Harry, like Jackson, flirted just because he could. Because they didn't know how to *not* flirt.

"So, you and Natasha aren't together?" I asked instead, arching a brow. I remembered Vincent saying something about Harry and Natasha having known each other before, and a part of me wondered if that meant what I assumed it meant.

Harry rolled his eyes and *tsked* his tongue. "Natasha. What a gal."

"Which is a...yes? No?"

"It's a 'not anymore.'"

"Thank goodness," Vincent huffed, folding his arms over his apron. "It was impossible to get any practicing done with you two either flirting or at each other's throats."

Harry waved a hand as if to shoo the thought out of my

head. "Don't listen to him, Addy. We were the epitome of a cute couple."

"Then what happened?"

He leaned in, coming close enough that I could smell the woody scent that clung to his skin. "I realized being with her meant I was going to forever be stuck in the past. And I don't want to be. The past is a dark place. A place where the soul runs ragged. I wanted to be free of it."

I couldn't help but smirk. "No wonder you're a singer. You've got the tortured soul thing down pat."

"Tortured doesn't even begin to cover it, baby," he agreed, raising his mug to his lips and taking a long drink.

Vincent watched his friend for a long moment, an unreadable expression on his face. Before anyone could respond, the door chimed again. A very tall woman in a wool pea coat walked in, taking a moment to wipe the soles of her boots along the entryway mat.

Harry immediately stiffened as he spotted her, turning and leaning closer to me. "How do I look?" he whispered. "Be honest."

I thought about saying something teasing, but he looked genuinely nervous, that flirty look in his eyes completely gone. "You look nice."

"Respectable?"

The ripped jeans might've been a stretch, but I nodded. "Very."

He let out a little breath at that, flashing me a relieved smile before he slid from the barstool. And in a second, he flipped a switch, going from nervous and vulnerable to confident, his voice radiating it. "Lily, my dear! How've you been?"

Before they turned to walk into the lounge, I saw a smile pass over the woman's face.

"They know each other?" I asked Vincent, who was just finishing stacking the array of cups.

Vincent casually glanced over at them. "Yeah."

I watched them for another moment, watched Harry nervously wipe his hands on his jeans. "He seems really nice. Flirty, but nice."

"He's something else," Vincent said with a shake of his head, but his eyes were light. "He's had a rough time this past last year, but he's a good guy."

I figured as much, at his *tortured doesn't begin to cover it* comment. I rubbed my fingertips along my arm, leveling my gaze with Vincent's. "I know a thing or two about a rough time."

He hesitated before he spoke, as if weighing his words. The air felt charged as I waited for his response, and I held my breath. "Me too."

"You and your dad..." I said, but then trailed off, unsure how I wanted to finish that sentence.

"Picked up on that tension, did you? The shouting must've given it away."

I looked at him sheepishly. "I didn't mean to eavesdrop."

"It's not like we were being that quiet." He let out a sigh, leaning his elbows onto the countertop. "He and I aren't seeing eye to eye—not like that's anything new.

Apparently his health isn't as important to him as it is to me."

"What do you mean?" I asked, hoping I wasn't prying too much.

If I was, Vincent didn't seem to mind. "He's supposed to have an aide with him now that I'm back in school, at least for a few hours. To help with physical therapy, make lunch, those kinds of things. I keep hiring them, and he keeps sending them home."

The frustration in Vincent's tone made my shoulders slump. I couldn't even imagine being in a situation like that, worrying about someone all day. "That's why you wanted to go home and check on him."

I understood how it could've been hard to accept help when you just wanted to be okay. I tried to picture how my dad might have reacted to a nurse helping him throughout the day. No doubt Dad would've sent them home within the first hour, too.

But I also understood how hard it'd be in Vincent's shoes. Not knowing whether his dad was with someone who could help him, not knowing whether his dad was okay or sitting on the bathroom floor, unable to stand up.

"Did he recover well in the hospital?" I asked. "He was sent home a bit early, wasn't he?"

That got a scoff from Vincent, a harsh noise that surprised me. "He wasn't sent home—he *left*. Against medical advice. Thought he didn't need physical therapy. Thought he could just heal on his own. Too freaking stubborn for his own good."

"I'm so sorry," I said, sadness pinching in my chest. "I can't even imagine."

The vulnerability in Vincent's eyes caused the sympathy in my chest to expand. "We've had a rocky relationship for a while. I was always a jerk, always doing the wrong thing."

"Like?"

"Like going to too many parties." Vincent shifted backward and then stood straight, unable to stand completely still for too long. "I sound like a loser, don't I? Complaining about my dad who's in a freaking wheelchair when your... I'm so sorry."

Without even thinking about it, I reached across the counter and laid my hand on his arm, the long-sleeved shirt soft beneath my fingertips. "Hey," I told him gently. "You're allowed to feel whatever you want."

The tension in Vincent's body lessened as soon as I touched him, the tautness in his arm relaxing underneath my grip. I could see he was struggling to figure out what to say, but was there anything *to* say? There was no shaking the understanding that existed between us.

We were on the same wavelength, the same past tying us together in a way words couldn't quite cover.

But knowing Vincent carried such a burden, so much worry and stress, made me desperately want to change the circumstances.

Sitting on the barstool across from him, I felt so *normal*. I didn't feel nervous about hanging out with him; I didn't feel worried that he'd seen a side of me that no one else had seen. The tightness in my chest was gone, and I felt like I could finally breathe.

I hadn't realized we'd been staring at each other, unspeaking, until the door chimed, and more customers came inside. Vincent straightened, pulling his arm from me, and went to face the first in line.

When I picked up my pen to continue planning out my journal spread, I was surprised to find my fingers trembling.

*B*efore too many people came in Friday night to see Untapped Potential, I claimed the booth closest to the stage. Even as eager music fans piled in, they couldn't quite block my view. Natasha plugged her guitar into the amp as Harry stepped up to the microphone, and Vincent sat down at the drum kit. He'd obviously ditched the teal apron, but he still wore the same clothes.

Harry shot a wink in my direction, and I found myself shaking my head. "How's my lovely little café doing tonight?" he said into the mic.

The lovely little café cheered in response, causing me to smile. The energy coursing through the crowd was infectious.

Vincent twirled his drumsticks in his hand, but the act didn't look performative. It just looked like second nature. Since I had a clear view of him now, I could see that there wasn't a microphone set up anywhere near him. That was why I hadn't heard his voice last week—he didn't have a mic to sing into.

"Let's start off with a little bit of a bang tonight," Harry went on, glancing toward Natasha.

Her band tee clung tightly to her curves, her eyes rimmed with heavy liner that exaggerated their shape. When they locked eyes, she gave him a sultry grin. *Huh*, I mused. *Wonder how long ago they broke up?*

Without waiting for him to say anything else, Natasha cued up the song with one long electrical tear, and just from a single note, Untapped Potential lovers immediately knew what song they were playing. Vincent, after finishing one last rotation with his drumstick, slammed them down in an earthshaking beat.

They were meant for bigger things, I knew. Bigger than this coffeeshop. The soul in the words Harry spoke, the passion in every strum of the guitar and clang of a drum, was almost too much for this café. They deserved to be playing in places designed for live bands—*specifically* for live bands.

I'd had this conversation with Jonathan last week, but I'd never been overly attracted to people in bands, but there was something about the atmosphere tonight. As I watched Vincent, heard the sound that came from each slice of his drumsticks, I could feel my heart beat a bit faster. His movements were controlled, practiced, fluid. He wore a short-sleeved shirt, so I could see his forearms flex from the power behind each strike of a drum.

Looking away from him was impossible.

"Hey!" Stella shouted over the music, sliding into the booth across from me. Her black bangs hung a little long, pin-straight and dangling down in her eyes. "Got yourself a front row seat, I see."

"Yeah," I said, but couldn't help but squint a little at her. That girl from the gas station had looked so much like her, but now I was second-guessing it. Stella's cheekbones looked sharper, lips fuller. Their hair was so different, the girl's being brown and curly and Stella's being black and straight.

Stella turned away from me to face the stage, but the action almost seemed deliberate. "Are you turning into a fan?"

"Hard not to. They're good." *Really* good.

Stella began to sing along with the song, her voice a beautiful lilt pairing with Harry's. She sounded better than Natasha did as his counterpart. Only I could hear her—and barely, over the noise—but Harry's eyes coasted from the crowd to me to Stella, snagging there.

It was almost as if they were singing to each other, in a way that made me feel almost like I was intruding on a moment. Like everyone here in the crowd was intruding on a moment.

They would be such a cute couple. Sure, Harry had coffee with that woman earlier today, but that didn't mean they were together. He and Stella were a much better fit.

Harry turned away, breaking the moment apart, but he frequently glanced back over at our booth. Never at me, which made me grin for Stella's sake.

"This is my favorite way to spend weekend nights," Stella told me, nodding to the next song. "Listening to good music, drinking good coffee, looking at good-looking boys."

My gaze flicked over to Vincent. "Sounds like a perfect weekend to me."

"So you and Vincent—you're *not* a couple?"

"No," I answered immediately, nearly snorting at the thought. "Just friends."

I could use that word a little more confidently now, especially after this afternoon. He'd wrapped his arms around me without question, holding me through sob after sob. I could still feel the heat of his body against mine, how perfectly my temple fit against his collarbone. Could still smell his honey scent tickling my nose, comforting me.

"He's got the broody air to him, doesn't he?" Stella said as she eyed him. "I've never actually gotten to talk to him. I only see him when he's on stage."

"He's definitely got layers."

As though he could hear us speaking, Vincent's gaze cut to us. Once again, that flutter in my chest made an appearance. It was weird, but not uncomfortable—I couldn't figure out where it was coming from.

When I turned back to Stella, I caught her smirking at me. "Right," she said, nodding like she knew something I didn't. "I bet he does."

By the end of the night, I was dead tired. It was just a little after eleven o'clock, and the café was silent. Everyone had cleared out a while ago—even Stella had disappeared once Untapped Potential wrapped up their final song. Vincent and Jonathan worked in steady rhythm, cleaning up the lounge area, setting up the chairs again, and wiping down the surfaces. They had their routine memorized, barely speaking to one another while they worked. They barely spoke to me either, which was fine by me, because I was barely awake.

For a while, I'd been drawing in my bullet journal, working on next week's spread, but my brain started to feel like mush not too long after the café fell quiet. I'd been running on coffee and fumes and good music, but now I felt drained. The sob session from earlier had taken its toll on me, and all those weeks without sleep were catching up. I laid my head on my arms, my hair creating a curtain around me.

I didn't know how long I'd had my head down when Vincent spoke. "You ready, Adeline?"

I made an affirmative noise, swiping up my journal and weaving through the tables. Vincent finished closing everything down as Jonathan hovered by the back door, and even he looked tired. The quietness of Crushed Beanz turned almost haunting as Vincent flipped off the last light, sending the café interior into darkness.

I reached out just enough that I could ease the door open. The soft hush of snow falling at a steady pace filled the air, the winter chill blasting through that small crack. It was so *calming*. Beautiful. I wanted nothing more than to go out and stand in it, let the snow fall against my warm skin, feel it melt.

The snow fell from the sky in even sheets, the blanket so thick that I could hardly see across the employee parking lot. I couldn't even see the blacktop of the road, and only two tire tracks cut into the snow—it hadn't been plowed clean yet.

There was no way I'd make it out of the school parking lot once Vincent dropped me off.

Jonathan and I stepped out the back door and into the snow, and Vincent set the alarm before following behind us.

"Dang, it's not even slowing down, is it?" Jonathan asked as he peered up at the sky, almost looking disgusted. "Fantastic."

"I'll call you tomorrow," Vincent told him, zipping up his jacket. "We might close down for the day, depending if it carries on like this throughout the night."

Judging by the layers of snow now, it didn't seem like it was going to be stopping. "Sounds good. Drive safe, you two." Jonathan headed across the lot to where his car was parked, and I could hear his feet slumping through the snow, creating little footprints that would soon disappear.

Vincent and I made our way to his truck, and I was careful on the slick sidewalk, the dampness starting to seep into my shoes.

Vincent plugged an AUX cord into his phone once we climbed into the truck, playing a song very low. Low enough that we could've talked over it, but I was too tired to try to come up with a conversation topic.

As Vincent eased out of the Crushed Beanz's back parking lot and onto the road, he said, "I can take you home."

I blinked at the road, my eyes having trouble focusing. "Where else would we go?"

"I mean, I can drop you off at home. Leave your car at school."

Was I so tired that logic wasn't making sense? "How would I get my car the next day?"

"I can pick you up tomorrow and we can get it."

He'd spoken the words so simply, as if this were normal. Normal for him to drive me home, normal for him to go out of his way for me the next day. Two friends, helping the other out.

"I would just feel better...if I could drive you home."

I tried to appear nonchalant even though his words were so serious. For some reason, the breath I pulled in tickled my lungs. "Feel better?"

"I'm not trying to hate on that beauty, but not totally sure it would get you home safely. Least not in a storm like this."

Yeah, he probably wasn't wrong. I'd been concerned about the same thing. It was strange, though, knowing we were both concerned about the same thing: my safety.

Vincent glanced over at me, waiting for me to answer. Waiting for me to accept or deny.

I picked at the sleeve of my coat with my fingertips, pulling the fabric over my hands. "As long as it's not too much trouble," I said finally.

The tense look vanished from his expression, and it was only then did I realize that tension was there. "Not a problem at all."

Vincent fell quiet again as he turned onto the road that led out of Hallow. This main road had been recently plowed, as indicated by the buildup on the shoulder, but enough snow had fallen that it was starting to accumulate again. Fortunately, Vincent's truck tires easily blew through it.

Given the conditions, I was a little nervous riding with him, but Vincent was a safe driver. He kept both of his hands on the steering wheel the entire time, though his knuckles remained their normal color. He drove under the speed limit, took his turns slow, allowed enough time for braking at stop signs. A fabulous driver. I bet his insurance company loved him.

That thought hadn't settled in my mind for more than a second before I thought about the accident.

"You guys did so well tonight," I said in a quiet voice, if only to speak over the thoughts in my head that had grown so loud. I pinched my fingers in my lap, watching the strange way the headlights lit up the falling snow. Almost like we were in space. "I really like listening to you guys play."

"Harry's been itching to change things up. We've been wanting to play at bigger venues, but it's hard to find an open slot."

"What are your thoughts on that?"

Vincent reached up and traced a finger along the hollow of his temple. "I think it'd be fun playing at a place other than Crushed Beanz."

I leaned my head against the headrest, my eyes drooping low. "And I bet as a drummer, it'd be super fun to play something with more of an edge."

I only caught the side of Vincent's smile since his head was turned, but the soft laugh that came with it—I heard it in full, and it made me feel funny. "It'd drive my dad insane, though. He's always complaining about my practicing being too loud as it is."

The clock on the dashboard read 11:21, which I couldn't believe. It felt like time had flown by tonight, and I wasn't even sure why. I had the stupidest urge to check my phone, to see if anyone had texted me, but I kept my hands in my lap.

"Do you have any tattoos?" I asked him suddenly, remembering the rumors I'd heard about him once upon a time. That he had a lip piercing—which he did. That he had tattoos. That he did drugs.

"Tattoos?" he echoed, sounding very confused. "No. Do you?"

I laughed at that. "Of course not. Where would I even have one?"

That question came out sounding much more flirtatious than I'd intended, and maybe it was because it required Vincent to actually *think* about my body. Which was...weird. And made the cab feel much warmer.

Vincent must've thought that it was a rhetorical question, thank God, because he asked me a question, cleaving through my thoughts and bringing me back to the present. "What's one thing that brings you joy?"

He looked over at me, and though the interior of the cab was dark, his eyes were so vibrantly green. It was almost jarring. Or maybe the intensity in his gaze was the thing that was jarring, because that shifting feeling was back, making me swallow hard. *Why does that keep happening?* "Thing that brings me joy. Hmm...oh!" I gestured at the windshield. "Snow."

"Snow."

"Snow," I insisted. "It's beautiful. Unique. So, so peaceful. If you were to roll your window down right now, you'd be able to hear it blowing in the wind, that sound it makes as it falls onto the ground."

Vincent shook his head. "If I were to roll my window down right now, we'd both freeze."

I reached out and swatted at his arm, and then instantly recoiled. It felt weird to be so casual with him. "It brings me joy. Building snowmen, snowball fights."

Vincent thought for a moment. "You know, that's the opposite of what I thought you'd say about snow."

"Why?"

"November was the last time we got a storm like this. When...when your dad died."

I drew in a slow breath, not to combat his words, but to pull them in. Feel them. Immediately, I wanted to cry again. I blinked, completely and utterly shocked by the bluntness of his words. *Your dad died.* And there was no emotion underlying the words, no maliciousness intended. He'd spoken the words normally, as if stating a fact. And he *was* stating a fact. A simple one. An obvious one. *Your dad died.*

Vincent cursed as my silence prolonged, the word slipping quickly from his tongue. "Adeline, I'm so sorry—"

But that little swear word—it was like a shot of energy to my soul. I pressed my hands to my face to suppress a laugh.

"Are you—are you crying or are you laughing?" Vincent reached over and laid his hand on my knee, five fingers pressing against the thin fabric of my tights. "It's so dark that I can't tell."

"My friends are goody-two-shoes," I told him through my fingers, voice muffled. "Mollie's dad would literally wash her mouth out with soap. I'm sure Bryce does it, but he's never done it around me."

"Done...what, exactly?"

"Swear." I pulled my hands away to peer at him, nearly laughing again from the worried expression on his face. "Especially not *that* word."

Such a strange look crossed over Vincent's face that I actually did laugh out loud this time. But when I moved my hands, my left one came down right on top of Vincent's right one, the one that still rested on my knee. His skin was so smooth, so *warm*.

And why...why didn't I immediately pull away?

"I didn't mean to say it like that," he said softly. "What I said about...the snow."

"I needed you to say it." And once I spoke the words aloud, I knew they were true. It was a subject everyone tiptoed around, a subject that had never been spoken about so bluntly before. "Thank you, Vincent. For helping me through...all that today."

He shook his head. "I just held you."

"That was enough." More than enough.

My hand was still covering over his, and all I'd have to do to take his hand into mine would be to push his fingertips apart with my own. All he'd have to do would be to turn his palm up and hold on. That thought caused the humming to kick back into my chest. Vincent didn't strike me as a hand-holder, but would he hold mine? Or was he waiting for me to let go?

Suddenly, a loud ring filled the cab—Vincent's ringtone. I jerked my hand back before he could pull free, and he fished his phone from his coat pocket. Without glancing at the screen, he accepted the call and turned it on speaker. "Hello?"

"Vincent," a male voice breathed, and even from the one word, I could tell the person was frantic. And vaguely familiar. "I didn't know who else to call, and I just needed someone to talk to."

Vincent frowned a bit. "What's wrong, Jackson?"

Jackson. That was why the voice sounded so familiar. "I'm at the hospital on Main. We went for a walk and she— I think she had some kind of asthma attack, and she didn't have her inhaler—"

I sucked in a breath before he'd even finished speaking. "Who are you talking about?" I demanded, not caring if it was rude to butt into Vincent's call, not caring if it was rude to cut Jackson off. I only knew one person with asthma, but she was so diligent with her inhaler, making sure she wasn't out in the cold for too long. She would never, *ever*, risk it. For the entire time I'd known her, she'd never had an asthma attack—hadn't had one in years.

But Jackson proved me wrong. "Mollie."

Seventeen

*V*incent didn't even have to wait for me to tell him. He flipped on his blinker and turned onto a road that would lead to downtown Greenville. I pulled out my cell phone, opening it to find a slew of messages. I only looked at the messages, not the senders, and most of them could be summed up in one sentence: **Call me back.**

Without waiting for Vincent to finish his call with Jackson, I dialed Vesta. Our feud went out the window. She answered on the first ring. "Mollie had an asthma attack and didn't have her inhaler," she said by way of greeting, pulling in a breath. "Jackson called me once they got to the hospital because he didn't know what her home number was. I called her parents—they're here."

"You're at the hospital?" I asked, the panic causing my voice to tighten. "Is she okay? How serious was it?"

"We're not allowed back to see her. Her mom came and said she was okay, though. I think Mr. Brooks talked them into keeping her overnight just to be safe."

I pressed my hand to my forehead, trying to breathe.

I didn't even know what to say. Why would Mollie be with Jackson? Sure, Mollie had mentioned Jackson, but I'd never gotten the impression that her opinion of him was favorable. Yeah, he asked her to the dance, but she said no. Didn't she? She'd never mentioned it. Never mentioned that she went to the New Year's Eve party, either. Vesta had never mentioned hanging out with Bryce and his friends outside of school. All of the secrets weighed on me again.

You never mentioned Vincent to them either, a voice whispered in my ear.

"Is it just you there?" I asked, shoving the voice and its words away.

"No, Bryce is with me." Before I had a chance to think about that, Vesta continued, "Jackson's here too, but he's not sitting with us. He's off in the corner of the waiting room by himself. I don't think he wants Mr. and Mrs. Brooks to know he's here for her."

I seriously could've murdered that boy. He did exactly what I'd told him not to—he'd messed with Mollie, and now she'd ended up in the hospital. "Did you hear how it happened?"

"Mrs. Brooks said that Mollie went for a walk without her inhaler and the cold triggered an attack. She thinks someone just saw Mollie and took her to the hospital. They didn't know it was Jackson."

Knight in shining armor, that Jackson.

Vesta let out a breath. "We'll probably head out soon, since she can't have visitors."

"I'll keep my phone on me. Call me if you hear anything?"

In response to my words, Vincent let up on the gas.

"Of course," Vesta answered, and hesitated before she spoke again. "I'm so, so sorry for everything, Addy."

"I know." I sighed, rubbing my hand over my mouth. "Me too."

As soon as I hung up, Vincent turned to me. "You don't want to go to the hospital?" he asked.

"If I go to the hospital, I might strangle Jackson."

And if Mollie couldn't have visitors and was okay, then being there, sitting in a chair, wouldn't have been great. And, though I didn't want to admit it out loud, the longer I thought about it, the more I really didn't want to go to Greenville's hospital. I'd faced enough memories today.

"Vesta said Mollie will be fine, so I didn't need to come down. And it's been a long day."

In response, Vincent took the nearest road to head toward my house.

He never reached back over, and so my hands never ventured out of my lap to find his. That strange tension was broken between us, and it made it almost easier to breathe. But a small kernel of disappointment welled in me, and I couldn't guess why.

Only the hum of the music kept us company the rest of the ride.

It was absolutely silent as I unlocked the door, the deadbolt flipping over seeming to echo in my ears. The darkness was so thick that it was almost tangible, and I shuffled inside as quietly as I could, stomping my feet to get any clumps of snow off my shoes before toeing them off. Simply slipping off my shoes had me sagging in relief—I couldn't wait to get under the covers.

But as I stepped into the kitchen, all thoughts about my tired body fled my mind.

It was still dark, but there was no missing Mom's outline at the breakfast bar, arms folded over the marble counter, body facing me. I switched on the lights, fearing her expression—and rightfully so. With the light on, I got full a view of Mom's glorious amount of anger.

Her voice was deadly quiet. "Where have you been?"

Abort mission, my brain screamed at me, and I suddenly wanted nothing more than to go back outside and chase Vincent's truck down the street. Anything to get away from here.

"What are you doing up?" I asked, trying to put off her question long enough to craft a believable answer. My brain was sluggish, slow to help me come up with a lie.

"Waiting for my teenage daughter, who is out during a *blizzard*, driving a car that's *not* made for snow, to come home. Or to call. Or to text. Or to do *anything* to let me know she's okay."

I let out a sigh. Even though we were supposed to technically be in a fight, I couldn't muster up enough anger to snap back at her. "Mom—"

"I called you several times. Where have you been?" Each word was enunciated.

"With Vesta."

Her stone-etched expression didn't change. "Vesta called the house looking for you, Addy. You weren't with her. Try again. Maybe, in your answer, include whoever owned that truck that just dropped you off."

I am so screwed. Why hadn't I thought about Vesta calling the house? If she couldn't reach me on my cell, of course she would've.

As a second passed, I considered telling Mom the truth. What would it hurt?

"I was out with a friend," I said slowly, trying to hold her gaze with an unflinching look of my own. "We went to a coffeehouse in Hallow. There was a band playing tonight—we were just listening to music."

"Your friend's name?"

A face came to mind a second before I spoke. "Stella." Well, there went telling the truth.

The interrogation wasn't over. "And that was Stella's truck outside, dropping you off?"

"It was her boyfriend's truck," I told her. "They saw how bad the snow was getting and offered me a ride. They're going to take me to get the car tomorrow."

Mom's eyes narrowed at that. "And where *is* the convertible?"

"Stella's house." Each lie wrenched my stomach tighter and tighter, making me feel sick. "Are we done? I'm tired."

Mom just watched me for a long, long moment, not wanting to give up my attention just yet. I could tell she was trying to figure out what to do, whether to punish me, how to respond. Our silence dragged on, and I considered telling her about what had happened today, that major breakthrough and breakdown. I even considered telling the truth about the night of the accident to her. She didn't know how cruel I'd been to Dad, didn't know I'd let him drive when he wasn't supposed to. Vincent said it wasn't my fault, but there would be no shaking that truth.

What would Mom say? Would she hold me? Would she repeat Vincent's words? Would she storm off to the guest room, angrier with me than she'd ever been? I was so, so afraid to find out, so I didn't open my mouth.

"You're grounded," she decided then, holding her hand out to me. "Your phone, please."

I didn't even fight it. Exhaustion had its claws too deep in me, and in some part of my brain, I knew I deserved this. I'd been pushing and pushing the curfew, and tonight, when the roads were bad, I never called.

I couldn't imagine what Mom was feeling. From the look on her face, I wondered if she'd expected more shouting, refusals.

But without a word, I handed it over, and headed toward the stairs.

For the first time in the few weeks that we'd been home, I let myself lift my chin as I moved up the staircase, finally facing the family portraits on the wall, finally facing the memories I'd attempted to bury deep. One of the pictures was of Mom and Dad on their wedding day, both donning smiles that screamed of happiness. Mom clung to Dad, and even though they were supposed to be looking at the photographer, he was looking at her.

The next photos were a series of family vacations, and one of them was as recent as this past summer. We'd gone to a beach in Florida, lounged around and soaked up as much sun as we possibly could. I wasn't smiling in the photo, probably because Dad was sipping on a margarita and Mom was already tipsy from her mimosa. Our last family trip together, last family photo, and I didn't smile.

My pace quickened on the last few steps, and I sealed myself in my bedroom. Getting ready for bed kept me distracted if only for a few moments, as I brushed my teeth and changed into my pajamas. But once everything was done, my mind once more traveled down the rabbit hole, peering inside the box again.

And then I lay down on my bed and let it all out once more. This time, there was no one to hold me together, no one to tether me. After keeping the box sealed for so long, I wondered if there'd ever be a time where I wouldn't fall apart after falling inside.

Maybe one day, but not tonight.

Despite being thoroughly exhausted, I didn't sleep restfully at all. I had no trouble slipping into unconsciousness, but bad dreams quickly invaded.

I dreamed about Mollie dying, gasping for air.

I dreamed about Dad dying, amidst shattered glass.

I dreamed about Vincent dying.

Didn't even know where *that* came from.

Mom had to pick up a shift at work today, a Saturday morning when it would've been her day off, so I was once more stuck in this house by myself. I definitely wasn't one of those teenagers who needed their phone to survive, but as the morning dissolved into afternoon, I found that I was so. Freaking. Bored.

The silence, though, almost felt bearable today. It didn't feel as crushing, probably because I wasn't trying to escape it anymore. There was no desperation to be anywhere else. For the first time since we'd come home from Rickett Falls, I was content where I was.

The snow had stopped falling sometime last night, leaving an eight-inch blanket across the city. Our back deck was completely covered in snow, so much that even though the deck was off the ground, the way the snow had drifted made it impossible to tell where the deck ended and the ground began.

Once again, the urge to build a snowman was strong.

At noon, as I was thinking about going outside and caving to that desire, a car honk startled me. It sounded close. I pushed to my feet from the couch to go peer out the window, expecting to see an accident in front of my house or something.

Except when I went to inspect the sound, I found my red convertible sitting in the driveway, Vincent behind the wheel.

Everything in me jolted, mind going into overdrive as I did a mental check of my appearance. I hadn't showered yet today—heck, I'd barely run a brush through my hair. My teeth were scrubbed, thank God, but that was as far as proper hygiene went for me. I didn't even have a *bra* on.

I snatched a blanket up from the couch as I hurried toward the door, wrapping it around my shoulders. *Be cool,* I told myself. Everything in me trembled, especially as

Vincent eased the car into the garage. Through the glass, I could see him, sunglass shielding his eyes. *Be cool.*

Once he killed the engine, Vincent hopped out, jingling the keys. "One shiny red convertible, at your service," he said in greeting.

"You didn't have to do this," I said. "You shouldn't have gotten out in this snow."

"I was already out." He jerked his thumb toward the road. "Harry's coming behind me in my truck. Should be here any second."

I nodded, pulling the blanket tighter around me as we fell into silence.

Vincent shifted on his feet, lifting his sunglasses to glance around the garage. "How's Mollie?"

"She'll be okay." I didn't have my cell so I couldn't check on her personally, but her mom called the house this morning and left a message. "That must've been so scary, though."

His eyes traced me up and down. "How are *you*? You look tired."

"I didn't sleep well," I admitted, shrugging as if the admission wasn't a big deal. "I haven't been for a long time."

He slipped his sunglasses along the collar of his shirt, processing my words. When he spoke, he kept his voice light. "Did you still want to come over sometime to watch the movie? I mean, I don't know about you, but I'm eager to watch an evil baby...kill people."

I grinned. "You're excited about that, huh?"

His voice sounded flat, but I could see him struggle to conceal the amusement. "For sure."

A part of me wanted to ask him what he was doing now —maybe I could just go inside and get ready, and we could go back to his house—but logic quickly interfered. I was still grounded. Harry was coming to pick up Vincent, which meant they'd been hanging out. And it wasn't like watching *Evil Killer Babies* with Harry would've been a bad thing, but I just...I found myself wanting it to be just Vincent and me. I wanted to be able to see his expression, poke fun at the gory bits, hear him laugh.

It was almost weird how desperately I wanted to hear him laugh.

"What are you doing Monday after school?" I asked him, bringing the blanket to my chin. "Do you work?"

"Monday's are our slow days," he said, taking a step closer to me. "I'm sure they can survive without me."

Vincent reached out and picked up my hand, which I'd pulled to my chest. His hands were so warm against my cold skin, almost shockingly so. Or maybe it was shocking that he'd picked my hand up so easily, so carelessly, as if it weren't that big of a deal. It reminded me of the night before, with his hand on my knee and my hand on his, wanting nothing more than to take his fingers with my own. That heat filled my chest again, but it only lasted a moment.

He pressed my car keys into my palm. "Is this something we'll need popcorn for?"

"Of course," I said, putting on a playful tone to hide the shaking of my voice. "With extra butter."

Harry pulled Vincent's truck into my driveway then, the rumbling vehicle cutting into our conversation. I glanced at the truck with a sharp breath. I didn't want him to leave yet. Instead, I found myself wishing he'd pick my hand back up.

Vincent, too, looked at the truck, taking a step back from me. "I'll see you on Monday, then?"

"Yeah," I said, disappointment welling, though I couldn't really pinpoint why. "See you Monday."

Vincent didn't say anything as he walked back to his truck. Harry must've scooted over into the passenger's seat, because Vincent climbed up into the driver's seat with ease, closing the door behind him.

Even though he was gone, I could still feel the tingling pressure of his fingertips.

eighteen

I'd just gotten out of my car Monday morning when I saw Mollie's dad's dark blue truck pull into the parking lot, tires crunching through the slushy snow. The school had done an okay job clearing the snow off the blacktop—could've been better, if anyone asked me —but it was still slick as I hurried across it, trying to catch Mollie before she disappeared inside.

She was slamming the passenger door shut by the time I made it to her. "I'm the worst friend," I gasped, immediately latching onto her arm. "I was going to call, but Mom took away my phone—"

"My parents took away mine too." Mollie shouldered her backpack up higher and dragged me toward the school, not giving her dad a second glance. Her gaze was stony, as angry as I'd ever seen it. With her free hand, she pulled her scarf up to her mouth, blocking as much cold air as possible. "I'm officially grounded for the first time in my life over what happened."

I couldn't even hide my shock. I knew Mollie's parents

never held back at grounding her older sister, Jess, but the idea of innocent Mollie getting grounded was almost unbelievable.

"So what *did* happen, anyway?"

Mollie sighed, expression darkening further. "I went for a walk and forgot my inhaler. *Stupid*, I know. You don't have to tell me—I heard it enough times this past weekend."

"Hey." I tugged on her arm, pulling her to a rough stop in the middle of the sidewalk. A few girls trailing behind us had to abruptly cut around us. "I wouldn't have said that."

Her eyes were fierce, the color of Friday's storm clouds. "If I could go back and redo Friday, I would. Trust me. I never should've left after curfew."

"Why did you?" I asked, batting hair from my face. "Why did you go out with Jackson?"

Mollie opened her mouth to answer when a dark green SUV drove past us. She watched as it pulled into the student parking lot. "I need to get out of the cold," she said, pressing her scarf firmer against her mouth and heading toward the double doors.

I hurried after her, not wanting to let go of the conversation yet, but I had a feeling that the proverbial door had slammed shut.

"My lovely ladies!" Vesta's voice came a second before I felt something slam into me from behind, and Vesta was there, arms slung over our shoulders, squeezing into the middle. "My ladies who don't know how to use a cell phone, mind you. I was worried you were abducted by aliens."

"We were both grounded," I told her, feeling a little on edge.

"I knew Mollie was, but why were you?" Vesta asked, and I could feel her gaze probing into the side of my head.

"Mom and I got into an argument." Not really a lie.

We got to the area where the sophomore lockers were located, and Mollie ducked underneath Vesta's arm. "I'll see you guys at lunch," she said, heading off in the direction of her locker without another word.

"So did you call Bryce when you couldn't get a hold of me?" I asked Vesta, heading in the direction of the junior lockers. I didn't want to talk about Mollie, didn't want to ask if they'd sorted things out yet. I wasn't in the mood to get into another argument over that, not this morning. "The other night, I mean. You said you two were together at the hospital."

She didn't look at me, but her expression almost looked nervous. "Yeah, but you weren't with him. He came down and sat with me, though."

How sweet, I thought, but I was surprised it wasn't bitter. That *was* kind of him to go sit with Vesta. If he had done something similar for me back in November, my heart would've been a puddle of goo.

The memory of him reaching over the seat and touching her arm came to me, the way her hand had immediately covered his.

"I'm going to drop my stuff off," Vesta said, interrupting my thoughts. She stripped her beanie from her head, already taking several steps back. "It's already close to the bell. I'll see you in homeroom? Hopefully no dance-posals are in front of my locker today."

After Vesta hurried off, I fiddled with my locker dial. My mind was still whirring fast, though, imagining Vesta and Bryce together. *Vesta and Bryce.*

I tried to take stock of the emotion coursing through me, but I couldn't pinpoint it. There was no red-hot anger, though.

I waited to see if Bryce would appear, but students came and went with that particular boy never showing. Even if he did, I had no idea what I'd say. Would I have demanded if I was right, that he and Vesta *were* flirting? If I *had* been right, wouldn't Vesta have told me?

Even though I didn't see Bryce, Jackson, however, was a tall guy I couldn't miss as he unloaded his backpack across the hall, his dark hair untidy, as if he hadn't brushed it.

Gosh, I so badly wanted to just go over there and interrogate him. Hit him over the head with my textbook. Because encouraging Mollie to sneak out? *So* didn't match up with the "leave her alone" speech I'd given him.

During my mental ranting, Jackson lifted his gaze from the inside of his locker and looked in my direction. Only a second passed before he shut his locker, striding straight to me.

"Is Mollie okay?" he asked when he was a few steps away, the worry in his eyes clear as day. It threw me off for a moment, because I hadn't expected *concern.* It was disarming. "I tried texting her, but she didn't answer all weekend."

"She's grounded," I told him, raising an eyebrow at him. "For sneaking out."

Jackson reached up and tore a hand through his hair, and I realized that was why it looked so untidy. He'd been combing his hands through it, possibly from nerves. "Is she okay, though?"

I'd never witnessed Mollie going through an asthma attack, but I'd seen enough portrayed on TV to know what one looked like. Gasping for air, not getting enough, not until an inhaler was used. And knowing she didn't have an inhaler... "She's at school today. You could ask her."

"I—I know. I saw her standing on the sidewalk." Gone was the jovial captain of the basketball team. The Jackson in front of me was worried, almost looking guilty, and it prickled my insides.

"Do you really care about her?"

Jackson was silent as he stared at me.

"Because if you don't," I went on, gathering my psychology book and shutting my locker door, "then you need to move on. She doesn't deserve some guy playing with her feelings, and you know it."

I turned on my heel and walked toward my first period before he could answer, my spine straight. The fingers clutching my book were curled tight, almost to the point where it hurt. I didn't know what was going on with Jackson and Mollie, but I'd always have her back. And if a guy like Jackson was just using Mollie because he needed a distraction, then I wasn't going to let that happen.

When I got to Mr. Walker's classroom, I could hear him talking to someone, and froze as I heard my name. "This is me not-so-gently telling you that if you want to pass, you need to ace the project with Addy, Vincent. Unless you want to repeat your senior year."

If Vincent responded to that, I couldn't hear it.

"I mean it, do you understand? No more handouts. I was hoping that maybe she'd be a good influence, but if you don't turn in the assignments, there's nothing I can do for you."

A boy breezed past me before Vincent had a chance to reply. I heard Mr. Walker sigh quietly. "Meet me after school and we'll discuss this more."

Several students filtered in from behind me, and I followed their current to my seat. As Vincent slid into his own desk, our gazes locked. And it was the weirdest, weirdest thing.

Instead of quickly looking away, pretending to not have seen me, one corner of Vincent's mouth tipped into a small, tired smile.

A wave of butterflies shifted in my stomach, and even though what I'd just overheard wasn't good, I couldn't help but smile back.

Since it was the Monday before the Snowflake Dance, things had kicked into high gear. All of the final details were being ironed out, and everyone who'd put off buying tickets until the last minute flagged me down today, asking where they should go.

It felt good on my end, knowing I'd checked everything off my list. Faux snow, the arch, the ribbons, and paint—all retrieved. That was one of the things I loved about keeping checklists. When I got to check everything off, I felt like a superhero.

At the end of the day, I loitered by my locker, taking my time counting my books, reorganizing my locker setup. Anything to waste time until Vincent retreated out of Mr. Walker's classroom, which I'd seen him go into five minutes ago.

There were hardly any students in the hallways now, everyone trying to get out of school as quickly as they could on a Monday. Honestly, I didn't blame them. With *Evil Killer Babies* in my backpack, I was excited to leave the building myself.

"Hey."

I whirled around to find Vincent coming out of Mr. Walker's room, his backpack slung over his shoulder. He had his winter jacket over one arm.

"There you are," I said, curling my fingers into fists so they wouldn't shake.

Vincent hooked his fingers under his backpack strap, opening his mouth to speak before his eyes shifted to a spot behind me. And stayed there. Curiosity got the better of me and I turned too, looking straight down the senior locker hallway.

Bryce stood in front of his open locker, but it was obvious that there was someone standing between him and the locker, just barely hidden by the open door. His smile was so easy and full, and I realized that I hadn't seen it in so long. He hadn't smiled at *me* like that in so long.

The person he was looking at leaned forward just enough that I could see the vibrancy of their red hair.

I moved on impulse. I grabbed Vincent's upper arm and pushed him to the spot behind the end of the lockers, the little space that was just out of sight of the senior hallway. His back hit the wall and my chest slammed against his, my heart hammering.

Vincent sucked in a quiet breath as I froze against him. Even though I wasn't looking anymore, I could still see them. Vesta's wide grin at Bryce, him leaning in with his wide, boyish smile—their laughter, swirling and mixing together like two pretty shades of paint.

Well, I guess that answered *that* question.

I wasn't surprised by the twinge of pain in my chest, but I was surprised by *why* I felt the pain. It wasn't because Vesta, my best friend, was embracing Bryce, the guy I'd been crushing on—it was because she hadn't wanted to tell me about it.

Did Mollie know? If she did, that would've made everything ten times worse.

One of Vincent's hands pressed against the side of my hip, jolting me from imagining what Vesta and Bryce were saying and bringing me back to this moment. To the moment where I was pressed up against the length of Vincent Castello, who looked down at me with wide green eyes. That honey scent was everywhere, heady in a way that made my mind swim. His lip-ringed mouth was inches from mine, and if I had been an inch taller, our lips would've been even closer.

Move away from him, I commanded my feet, but they didn't listen right away. My hand was still curled around his arm, each one of my fingers pressing into his warm bare skin.

Clenching my jaw tight, I forced myself to step back into the hallway, looking where Vesta and Bryce had stood a moment ago. They were gone now, almost like they hadn't been there to begin with.

"Adeline—"

I cut him off, turning so he couldn't see the heat racing to my cheeks. I peeked down the senior hallway, but everyone had cleared out by this point.

"What did Mr. Walker want?" I asked, my voice surprisingly even, acting as if I *hadn't* just pressed the length of my body against his. Acting like I hadn't just seen what I knew I had.

"We were talking about the assignment. He wants to make sure I'm turning it in."

I started moving as soon as he spoke, heading back to my locker to gather my coat and slamming the door shut. The actions felt mechanical. "Why wouldn't you?"

"Well, I've sort of been...slacking in the homework department."

"In psychology?"

"Uh, and physics. And English."

My eyes widened. "Vincent."

"I just don't have any time," he said a little defensively. "Between a job and making sure my dad doesn't fall and hit his head, there's not a lot of time to analyze sonnets."

Vincent held his hand out to me, and it only took me a moment for his past words to echo through my mind. *Give me your bag so you can put your coat on.* "I can't come over today," I decided, passing over my backpack, weaving my arms through my sleeves.

"What? Why not?"

"You just said you have a lot of homework to catch up on." I fastened the last button and reached for my bag. "I can't distract you when you have so much due." Especially since Mr. Walker said something about Vincent passing his senior year. No way would I be one of the reasons he didn't get his homework done. "Besides, I should probably be studying for my midterms anyway."

When I grabbed the bag strap, Vincent didn't let go. "What are you doing tomorrow?"

I pressed my lips together, fighting to keep my expression serious. "Careful. You seem genuinely excited to watch a bad horror flick."

"You're the one who hyped it up," he pointed out. "Maybe *you're* just afraid that I'll think the movie's garbage."

"Don't you have to work tomorrow?"

"I have Tuesdays off."

Now I raised an eyebrow. "Since when?"

"Since just now. Perk of being the owner's son."

It wasn't as if I didn't want to watch the movie with him —I'd so rather do that than go home. But I'd be a good friend today. "Tomorrow," I agreed, quickly adding, "If you finish all of your homework. I don't need Mr. Walker thinking *I'm* the bad influence."

He raised an eyebrow and released my backpack. "Oh, so I'm the bad influence, huh?"

"Out of the two of us, who's more of the partier?"

Granted, we'd never talked about Vincent going out to parties. That topic of conversation had only come up once, not long enough for me to question him about it. Even though Bryce and Vesta were convinced that Vincent did nothing other than party. But as I said it now, the words felt wrong in my mouth.

The amusement in his gaze dimmed a bit, but he said, "You're probably right."

Vincent and I walked out of the building in silence, and I had the feeling that I'd said something wrong. Maybe I'd offended him with the bad influence comment. Honestly, if someone had said that to me, I'd be a little miffed too.

As I scrambled for an apology, he asked, "What's the worst lie you've ever told?"

"The worst lie I've ever told?" I repeated, frowning a little. He held open the door so I could pass through, and I huddled deeper into my coat. I couldn't help but scan the parking lot, trying to find any prying eyes. There was the green SUV from this morning parked in the lot, and even though I could see movement through the tinted windows, I couldn't make out any faces. "Oh, I know. I told Bryce that he was my first kiss."

Vincent's lips spread, a grin so wide that I almost thought I'd said something else. Surely he wasn't smiling at my confession. It wasn't *that* scandalous. "You told him he was your first kiss?"

"I know, it's lame." But also kind of horrible. "We kissed in a game of Lip Locker last October—that game where you kiss someone in a closet? After, he asked if he was my first kiss and it kind of just came out."

"You *would* think that's a big lie," Vincent said, but his slight chuckling continued. "You never told him?"

"Never. I doubt it'll ever come back up. Especially not if he and Vesta..." I sighed, feeling conflicted.

Vincent had lost the smile, sticking his hands into his pockets. We were halfway across the parking lot now, nearing where I'd parked the convertible. "Maybe it's a sign that kissing someone in a closet game wouldn't work out."

"I don't know. I'm sure it's worked out for someone before." I glanced sideways at him, gaze catching on the lip ring. "Have *you* ever played?"

"Please. Can you imagine me playing that?"

I could. The image fluttered to my mind with relative ease. I could imagine a blindfold tied around his eyes, imagine his hands on someone's hips—like they'd been on mine moments ago in the hallway. When he kissed them, they'd have to know immediately who it was by the lip ring. How would they react?

How would *I* have reacted if it was Vincent in that closet instead of Bryce?

Suddenly, the air felt too cold to inhale, nearly burning my lungs.

Vincent didn't wait to hear me answer his question—which was a good thing, because I hadn't thought of a good answer. Instead, he crossed the parking lot to his truck, a few spaces down from mine. There were a handful of cars in the lot, but they most likely belonged to athletes at after-school practice, because there was not a student in sight.

"So tomorrow," Vincent threw over his shoulder, not fully looking to find me frozen beside my car, the mental image of Vincent playing Lip Locker still dancing in my brain. "I'm holding you to it this time, Adeline."

"Don't forget the popcorn," I called after him, finally managing to pull open the door.

Vincent tugged on his own door handle, turning to regard me once more. "How could I?" he asked, hauling himself inside his truck without waiting for an answer.

I wrote it all out in my bullet journal, a nice little list that I'd been ready to tackle.

Tell Mom about how I blamed myself for the accident.

Figure things out with Vesta and Bryce.

Talk to Mollie about Jackson.

I figured I could talk to Mom first since I'd see her first. Of course, that was the most daunting one.

I could catch Vesta tomorrow after school. Mollie would be trickier to pry the truth out of—unless she was 100 percent comfortable, she wouldn't spill about Jackson, and she wouldn't spill about what was going on with her and Vesta. She wouldn't talk at school where there were distractions. Since she was grounded, I also couldn't show up at her house. That one might have to wait to be checked off.

After making that list, I started studying for my midterms, focusing on math, since it was the class I was the most concerned about. I knew I'd pass, but I really wanted to get a good grade.

"Hey, Addy," Mom called as she clattered inside, her car keys jangling. She brought a symphony of sound with her, filling the silence that had been there moments before. "Are you hungry?"

Her curious tone made me wary. "A little."

"I brought home some takeout from Mary's Place," she told me, and as she stepped further into view, I saw she carried plastic to-go bags, setting them and her purse on the kitchen counter.

That cautious part of me grew stronger as I stood from the couch, pushing my textbook and worksheet to the side. "What'd you get?"

"I got a chef's salad for me and pig pancakes for you. I wasn't sure what to get, but I remembered that you always loved those as a kid." She started to place the to-go containers at the breakfast bar, like she wanted to eat together. Spending time together was new. When we ate our meals, we did it separately. Once she got home from work, she usually went into her bedroom and sometimes wouldn't emerge for the rest of the night. "I made sure to ask for no bananas."

Right, Mary's Place always put two slices of bananas on their pig pancakes. It struck me then—Mom had remembered I didn't like bananas. "Thanks."

"I had the kindest patient today," Mom said as she pulled silverware from the drawer. "She was a little old lady, she's new. Sweetest thing. In there, recovering from a hip replacement and was just as positive as could be."

I listened to Mom talk about her day as I sat down on the other side of the breakfast bar, opening up my box. Sure enough, a little pancake designed like a pig sat before me, with no eyes.

"It's been a while since we've caught up." Mom sat down across from me. "Tell me. What's new with your friends? How's Mollie? When Vesta called, she mentioned the asthma attack."

"Mollie's better—she was at school today. The girls have been...a little distant lately." I didn't really want to get into all the details, unsure what kind of response she'd give me. "The Snowflake Dance is Saturday, so I've got a lot coming up with the dance committee."

"And your midterms," she added, cutting up the larger pieces of her salad. "I read the newsletter the school emails out."

The lulls in the conversation came, like I knew that they would, but they didn't feel nearly as painful as I worried they might. With Mom, the silence almost felt comfortable. We both had reasons to be quiet, to linger in our own thoughts.

We hadn't eaten dinner together since Dad died. Was that on her mind, too?

Thinking of Dad made Vincent's face pop into my mind. I felt my face grow warm as I remembered how he'd held me in front of his house last Friday. Or even today, when I'd pressed him against the wall to hide from Vesta and Bryce, how his hands had fallen to my hips to steady me. It was a simple touch, but if I focused on it, I could still feel the pressure of each fingertip through the fabric of my skirt.

It'd been forever since Mom and I had talked boys, but

I found myself wanting to broach the topic of Vincent. Maybe not the full truth—I'd definitely omit the last name —but just a bit of it.

"Have you heard of Crushed Beanz?" I asked Mom as I poured the syrup over my pig, nonchalantly testing the waters without paddling out too far.

But it seemed even that was too far. Mom's head whipped up, eyes narrowing. "Why?"

"I—I'm just curious." The tension in her face threw me off, and I found myself lying. "Vesta got coffee from there the other day, and it was really good."

Mom turned back to her salad, her expression much, much stonier than it'd been a moment ago. This new silence was different. Heavier. It had me feeling like I needed to hold my breath, that breathing in or out would result in some cataclysmic event that would leave this moment uninhabitable. But it wasn't something I could let go.

So, staring down at the river of syrup, I asked, "Why don't you like Crushed Beanz?"

Her tone was brusque. "I just don't like who owns it, that's all."

So she knew who owned it. She knew it was Mr. Castello "Why not?"

"*Because.*" Her jaw was clenched tight, a livid line. "If you knew who owned it, you wouldn't like them either."

"You mean the Castellos?"

It was a name never to be spoken in this house, but I just crossed that line. Obliterated it. A part of me wanted to watch Mom's expression but the other part of me was afraid to look.

"The accident wasn't Mr. Castello's fault."

Stupid, stupid, stupid. I was stupid. So beyond stupid. I was crossing another line, one that I immediately wished I hadn't. In fact, her expression collapsed entirely, making her look torn between horrified and anguished.

My heart started beating faster at the pain in her gaze, but my mouth didn't take the hint. "It *was* an accident. There was so much snow."

"Stop." Her voice was fierce, cutting, just as sharp. That pain had been consumed by a bigger flame: anger. She stirred her salad around with violent jabs of her fork. "Just stop."

"Don't you think Mr. Castello is suffering enough?" I demanded, clenching my fork so tightly that it hurt. "He was a runner, did you know that? He used to run races, and now he'll never run again."

"You don't—how would you know that?" She'd abandoned the pretense of stirring the dressing in her salad now, abandoning her fork in the to-go box. "Are you just saying that to make me feel worse?"

Wait, make *her* feel worse? What did she have to feel bad about?

Before I had a chance to ask, Mom shoved to her feet, snatching up her salad. "I'll be taking my meal in my room," she told me, the fierceness returning to her voice. "Once you finish your pancakes, you can go up to yours."

And with that, she stormed down the hallway. A moment later, I heard the guest room door slam shut.

I sat there for a long moment, listening to the sound ring in my ears, before I grabbed Mom's purse off the counter island. I couldn't stay there any longer and do this dance. Couldn't let her hide in her room while I hid in mine. Couldn't just go up to my room and cry—because I knew that was what I'd do.

Mom had stuffed her purse so full that I had to shuffle through lipstick tubes, receipts, and other random odds and ends before I found my phone.

My hands also brushed her car keys, which I snatched up. They fit perfectly into my hand, spurring me on. After quickly grabbing my own purse and coat, I let myself out into the garage, knowing exactly where I'd go.

A darkness fell over Greenville that was abnormally shadowy, like every single star in the sky had been snuffed out with one blow. The moon was absent from the sky, whether obscured by cloud cover or a new moon, I wasn't sure. I didn't care, either. I just followed where the headlights led me, and for once, I was roasting.

The sedan grew much hotter than the convertible ever could, and though I was practically sweating, I didn't turn off the heat. Instead, I rolled down the windows, letting the chill in as I raced down the road.

I didn't care until I pulled in front of a familiar house, my headlights illuminating the garage door. Quickly, I pulled out my phone.

Me: ***I'm out in your driveway.***

I stared at my phone for several long moments,

wondering if I'd get a response. Wondering if I'd driven out here for no reason. Wondering if the front door would even open.

And then it did.

Bryce poked his head out as if to confirm that I was, in fact, in his driveway before he fully came out. He didn't have a coat on, his arms bare, as he hurried across the yard. He slid into the passenger's seat, rubbing his hands together. "Well, this is a nice surprise. I just got home from tutoring, actually, so good timing." Bryce looked at me closer. "Though, can I ask *why* you're in my driveway?"

"Have you asked Vesta to the Snowflake dance yet?"

His body angled toward me, but I hadn't taken my gaze off his garage door. "I—"

"You should do it in a cute way," I went on. "With a sign and everything. She'd really like a sign."

"I don't—has she talked to you about...that?"

"No, but it was pretty clear when I saw you two in the hall today."

I wasn't sure why I was confronting him about this instead of Vesta. Maybe it was because this conversation was long overdue; maybe it was because I needed to clear the air between us. Talking with Vincent about my lie to Bryce had him on my mind, had me wanting to let everything out. The fact of the matter was that things hadn't been the same since the new year. And it was time to face it.

"I swear, nothing's really happened between us," he said quickly. "She claimed it was girl code. But...I *do* like her, Addy. And I liked you, I did, I—"

"I get it," I cut him off gently, though I couldn't muster up an appropriate expression. "Sometimes you're with someone and you just *know*. I get it."

He still watched me. "Are you just saying that?"

Finally, I turned my head to look at him, at those blue eyes and brown hair. His shirt hugged his frame in a way that complemented his football player build, and his expression was wary, nervous. "This is the first time we've spoken outside of school in weeks, Bryce. And I didn't mind that. I didn't mind the idea of *not* seeing you, as rude as it sounds. Did you mind that you never saw me?"

Bryce's lips pulled into a frown, one filled with a somber sort of sadness. "I missed you, but not...not like that."

Not like that. We regarded each other, that wishy-washy label of "more than friends" dissolving on the spot. A new label branded us: *friends*. I dug around in my emotions, trying to find any sadness there, but there was none.

"You weren't my first kiss," I admitted to him, stupid that of all things, I felt like I needed to say *that*.

He let out a shocked laugh. "Thanks for being honest. I had a feeling." Before I could ask him what that mean, he went on. "And...thank you for coming and saying all of this. I didn't want to be the one to say anything."

"Because you didn't want to add to my mountain of worries?" I guessed, recalling what Mollie and Vesta had said about not wanting to burden me.

"I just didn't want to ruin things between you and

Vesta. She was worried that if you found out, you'd never forgive her."

I coasted my hands down the sides of my steering wheel, feeling the leather underneath. Heat still spilled from the vents, and since I wasn't moving, the air from the window wasn't quite enough to keep me cool anymore. "Life's too short."

Bryce reached over and grabbed my hand, giving it a squeeze. "I am sorry, Addy. For Vesta, for this, for...for your dad."

Breathe, I caught myself thinking, but squished the thought as if I'd stepped on it with my flat. Instead, I gripped his hand back, giving him a sad smile. "Me too."

I held his hand for a bit longer, struck by the stark difference between holding his hand and almost holding Vincent's. When my hand had been on top of Vincent's, my heart had been beating much faster, much more nervously than it was beating now actually holding Bryce's.

"You have my permission," I told Bryce, letting go. "Ask Vesta to the dance. Make it epic."

Bryce's smile stretched so wide as he opened the passenger door, as if knowing, too, that our conversation had come to a close. "I promise that I will."

"And don't tell her that we talked," I called before he pulled fully from the vehicle. "I...I want to have that conversation with her, okay?"

"Don't wait too long—I'm running out of time to do an epic dance-posal."

I rolled my eyes, a rueful smile springing to my lips. "I'll talk to her tomorrow."

He made his way back to his front door, turning to lift his hand in farewell before disappearing inside. Even though he was gone, I sat there for a long, long time, listening to the hum of the heater, feeling sweat gather at the back of my neck.

I let myself wonder, for the first time, what Dad would say if he were here. Would he say something comforting? Offer to make me a milkshake? Not know what to say, and just hold my hand instead?

I didn't know the answer. I didn't know him well enough to be able to guess.

And with that thought and tears in my eyes, I shifted the car into reverse, ready to go back home.

twenty

For the first time in a long time, I slept soundly and through the night. No nightmares clung to me, refusing to let me out of their grasp. I didn't toss and turn, and I didn't have a hard time falling asleep. Peaceful, dreamless sleep gathered me in its arms quickly, holding me for the night.

My pillow felt like velvet against my cheek the next morning, my comforter swaddled around me, keeping me warm. So warm that I didn't want to move an inch. I didn't want to give up the sweet quiet of unconsciousness. I knew if I moved too much, if I opened my eyes, sleep would ebb away quickly, and I didn't want it to. The warmth my covers provided was safe, comfortable, and I never wanted to move.

Except it was *really* bright, which didn't make much sense. When I woke up normally for school, the sun was barely rising. Had I left my lamp on last night? Didn't really sound like me, but maybe I forgot. I opened my eyes to just slivers, finding my lamp turned off. Then what—

I glanced a smidge lower, to the alarm clock on my nightstand, the one that wasn't going off.

11:04.

Oh. *Crap.*

I flung myself up and out of bed, kicking my comforter away and scrambling to my feet. Fudge, fudge, fudge. I was *never* late. Ever. Granted, I usually used my cell phone for alarms, not that clunky, ugly thing I'd dragged from the depths of the closet. Who used actual alarm clocks anymore? No one, because *of course* it hadn't gone off. Of flipping course.

I got ready for the day at a rapid pace, nearly tearing a hole in my tights in my attempt to shove my legs into them. My hair was easily coaxed up into a bun, mascara quickly swiped on, and I snatched a tie from the top of my dresser, hurrying to loop it around my neck.

Of course all of my lack of sleep had caught up to me, but did it have to be on a school day? I'd missed all of my morning classes, wouldn't arrive until the tail end of lunch. A part of me wondered if it was worth it, but with midterms so close, I couldn't risk it.

So I drove all the way to Greenville High, taking Brewer even though it made me a bit later. Every close parking space had been snatched up, leaving me to park all the way in the back. I just couldn't catch a break.

Everyone in the cafeteria was almost done with their lunches by the time I got there, after having ditched my stuff at my locker and signing in with the office. I made a beeline for my table, and Mollie turned her head as she noticed me. "Where were you this morning?"

"I overslept," I sighed as I sat down, noticing the absence on the other side of Bryce. "Where's Vesta?"

Bryce's gaze met mine, heavy with meaning. "She had a doctor's appointment this afternoon, so she left after last period."

Of course. That was my motto for the day, apparently. I felt guilty then, especially since I'd promised Bryce I'd talk to her today. I gave him an apologetic look.

"How long are you grounded for?" I asked Mollie, watching as she stuffed the to-go container for her soup back into her lunchbox. "I want to stop over soon and talk to you about something." *Like someone named Jackson Mannerfield.*

Mollie's gaze dipped past me. "Until tomorrow."

That would work. I could take her home after school tomorrow. After tomorrow, my days would get busy. Thursday after school there was a committee meeting to make sure all our ducks were in a row, and then Friday we were moving all the decorations into the gym. I'd promised Mrs. Keller I'd be there both days, and of course I'd be there to help set up on Saturday.

I'd be dateless to the dance, which was okay. For so long, I'd been obsessing about a potential ask from Bryce, but I found that I was actually content at the idea of going alone.

"Have you finished your peer interview thing for psychology yet?" Bryce asked me. When I gave him a questioning look, he added, "Vesta's been stressing about it. Apparently Kyle's a hard guy to get to focus."

"I need to start writing the report tonight." I couldn't

use what I'd written before. All those hateful things about Vincent were untrue, and now that I'd gotten closer to him, my opinion had totally changed. "Honestly, I should've started it earlier, but I've been a bit distracted."

"It must be hard to get Vincent to talk about himself," Mollie said, but she was looking at her hands.

My breath caught in my throat. "I'm not partnered with Vincent."

Hadn't I told her that lie too? I thought she'd been there when I said it.

And then I remembered how Jackson had called Vincent Friday night when he took Mollie to the ER. He'd called *Vincent*, meaning they were close enough to have swapped numbers. Close enough to call each other. Close enough to tell each other partners they might've had for a school project.

Mollie didn't press the question, didn't call me out for lying—if she even knew. She merely tipped her head, rubbing her fingers over her nail polish. I couldn't tell if she brushed the subject off easily or was still thinking about it. Either way, nerves ate at me.

As lunch wrapped up, I found my gaze drifting to the table in the back corner, looking for a certain lip-ringed boy. Of course, though, he wasn't there.

I was hoping I'd catch Vincent in the hallways, if only so he didn't think I hadn't come to school at all today. He would've been wondering, wouldn't he, since I'd missed first period? Or maybe he wouldn't care. Each time the bell rang at the end of a period, I lingered by my locker as long as I could, hoping he'd swing by his.

At the end of the day, I packed my things quickly, hoping I'd go out and find his truck. I hadn't even buttoned my coat before I slammed my locker door shut, turning to hurry down the hall.

"Addy? Can you hang on a second?"

I halted at the sound of my name, finding Mrs. Keller a little ways behind me with a clipboard in her hand. Impatience tore at me, making me feel jittery. "Yeah, sure."

"I just wanted to clarify that we were still set for our meeting after school Thursday," she said as she came closer. "And Friday after school, we're still planning to start to set up, correct?"

She said *we*, but she was really asking about *me*. I knew her nerves came out when things got closer and closer, but she should've trusted me—I was the chair of the committee. "Of course. I've got a nice task list set for Friday, so hopefully everyone shows up. And I'll be here bright and early Saturday morning to finish everything off."

A wave of relief passed over her face. "Great, great. You make things so easy for me."

"I live to make your life easier," I teased, but took a deliberate step backward, hoping that the conversation was over.

When I took another step, I walked right into someone, feeling their hands come up to my arms at once to steady me. The honey scent hit me before I could even turn around, and my heartbeat kicked into high gear.

Vincent released me, sticking his hands into his pockets. "You should really watch where you're going," he said, but the amusement in his eyes was as clear as day.

"You shouldn't have been right behind me," I countered, and then turned back to Mrs. Keller. She was looking at Vincent with a strange expression—no, looking at *us* with a strange expression. "Don't worry about anything, okay? I've got all the heavy lifting covered."

"I trust you," Mrs. Keller said. "See you tomorrow, Addy."

"Heavy lifting?" Vincent questioned as we walked away. The rapid pace of my heart hadn't slowed. Maybe it was because I was excited to watch the movie. Maybe it was because I could still feel the imprint of his hands on my arms. "You and Mrs. Keller talking about weightlifting?"

"We were talking about the Snowflake Dance," I clarified, fingers shaking as I buttoned my coat. "I have recruits to help us on Friday. There are a lot of things we have to get from the basement."

Vincent looked mock-offended. "And you didn't feel like you could ask me about heavy lifting?"

I raised an eyebrow at his bicep. "You've got muscles?"

He nudged me, causing a laugh to slip past my lips. "I guess if you've got to ask, that's a bad sign."

"Your muscles *do* look like they could use some work," I told him with a wink, recalling words he'd once spoken to me. But I really wanted to tell him he had nothing to worry about, that I'd seen the strength in his arms when he played drums last Friday. I kept my mouth shut. "So, I should probably drop my car off at home before we go to your house."

Evil Killer Babies was almost a two-hour movie, meaning that Mom could get home before I did. If she saw the car in the garage, she would leave me alone, assume I was up in my room. Sneaking in might get tricky, but not impossible.

"Can you follow me home and we can go from there?" I said.

"I live to make your life easier."

It sounded so much weirder, those words coming from his lips. They were much lower than how I'd spoken them to Mrs. Keller, as if he were trying to caress my ears with the sentence.

I gave him a look. "Did you get your homework finished?"

Vincent reached up and pushed his hair from his eyes, tucking it behind his ears. "You should've seen the look on Mr. Walker's face when I turned in those missing assignments. He probably thought I paid someone to do it for me."

I was surprised by how warm the air felt outside. Maybe it was because the sun finally had a chance to peek through the clouds, its rays beaming down and lending heat to this cold winter.

I stopped beside the door of the convertible, fingers curling around the handle. "Would you have?"

Vincent hesitated on his trek to his truck. "If I were desperate."

"Almost failing psychology doesn't count as desperate?"

Vincent smiled, just a little, and it felt like the rays of

sun shined a bit brighter. Before he turned fully, he said, "It's the *almost* part that made everything okay."

Our conversation was put on pause for the ten minutes it took to get to my house from the school. It was weird to look up in my rearview and see Vincent behind me, close enough that I could see his face but far enough away that I couldn't make out his expression. Just knowing he was there had me driving more carefully. As if he were judging my every turn or brake.

It wasn't until I dropped the convertible off in the garage and hopped in the truck that he asked, "Also, I thought of something on the drive over. Who's the bad influence now, skipper?"

"I *overslept*. There's a difference." Still, I couldn't help but smile as I pulled the seatbelt across my chest. "I'm surprised you noticed I was missing."

"Well, when Mr. Walker called out a certain Adeline Arden, and a certain high-pitched voice didn't respond, I noticed." He put his hand on the headrest of my seat to turn and see behind him as he carefully backed down my driveway.

"He doesn't call me Adeline," I pointed out. "He calls me Addy. Everyone does. But you."

Vincent blinked at that, as if he'd just made that realization. "No one else calls you Adeline?"

"Almost never. Not even my mom. I used to tell people I'd never speak to them again if they spoke my full name."

"So does that mean you want me to stop saying it?"

It was such a mouthful to hear. *Adeline.* I didn't feel much like an Adeline. It was a sophisticated name, old-fashioned. Not at all like me. But when Vincent said it, I felt the complete opposite. It didn't feel old-fashioned or stuck-up or anything like that. When he said it, it just felt like *me*.

Before, I hated when he'd said it because it reminded me of Dad. But now, whenever Vincent spoke my full name, it felt like I could finally take a deep breath.

"No, you can keep saying it," I tried to tell him in as casual as a voice as possible. "So, I need to be home before six-thirty. I know that doesn't give us a ton of time."

"Plenty of time for evil babies." Vincent gently drummed his fingertips on the top of his steering wheel, as if playing to a silent tune in his head. "My dad'll be there, but he agreed he'd stay out of the living room while you're there."

"Oh, he doesn't have to," I said immediately, but I couldn't deny the little bit of relief. His dad's face was still clear in my mind, and I thought about how we'd looked at each other the other day, the sound of his raised voice still in my ears.

"Horror's not really his thing, anyway."

I shook my head at that. How anyone could *not* like horror was behind me.

"What's one moment from this past year that you would change?" he asked me. "Other than the obvious."

The obvious. I waited for the pang to come, of pain or sadness or guilt, but it never hit me. "I thought we weren't allowed to ask each other questions anymore?"

"I was being a crybaby that day."

That made me laugh aloud as the truck bumped over a

pothole, hitting it hard enough to make me bounce in my seat. "No, you weren't. Your reasons were valid."

He looked like he wanted to argue that, though his eyes glued to the road. "Your answer?"

I tapped my finger along my chin, thinking. I couldn't say *the obvious*—the accident. There had to be something else. When it hit me, I slumped a little in my seat. "There's a photo of my family on our last vacation, and I'm not smiling in it. I...I would've smiled."

Vincent was quiet for a long moment, and the hum of the heater seemed so loud. He didn't ask me why or try to pry further. He also didn't wait for me to ask the same question for him. "I wouldn't have gone to Keith Richardson's party."

I'd never been to one of Keith Richardson's parties, and for good reason. Vesta had been once and said that it was... crazy. Not the kind of high school house party with music and cheap beer. Keith's party had older people, harder stuff. They didn't play silly games like Lip Locker. If Vincent went to his parties, no wonder he rolled his eyes at the mention of the closet game.

I didn't know what specific party he was talking about, but I didn't want to ask. Not in that moment.

"You know, I can't picture you at a party," I confessed, squinting at him. Especially not the kind that Keith Richardson threw. "You just don't seem the type."

"Trust me, I was the type." He shook his head as if to shake out the memories. "But that's in the past."

I really wanted to ask him why it was in the past—ask

him what had changed—but I found myself unsure. I didn't want to push. "Really?"

His gaze was serious, his tone equally so. "Really."

Vincent's house wasn't that far from mine, so we ended up there pretty quickly. Thankfully, there was a white car in the driveway, one with a hospital emblem on the side, and Vincent visibly relaxed when he spotted it.

When I hopped down from the truck, I stepped in a snowbank, which reached the middle of my ankles. The snow compacted under my weight—perfect consistency for snowman-making.

Or snowball throwing.

After dropping my backpack in the snow beside me, I bent down to scoop snow into my palm, packing it tightly so it formed a ball. The cold was painful against my skin, but I only held onto it for a moment before I launched it.

My aim went wide, and the snowball sailed past Vincent's shoulder. He turned to face me, as if to verify that I had, in fact, just declared war.

"I missed," I tried to say, holding my guilty hands up.

Vincent bent down, and though his body was obscured by the front of the truck, I knew exactly what he was doing. "Yeah, well, I'm not going to."

That's when I started to run.

I'd picked the wrong shoes, my ballet flats doing nothing to protect my feet from the snow. I rounded the edge of his house for cover, quickly forming another small snowball.

As soon as Vincent followed around the corner, I threw my ball, hearing the victory of it splitting apart on contact. I didn't hesitate before hurrying toward the back of the house, bracing myself for the inevitable impact.

Vincent launched his snowball, but I saw it fly past me. "Why are you so fast?" he demanded, sounding like he was trying to keep from laughing. "I thought your shoes would have you at a disadvantage!"

"You thought wrong!"

Vincent's backyard was large, bigger than my own. The acreage spread out far back, with a shed near one edge of the property. I almost stopped to marvel at it, not having known there was land like this in town, but I kept moving, Vincent was hot on my heels.

Except after a few steps deeper into his yard, I felt the ground change, from crunchy snow to smooth glass. Ice.

"Wait!" Vincent called when he came closer, breathing hard. "Come back into the yard. You're standing on the pond."

I eyed the snowball in his hand, remembering the story Jonathan had told me about the pond, and took a small step backward. "I heard it wasn't that deep. Jonathan said it was four feet."

"But it's been warming up lately."

Still, it hadn't warmed up enough for it to completely thaw out. "Four feet, Vincent. Big deal."

I'd barely gotten the words out before he hurled the snowball at me, and I only just managed to duck in time, dropping to a crouch.

"Dang," he muttered, and started advancing closer, boots gliding effortlessly over the ice.

We went on like that for a while, scrambling to make

snowballs while the other launched theirs. I hit Vincent twice, whereas he didn't even manage hit me once. At one point, I'd gotten a collection of three snowballs, all balanced in the crook of my arm, rapid firing them at Vincent. The first two missed, but my last one hit him in his right shoulder with so much force that it had him spinning.

No, with so much force that it had his feet slipping out from under him, and he landed on his back with a loud *crack*.

For a second, neither of us moved. Neither of us spoke.

"You should've been a baseball pitcher," Vincent gasped out.

"Are you okay?" I tentatively crept closer. His hands were still at his sides, not making an attempt to build another snowball to ambush me. "Did you hurt anything?"

Vincent let out a groan. "Only my ego, I think. And my spine."

I smiled a little, coming closer until I was peering down at him. His black hair fanned out against the icy surface, his eyes pinched shut. "If it's any consolation, you had a few throws that could've gotten you on the baseball team, too." Even though none of them landed true, but I didn't add that part.

"Should've. We won the championship last summer."

"By a forfeit. Doesn't quite count, does it?" I extended a hand down to him. "Come on, soldier. Truce."

Vincent pried open one eye to gaze at me for a moment, as if trying to judge my sincerity. "I didn't even get you *once*."

"We can't all be winners."

He glowered at me before he slapped a palm into my hand. "Truce." He let out another groan as I pulled him upward.

My feet slipped on the ice as he got to his feet, but even once he was standing, he didn't immediately let go of my hand. In fact, he held on, and though my fingers were numb, I could feel the softness of his skin, the frigidness of his ring.

There was snow in his dark hair, glittering in the sun, and I wanted to reach up and brush it off. I was so used to Bryce's shortly cropped hair, and I found myself wondering what Vincent's would feel like. Would it be soft? It *looked* soft.

Vincent's fingers on mine tightened imperceptibly, and he drew in a breath as if to speak, to share whatever thoughts were dancing in his head. I really, really wanted to hear them.

Except before he had a chance to, there was a massive *crack*. One so loud that I felt it tremble underneath my feet, vibrate through my body.

"Vincent," I said warningly, but that was all I managed to get out before the ice broke underneath us, sending us plummeting into the pond.

twenty-one

That pond was *so* not four feet.

When Vincent and I fell into it, I quickly discovered that it was easily five feet deep. And for a girl who was barely five-five on a good day, a five-foot deep pond was *not* cool.

The freezing water was everywhere. In my mouth, in my eyes, filling my ears. My shoes nearly fell off, wanting to float away and disappear into the mucky sediment at the bottom.

Vincent's hands trembled as he hauled me out of the water, hands flexing over my arms. It was hard with my red coat weighing me down, and the ice he tried to pull me onto kept fracturing beneath our weight. Water poured from our clothes, our hair plastered to our skin.

"A-A-Are you o-okay?" Vincent reached up and shoved his hair back out of his face, but it'd already started to freeze in the air. My own was still dripping—every part of me was dripping. "C-c-come on," Vincent gasped, trying to draw me away from the center of the pond carefully.

If I thought my hands were cold before, clutching those snowballs, that had *nothing* on this sensation now. I was so cold that I could barely feel my body. The pins and needles pain was everywhere, all consuming. And I smelled like pond water. *Ew.*

Teeth chattering, he helped me up the back porch. My body started to stiffen up, and it was hard to bend my knees, but I managed to get up the steps.

"T-take off your c-coat," he got out, reaching for the zipper on his own jacket.

The back sliding door pushed open, revealing Mr. Castello on the other side, already clutching two towels. "I was watching through the window," he said, but the rest of his words were garbled, drowned out over the severity of my shivering. Could eardrums freeze?

Before I knew what was happening, Vincent reached out and started undoing the buttons on my coat with trembling, struggling fingers. After a second, he worked them free and shoved the heavy, soaking material from my shoulders.

Almost immediately after, Mr. Castello reached up from his chair and wrapped a towel awkwardly around my shoulders, and I latched onto it tightly. "Come in, come on," he ushered us, pushing his chair backward to give us a pathway.

For the first time, I noticed there was a man standing close to Mr. Castello's wheelchair. He was tall and watching our movements quietly. "You'll need to take your clothes off," he said after a moment. "You need to warm up gradually."

"S-s-so no sh-sh-shower?" I asked, because there was nothing I wanted more than to be drenched in hot water.

But the nurse shook his head. "No, that's the last thing you want to do. It'll spike your blood pressure, and you'll likely faint."

Jeez, he was spot-on. Fainting in the shower at Vincent's house? Yeah, no thanks.

Mr. Castello started wheeling backward toward the kitchen area. "Vincent, go get her some new clothes to change into. Layers."

Vincent made an affirmative noise in his throat and grabbed the hand that wasn't clutching my towel shut. I could barely feel his touch; every inch of me was so cold. He led me down the hallway and we turned into his bedroom, an area filled with an absurd amount of black and navy. It was fitting, though. Dark colors suited him.

He dropped my hand and moved over to his dresser, riffling around through the drawers, picking out clothes. "H-here." He passed me two shirts and a pair of sweatpants before swiping up a set of clothes for himself. "I'll ch-change in the gu-est b-bathroom," he told me, flashing me a quivering smile before shutting the bedroom door behind him, leaving me alone.

I immediately went over to the curtains and drew them shut, darkening the room further. But after that, I refused to move, refused to even let the towel slip an inch off my shoulders. He expected me to get naked in his *bedroom*? There was some sort of joke in there, surely. Because there was no way.

It only took a moment of me standing there, shivering

so uncontrollably that I could barely think, to wonder how cold I'd have to be to get hypothermia. Much colder than this, surely...right? If I stayed in these wet clothes, were my chances higher?

Gritting my teeth as tightly as I could, I stomped over to his bedroom door and pushed in the lock. *Don't think about it*, I told myself, letting the towel fall to the floor. *Don't think about it*, I chanted again as I drew my shirt over my head, feeling it squeegee off my skin. Quickly, I used the towel to dry myself off before grabbing the first shirt Vincent had given me, which was long-sleeved. It was a bit big on me, and the sleeves went down past my hands, but it was worth it.

The second shirt, though, was a black one I've seen him in often. As I brought it over my head, I was overwhelmed with the scent of him. He smelled so good.

Once my fingers stopped trembling slightly, I braided my hair back out of my face. I'd have to wash my hair anyway, since I smelled so strongly of pond water that it made my stomach turn. After I emerged from Vincent's bedroom, fully clad in clothes that were so soft and so warm against my skin, I found Mr. Castello in the living room, setting two bowls of water on the floor.

"They're for your feet," he'd said. "Trevor says that it helps warm you up at a healthier rate."

So I had Trevor, who was presumably the man loitering around, to thank for sitting on Vincent's couch, slipping my feet into a glass bowl of hot water. Awesome.

When Vincent came out of the bathroom, dressed in gray sweatpants and a long-sleeved navy shirt, his eyes immediately fell to my feet. "Do I have to do that too?" he asked, only chattering a little.

I was so distinctly aware of being dressed in his clothes. It seemed like such a personal, intimate thing. Like I was crossing some sort of line. The more I thought about it, the warmer I became.

"Yes, so sit." Mr. Castello directed Vincent toward me. "Sit next to her. Your body heat will warm each other."

It was a wonder I wasn't fully thawed yet, with how flaming my cheeks felt. Vincent, though, didn't hesitate before he sat beside me, grabbing ahold of the blanket that was draped over my lap and slipping under it too. We were so close that our thighs pressed together, and even though I could barely feel it, my breath still hitched.

"Trevor?" Vincent called. "Addy's backpack's out by the truck. Can you go grab it? Then we should be good for today."

Trevor sounded cheery, probably happy to be of use for our near-popsicle selves. "On it."

I was still shivering uncontrollably, even with the extra layers, my feet in a bowl of hot water, and a warm body pressed up against my own. Vincent's body heat *was* amazing though, and I pushed closer, eager to steal as much of it as I could.

"What a way to make an introduction." Mr. Castello chuckled as he wheeled in front of us. "I'm Vincent's dad, if you haven't already made that assumption."

I gave him a shaky smile, more than just the cold making me shake now. "Addy," I got out.

Vincent, though, quickly tackled on, "Arden. Adeline Arden."

Mr. Castello *did*, in fact, recognize the last name, because he paled. His eyes, I could see now, were a dark brown, and leveled with mine. "It's nice to meet you," he said, though his voice was less cheery than before. "I'm very sorry for your loss."

"I'm s-sorry too." My eyes traced the metal of his chair.

Color came back to his face then, or just to his cheeks, because they reddened. "Oh. Well. I'm the lucky one, Miss Addy."

Looking at him, hearing him say that, made the guilt come on again in full force. My brain threatened to travel down the rabbit hole of *this is my fault*, but I gripped the lifeline that dangled in front of me. *It was an accident*, I repeated, until the words themselves pacified the feeling.

Trevor returned with my backpack, and Vincent instructed his dad to put in the movie. "Well, this movie looks...interesting," Mr. Castello said as kindly as he could, popping the DVD into the player. "Let me make you two some hot cocoa to go with it."

"I better not get nightmares from this," Vincent breathed in my ear, the warmth of his breath making me shiver.

"I hope you d-do."

A smile split across my face as the opening credits rolled, the dramatic music flaring up higher and higher until the first scene began. Mr. Castello delivered the hot chocolates before heading off away from the movie, before the baby could even kill anyone.

"I can see where you get your drink-making skills from," I finally managed to say without stuttering, taking another long drink of the chocolatey goodness.

"He's got a gift, that's for sure. Good thing it's genetic."

Cradling the mug in one hand, I pulled my other hand out from underneath the blanket and pointed at the TV screen. "Watch, this is the part where the baby cuts the storekeeper's tongue out and eats it. Don't get too freaked out—I read somewhere that the tongue was actually taffy coated in cherry syrup."

Vincent looked at me from the corner of his eye. "I worry about you, you know."

"You're not watching!" I reached under the blanket and hit his knee. My fingers hadn't fully thawed yet, but they were getting there. "You're going to miss it."

The gory puppet on the screen attacked the woman's face with a vengeance, her high-pitched screams crackling over Vincent's television's bad speakers. Red spurted from the wound, too red to resemble blood very well, and looked more like paint than anything. I couldn't stop smiling as the puppet began to eat the lady's tongue, the sheer terribleness of the movie lightening my spirits.

My grin was so big that it hurt my cheeks. "Oh, that was so gross. I love it."

The next part was where the baby went off to find its next victim—a man in the middle of shaving—but as the music ramped up for the next kill, my heart stopped beating.

Like the moment had been put on slow-mo, Vincent reached over under the blanket and found my hand, curling his warm fingers around my own. The hard metal of his ring pressed against my skin, the edges of his hardened fingers gentle.

A heady pressure rolled over my chest, leaving me lightheaded and a little surprised. *He is holding my hand. Vincent Castello is holding my hand*, and it was something totally unlike him. Vincent Castello didn't seem like a hand-holder—no, trivial things such as hand holding were beneath him. Lame. Cheesy. But here he was, with his five fingers curled around my five fingers, and I was *so* not breathing.

From the corner of my eye, I could see his chest rise and fall evenly. "How is that woman still alive after losing so much blood?" he asked, voice as even and unbothered as I'd ever heard it. It was the way he usually spoke—off the cuff, as if he truly weren't feeling anything. "She'd be dead and gone. No way she'd have the strength to run across the street."

I forced myself to nod. "Adrenaline, man." My eyelids swept down, cheeks warming because I knew he was watching me, and I knew he was holding my hand, and I couldn't help but smile a little. "I'd bet you'd be running like that if a baby clawed its way through the roof of your taxi and ate your tongue."

Vincent laughed, such a musical sound that I felt it course through my body, a sound I'd memorize. This was it. The moment I'd been waiting for. I looked over to find him shaking his head, his eyes on the TV. In that moment, I didn't want to compare him to Bryce—to any of my friends —but I couldn't help it. None of my friends would've watched this with me. If they had, they wouldn't have lasted the first five minutes.

They wouldn't have held my hand, either, and I wouldn't have enjoyed it nearly this much.

He tipped his head on the side and met my gaze. "This is the worst thing I've ever seen," he told me, in a voice that made my insides feel like they were beaming. I felt warm all over, instantly defrosted.

"It's definitely at the top of your cheesy horror movie list," I countered, unable to look away.

He squeezed my hand once, that intensity never disappearing from his eyes. "Definitely."

The movie ended a little after five o'clock, with my cheeks hurting from smiling so much and my hand warm, still in Vincent's. I hadn't wanted him to pull away, but once the end credits rolled over the screen, he let go, stretching his arms. The coolness swept over my skin instantly, the loss impossible to ignore.

I'd never thought of how Vincent would look in sweatpants before, but now I couldn't stop noticing it. So much different than his dark jeans. His sweatpants had me thinking strange thoughts—like what he looked like late at night. Like what he looked like when he first woke up.

As soon as we got into the truck, he flipped on the heat as hot as it would go. "Are you still cold?" he asked, catching me shiver.

I hadn't been able to put my coat back on—all my clothes were in a plastic bag at my feet—but Mr. Castello had lent me one of his zip-up jackets. "Just a little," I lied, pressing my hands in front of the vent. Heat wasn't pouring out yet, but it was starting to trickle through the cold. "I didn't think it was warm enough that the ice would've broken."

He shook his head a bit, putting the truck into gear. "It wouldn't have broken if I hadn't fallen."

"You wouldn't have fallen if I hadn't creamed you in that snowball fight."

That caused a wide grin to split his face. "Yeah, you're the snowball queen."

"I'll take the title," I said in a haughty voice, eyes lingering on where his hands gripped the steering wheel. "Are you fingers as cold as mine?"

Vincent held out his hand to me, as if wanting me to see for myself.

So I did. He let me pick up his hand, let me press it between both of my palms. "Not bad," I decided, feeling silly, stupid, because I had to be see-through. The worst flirt ever. Harry and Jackson needed to give me some tips. "I think mine were colder."

He didn't say anything in response, and when I looked at him, I found his gaze laser-focused on the road.

I could feel the callouses on his fingers where he usually gripped his drumsticks, but beyond that, his skin was soft. Barely breathing, I traced a fingertip along the backs of his knuckles. I was too afraid to look at him.

We drove the rest of the way in silence, half because I had no idea what to say, half because I thought if I spoke, he'd pull away. Instead, I just looked out the window, at the spot where the sun was beginning its descent below the horizon. The colors became more and more vibrant with passing each minute, and I looked at the spot where darkness was chasing the daylight. In a little over an hour, Greenville would be very, very dark.

When I saw that we were coming up to my road, I released Vincent's hand, and he placed it back on the steering wheel, getting ready to turn it. "Have you written the report for psychology yet?"

"I'm working on it," he said. "You?"

"I'm having trouble organizing my thoughts," I confessed, thinking about the paper. I'd thrown the old one away, of course, but now trying to articulate my thoughts about Vincent felt impossible.

"About me?" Vincent's lips tipped into a smile as he eased into my driveway. The garage door was shut, and from the outside, I couldn't see any lights on. "I'm flattered."

I let out a breath, pressing my hand against the seat between us. "You should be."

I realized then that we were both talking quietly, as if we were trying to avoid breaking the moment in two with our words. Afraid that if we spoke too loudly, the moment would be shattered, and Vincent would go home. Or, at least, that was what I was afraid of.

My hand was still lying on the bench seat between us, five fingers splayed on the fabric, and Vincent reached over and rested his hand on top of mine. For a moment, it was just his warm skin against my cool fingers, and then his ringed fingers traced the outline of mine. Like a cursive sort of script, written in a different language. Tingles danced all over my hand, creeping up my arm, flowing through my body.

"What's a moment from the past year that you *wouldn't* change?" he whispered, calling back to the question he'd asked before, only in a slightly different way.

"You first."

"I wouldn't have changed falling through the ice," he murmured in the quiet, and his voice was nearly drowned out by the furious thumping of my heart. Before I could ask him *why*, he turned to me, gaze soft. "What's your moment?"

He was so, so close, and his scent was everywhere. Honey and sweet and I couldn't think around it. I didn't want to think around it. I was hyperaware of his hand on mine, his touch both electric and soft. "The same," I said in response, but that wasn't true.

This one, I wanted to say. *I wouldn't change this moment.*

I looked up and found his green eyes already on me, so deep and serious that I could fall into them and never emerge. My eyes were drawn to his mouth, the lip ring against the corner. Seeing it caused lightning to course through me. I'd never asked him why he got the piercing. What would it be like, I wondered, to press my lips against it? What would he say?

I hadn't realized I'd been leaning in until Vincent's mouth met my own halfway.

twenty-two

$\mathcal{I}$t happened so fast that I couldn't believe I was doing it. Kissing him. His lips pressed against mine, the cool metal of his lip ring against my mouth, and some sort of sharpness behind my ribs exploded, a near painful sensation.

Vincent's mouth was so, so soft underneath mine, gentle, warm. But I didn't want soft and gentle—I wanted closer. I wanted to curl my fingers around his skin, feel his body against mine. I fumbled with the latch on my buckle, letting it go so I could slide into the middle of the bench seat. One of his hands came up and touched the skin of my throat, fingers curving around the back of my neck.

Vincent, I learned, was an excellent kisser.

It made sense. Just looking at him made me certain he'd never do anything halfway, but this was...*whoa*.

The cool metal of his lip ring began to warm as my mouth curved over it, a sensation that I'd never felt before. The moments when our lips parted were half-milliseconds in time. I reached up and threaded my own hands into his hair, feeling the silky strands curl over my fingers. As soft as I'd imagined.

I never wanted the kiss to end, but I ended up pulling away ever so slightly, drawing in a sharp, short breath. For a long moment, neither one of us moved, our breathing shallow and mixing together in the tight space between us.

A breathy chuckle came from him, tickling my insides. "Jeez," he murmured under his breath. "Did you kiss Bryce like this when you said he was your first?"

I wanted to laugh, but everything inside of me was shivering, jittering, wanting to pull his mouth back to mine. "I've never kissed anyone like that."

Vincent reached up and smoothed the hair out of my face. His lips curled up into the most beautiful smile I'd ever seen. So much emotion lay there, all for me to see. No more barriers existed between us. "He missed out."

A stupid grin spread across my face. "I'll get your clothes back to you tomorrow, okay?"

"They look better on you anyway."

And so I leaned in again, pushing up against him, catching his mouth with my own. I felt bold, and maybe it was because I was wearing his clothes, or maybe it was because our lives were already intertwined. Either way, I felt bold, bold enough to slip my fingers between the material of his shirt and his side, to feel the warmth of his skin there. In response, he kissed me deeper, and the cycle of feelings started over from the top.

Until the passenger's side door pulled open, flicking on the cab lights and illuminating my mother's stricken face.

I almost thought I imagined her standing at the open

door, wearing her work-issued scrubs. She had her coat on, but unbuttoned, and her purse was settled in the crook of her elbow.

"Addy Annabelle Arden," she said—or growled, really —voice barely audible. Her words almost didn't register. That, or my brain was still cast in the haze from Vincent's mouth. "This is Stella's *boyfriend*, huh?"

I just blinked at her for a moment, unable to think. "No," I said instead, voice stupid in my ears. "This is Vincent *Castello*."

As soon as I said his name, I regretted it. Instantly. I'd spoken his last name with such emphasis, but I really hadn't even thought about it, the name just falling from my mouth.

"Castello," Mom echoed, almost as if she didn't recognize the significance.

I was so close that I could feel Vincent stiffen beside me, probably hating the fact that he was caught in the middle of our mommy-daughter showdown. "What are you doing home?" I figured she'd either be home later—not *now*, at the same time as us.

"I told you my shift was different today. I told you I'd be home at five-thirty, or did you just block that out too?"

I honestly didn't remember her telling me any of that. She'd said something about picking up different shifts for one of her coworkers before, but not that she'd be home at five-thirty. Her shifts usually ended around six-thirty or seven.

The anger on Mom's face lit a fire inside me, one that made me feel indignant. I should've gotten out of the truck, but now that I finally had Mom's attention, I wanted to make her steam further. "I just was at Vincent's house watching a movie."

Now Mom was looking at me as if she didn't recognize *me*. "Excuse me?"

"Such a cringe-worthy movie, wasn't it?" I asked, but when I looked at him, he wouldn't meet my gaze. And all of my anger and frustration melted in an instant. Well, maybe not all of it, but a good amount. I hated myself for making him so uncomfortable, for making this entire situation so much worse.

"Get in the house. *Now*, Adeline."

And that was how I knew I was dead meat. *Adeline*.

I grabbed my bag of clothes and my backpack and stepped onto the driveway. With a voice that sounded more confident than I felt, I turned back to Vincent one last time and said, "I'll see you tomorrow."

Vincent didn't reply. He stared ahead, jaw set. A seed of unease unfurled in my stomach at the line of his jaw, at the stiffness to his shoulders, but I pushed it away as I turned toward the house, Mom trailing hot on my heels.

She didn't even wait to shut the door before she launched into it. "I don't even know what to say to you. I don't even know what you were thinking!"

"I'm thinking that I should've remembered what time you got off work," I grumbled, my fear disguising itself as anger. I kicked off my shoes, not bothering to place them against the wall.

"Yeah, I bet." Her keys slammed down on the counter, letting out a loud ring. "You are *grounded*, Adeline, remember that? And you do *not* associate with those people! You know better! And look at you—are you wearing his *clothes*? Oh, you are in so much—"

"*Those people*," I repeated, but continued toward the staircase, refusing to turn around. "You don't know him. You don't know either of them."

"Oh, I don't? He's a *Castello*! His father—"

"His father did nothing!" I shouted, surprising myself as the words echoed off the walls. It made everything in me shake, as if my soul was flinching at my anger. My frustration. Because everything was coming to a peak. All of the guilt and grief and anger and pain reaching a crescendo. "Mr. Castello did nothing, Mom. *Nothing*. He was driving. Minding his own business. Mr. Castello didn't kill Dad, and you know it!"

She recoiled as if I'd struck her, pulling her arm close to her chest. She held it almost protectively. "If *he* hadn't been driving, he'd still be with us," she told me, voice definitely not as strong as it'd been a moment ago.

I knew the second "he" she was referring to was Dad, but I couldn't keep my response from sounding harsh. "If *Dad* hadn't been driving, maybe Mr. Castello would have a normal life. Would have function of his leg. Would be able to do what he loves."

Then I hurried up the stairs, leaving her steaming behind me. I was half surprised she didn't storm up after me, or at the very least scream up the stairs at me, but she remained silent.

I slammed the door shut between us, breathing hard. For the second time that night, adrenaline was coursing through my veins. I sat down on the edge of my bed, unable to pull in a steady breath.

Heat swamped me, making me feel sweaty and shaky. After the cold shoulder with Mom for so long, yelling at her like that felt *horrible*. Like I'd been forced to eat something spoiled.

I flung myself backward on the bed, closing my eyes to try and recall the warm feeling with Vincent from earlier. I wanted that feeling to overwhelm me, not this bitter taste in my mouth. Touching him, tasting him. It had felt electric, static charging and filling the air. Had Vincent felt the same way? Was he driving home, thinking about that kiss?

To high heaven, I wished I could call him. Apologize. But with Mom still in possession of my phone, I'd have to wait for a full-on apology tomorrow. I'd have all night to craft it, because there was no chance of falling asleep anytime soon, not with Mom's angry voice ringing in my ears and not with the memory of Vincent's mouth pressed against mine.

I hugged a pillow to my chest, trying to breathe through the tears, but still some leaked out.

My relationship with Mom had sunk to an all-time low. I'd already lost one parent, and now I couldn't have a civil conversation with the other. And it wasn't just her fault— there was something about whenever we spoke that put me on edge. So long, we'd been avoiding each other, not wanting to even broach the topic of the accident, and it felt like we'd permanently changed something in the process.

❄

The warmth of yesterday had done a lot of thawing, so as the temperatures dropped overnight, everything turned into a layer of ice. When I got up for school that morning—the alarm clock actually working this time—I'd gotten fully ready before heading downstairs to where Mom had left a sticky note on the counter. **School's canceled for the day.**

I dropped my backpack in the middle of the kitchen in utter disbelief. She couldn't have *knocked*? I mean, at least she told me before I got my keys, got all the way to school, and...

Wait. No way. The convertible keys weren't in the dish I always put them in. Had she seriously taken my keys? So my phone wasn't enough—she had to make sure I couldn't leave the house, too. What was next, barricade me in my bedroom so I couldn't get out?

Joke was on her. I walked over to the mudroom and slipped on my snow boots, grabbing a spare coat and bundling it tightly around me. I didn't have a car, but that didn't matter. I still had two legs.

Sure, Mollie's house was about five minutes away by car, which equaled many more minutes by foot in snow, but I'd get there eventually. She'd said she was ungrounded today, so I couldn't imagine her parents turning me away at the doorstep. And it wasn't like she had her license so she could come and pick me up, either.

I set off through the snowy Greenville residential area, passing Grisham Street and Walnut Street without a car. I shivered a little, watching the sun slowly start to rise from the horizon. It was mostly obscured by cloud cover, but it tried to peek out and say good morning.

As I walked, I found myself thinking about Vincent. What was he doing? Was he up yet or did he want to sleep in? Was he working on our peer interview report? I'd started writing mine last night after I'd managed to calm down, and finished about half of it before my eyes grew heavy. Was he almost done with his?

Once words started to flow, writing about him had been easy. I couldn't believe I'd written such horrible things before. No, it was easy to see how all of it connected. How he was quiet before, afraid to speak his thoughts. Afraid to display emotion. He'd wanted to keep to himself, share as little of himself as possible. Through the past few weeks, I'd broken down his defenses, gotten him to smile. Gotten him to *laugh*. I could still remember how the sound made me feel, all warm and tingly, like butterflies were filling my entire body.

I tried to imagine what Vincent would write about me, but thinking about him brought the memories of last night to mind. His warm hand against my skin. My fingers curling into his hair. His lip piercing against my mouth. I shivered, tightening my jacket further around me.

Mollie lived on Southerland Avenue, where houses looked a tiny bit like they did in Addison, only on a smaller scale. The red brick of her house stood out vibrantly against the snow. Her dad's car wasn't in the driveway—no doubt he already left for work.

It only took a few moments after I rapped my knuckles on the storm door for the interior one to open, revealing

Nicole, who was still dressed in her polka-dotted pajamas. She squinted at me. "What are *you* doing here?"

"And what are *you* doing answering the door?" I fired right back, holding my hand out in front of me, just above where her head rose to. "Aren't you a little short to be doing that?"

Nicole stuck her tongue out at me but unlatched the lock. "Did you walk all the way here?"

"My car's out of commission."

As I stepped over the threshold, Nicole wrapped her arms around me, all pretenses of being a brat evaporating. If only for a moment. She quickly let go, stepping back. "Ew, you're cold!"

"We just established I walked here, dork," I snorted, kicking off my boots, making sure not to get clumps of snow everywhere. "Where's Mollie?"

"Bedroom. She doesn't want to come out and face Mom."

"Addy, so good to see you," Mrs. Brooks called as she walked out of the kitchen, smiling at the sight of me. She was a short woman, barely coming up to my shoulder—and all of the girls except for Bree had definitely inherited that gene. "Mollie's been in a bit of a mood this morning. Maybe you can break her out of it."

Mollie in a mood? The idea still sounded so bizarre to me. I shrugged off my coat, hanging it on a peg near the door. "Is she bummed that school's canceled?" I asked ironically. "She could probably still have gone."

Mrs. Brooks smiled, though it didn't reach her eyes. "She's starting to act so much like Jess."

I thought of Mollie's older sister, who still lived under the same roof but was home as infrequently as possible. "Is that a bad thing?"

Her fingertips fluttered around the collar of her shirt, eyes betraying her words. "No, no. She's just...starting to shut us out, just like Jess did. We can't figure out why. It's been hard."

Though I had sympathy for the Brookses, I knew how they were. I remembered Mollie telling me all about how they treated Jess—forbidding her to do things, dictating when she had "car privileges." Not just strict—controlling. I thought about Mollie being forbidden to date, even though she was sixteen.

"I'll see what's going on," I promised Mrs. Brooks, rubbing my hand over Nicole's knotty hair as I walked past, stretching out of reach when she tried to swat my hand away.

Mollie was lying on her bed when I pushed her bedroom door open, staring up at her ceiling, still dressed in her pajamas. She wasn't under the covers, though, just lying on top.

"I said I'm not hungry," Mollie said, not even looking over.

"You're not?" I asked. "Because I am. I didn't have breakfast."

She sat up straight in bed, turning to me with wide eyes. She took in my skirt, tie, my no doubt red cheeks. "What are you doing here?"

"I was in the neighborhood." I shut the door before walking inside and sitting down on the edge of her bed.

"Mom took my phone and my car keys, so I had to walk over here."

"Why'd she take your keys? Why did you *want* to come over here? Now? It's barely eight o'clock."

"I was lonely," I said, and it wasn't quite a lie. "It wasn't like I could text anyone, and you live closer than Vesta."

Mollie didn't say anything to that, but merely patted the space beside her. She didn't have to tell me twice. I scooted up next to her and fell down on top of the covers, folding my hands over my stomach.

"So, are you ready to tell me what's actually going on with Jackson?" I asked her, staring at her ceiling.

Mollie covered her eyes with her hands. "Nothing's going on. He thinks he likes me, but he's wrong."

"Why's he wrong?"

"We all know what he's like. I mean, he broke up with Trish a few days before he decided he liked me? I just... Vesta says I should play his strings, whatever that means."

"No offense to Vesta, but you are *so* not the kind of girl who plays strings," I said with a small laugh. Just picturing it was ridiculous. "How come you two always seem to be talking, then, if you feel that way?"

Mollie turned to me. Her dark eyes looked so conflicted. "Anything to get out of this house, Addy. Away from the screaming sisters and annoying parents. And...the attention's nice, you know?"

I *did* know. I thought about Vincent's attention the past few weeks, more recently the past few days. His hand, curling around mine. His scent, filling my head. His eyes, and the way they lit up when he smiled. "I lied about my partner project for psychology," I told her, feeling that since she'd shared something personal with me, I needed to get on with it. Lay it out there. "I didn't get paired with someone else."

"I knew," she said, nudging me with her elbow. "I saw you getting into his truck one day after school. That, and Jackson said something about it. But I can't figure out why you lied."

I gaped at her for a moment, so many emotions battling at once. Guilt for lying. Relief that she wasn't mad about it. Amusement fluttered around in there too, because apparently I hadn't been as good at sneaking as I'd thought. "Why didn't you ask?"

She tilted her head to the side. "I figured when you were ready, you'd say something."

"Is that why you didn't tell me about Jackson?" I countered. "Because you weren't ready?"

Mollie gave me a sad smile. "I didn't want you to judge me."

"Which is *ridiculous*. I mean, sure, Jackson's a mega-flirt and you could do so much better, but I wouldn't judge you for it."

"I wouldn't have judged you either, you know." Mollie shifted, causing the bed to squeak and her hair to tickle my cheek. "I know the others judge Vincent, but I don't."

"Vincent's not as bad as everyone makes him out to be." It felt like something that needed to be said, something she needed to know. "He's really kind, Mollie. And funny. I never would've thought he'd be funny, but he's just so witty. He makes me feel like I can actually laugh again."

When Mollie spoke, I could practically hear the smile in her voice. "Sounds like you like him."

Putting those words to the emotion that's been simmering on a high heat over these past few weeks was a little overwhelming. *I like Vincent Castello.* They sounded funny in my head, but I didn't doubt that they were true.

I drew in a breath, staring up at her ceiling as I confessed, "I kissed him."

Her reaction was instantaneous. She once again flew up into a sitting position, looking at me as if I'd grown a second head. "*What?*"

twenty-three

"*W*hat?"

Vesta's voice pitched so much higher than Mollie's had, and her eyes bugged much, much wider. I'd braced myself for her reaction, but I still found myself feeling anxious. "Yeah, last night."

"You kissed him? Like, on the mouth? Was there tongue?"

Mollie made a face. "Ew."

"Did he kiss you *back*?"

I thought of Vincent's hand on my neck, the other that reached around my back, pulling me closer, closer. "Yeah."

"Oh my *gosh*." Vesta flopped down in the chair at the corner of Mollie's bedroom. She hadn't even bothered putting on real clothes before coming over here. Mollie had texted her the equivalent of a 911 text, and she'd rushed straight over. If I looked closely enough, I thought I could still see a bit of her nightly face mask by her jawline. "You and Vincent Castello. I just...my brain doesn't know how to process that."

"Have you two been getting close for a while?" Mollie interjected, knocking her head against the headboard.

"I wouldn't say *close*..." But there were those times where I found myself looking at him in a different way, craved his company, his scent. "I didn't plan on kissing him."

No, that was most definitely not written down in my bullet journal. Not on my list of to-do's. That had come from left field.

Vesta shook her head ever so slightly more out of surprise than disdain. "What are you going to do about it?"

Freak out, obviously. I really, really wished that I had a way to reach out to him, to see what he was thinking about it. *Was* he even thinking about it? Gosh, what if he wasn't?

Vesta was still watching me, waiting for my answer. "Bryce and I are just friends now," I told her, as if me kissing Vincent hadn't made that obvious.

Every inch of her froze—even the movement of her chest stalled. I could practically see her mind whirring, desperate to come up with a response. "Is it because of Vincent?"

I shook my head. "You should've told me you liked Bryce."

Her gaze whipped toward Mollie. "Did you tell?"

"No!"

"You should've." I gave each of them a level stare. There was no anger there, not anymore. The relief that we were finally getting to the root of everything was far too substantial. "You *both* should've told me."

Vesta stood up from the chair and came over, all but

falling onto the bed as she grabbed my hand. "I *swear*," she whispered, all amusement gone. "I swear I didn't plan on anything happening between us. *Nothing* happened between us...except..." She trailed off, as if admitting the truth was still too hard.

Mollie, from my side, helped her out. "They kissed. At the New Year's Eve party."

Vesta made a noise, a little bit like a kicked puppy. "It hit midnight and I just grabbed the person closest to me. I didn't realize it was Bryce until after, I swear."

I smirked a little, picturing the scene. "You have to admit, that's sort of romantic."

"Why aren't you more upset?" she whispered, eyes still glassy. "You were so excited about your Lip Locker kiss with him, and coming back from the worst month of your life, and I just—I didn't want to ruin it."

I squeezed her hand, glancing at Mollie. "How'd you find out?"

"I saw them." She wrung her hands together, as if she were waiting for a reprimand. "I was at the party too. I'm sorry that I kept it from you."

Vesta cast an apologetic look to Mollie. "I asked her not to say anything, and I shouldn't have done that."

I tried to imagine what might've happened if Vesta *had* said anything. If she'd come to me telling me about her feelings for Bryce right when I came back to school. How would I have responded? A part of me loved to think I'd have been understanding, that I'd have backed off, but I didn't even know. I'd been in a weird headspace then.

"I'm not mad. Not at either of you." With my free hand, I grabbed Mollie's. "I kept secrets too."

"But *I* broke girl code," Vesta objected.

Mollie added, "And I was an accomplice."

I snorted. "It'd be different if Bryce and I were actually dating, but we weren't. I came back and things were different." I pulled back from both of them, fiddling with the collar of my shirt. "I don't feel that way for him anymore. Any of those feelings are long gone."

"No, you like *Vincent*," Mollie let out a breath, shaking her head. "I never would've imagined that."

"That's why you should never keep secrets from me," I told her in a serious tone. "All that worrying for nothing."

Except I *had* been worrying about the entire situation, so I wasn't really in a position to say anything.

"I'm sorry for lying too," I said, letting out a breath. "I just...for the longest time, I didn't want to talk about everything, you know? I wanted to shove it all down. Pretend that Dad..." I cleared my throat, but it still tightened. "Pretend he wasn't gone. I was afraid if we talked about Vincent, we'd talk about the accident again. And I just couldn't."

Mollie leaned her head against my shoulder, and Vesta pressed in closer. "You can always tell us anything," Mollie said. "And if you tell us that you don't want us asking questions, that's okay too."

Vesta nodded. "Always. That's what best friends are for, right?"

I reached out and pulled them into a group hug, finally feeling like we were on the same page. It'd been so long since we'd hugged like this that I found myself closing my eyes and basking in it, in the embrace of my best friends. I was so relieved to have put all of that behind us, to have all our secrets out in the open.

"You and Vincent," Vesta said, arms still around us, trying out the words. "Weird."

"A bad weird?"

Vesta's green eyes met mine, not nearly as vibrant as Vincent's. After a quick glance at Mollie, she smiled. "Nah, it's good. Just weird."

When I got to school the next morning, I was on a stakeout. As soon as Vincent Castello walked down the hallway, I was ambushing him. It didn't matter if anyone saw us together anymore, not since my friends already knew the truth. Once I'd gotten home from Mollie's yesterday, I spent the entire day working on my report and an apology, one probably getting more attention than the other.

So as soon as I spotted him, I was going to attack him with my rehearsed spiel.

What I did the other night was so horrible. Seriously. I'm so sorry I put you in that position with my mom—I can't even begin to imagine how uncomfortable that must've made you. I'm so, so sorry. But...I'm not sorry about the kiss.

Okay, maybe that last line was a part questionable—maybe a lot a bit questionable—but I had no other idea how I was going to nonchalantly slip in that "hey, I really dug kissing you, let's do it again sometime" line. I wanted him to know that I was apologizing for my behavior *after* the kiss, not for the kiss itself.

Because that kiss? Wowza.

"When are you ungrounded?" Mollie asked as we waited at my locker. "We should have another girls' night—a real one this time."

"No idea," I sighed. In all honesty, I'd probably never be allowed out of the house again. Probably not even for my wedding day. Mom's hold on my phone had gone from "a week" to "indefinite." It wouldn't surprise me if she never spoke to me again.

It made my heart hurt so, so much. But I didn't know how to fix it.

"I have to get to class," Mollie said after she looked at her watch. "Maybe he'll come in before the bell."

"I hope so." If not, maybe later tonight I could sneak out and swing by Crushed Beanz and...be a stalker? Ugh. No, not a stalker. I needed to drop off his clothes—that was a good enough reason, right? Except I'd have to time it right to get out under Mom's watch. That is only if she put my car keys back.

Before I could head to Mr. Walker's classroom, though, I saw him. He was striding toward his locker, hadn't seen me yet, so I just stopped in the middle of the hallway, staring at him like a creeper. I couldn't shake myself from the grinning-stupor he'd thrown me in. I tried to keep the smiling and the stomach fluttering to a minimum, but it was almost impossible.

I clutched my backpack strap tighter, waiting for his

eyes to lift and meet mine. And when they did, it wasn't right.

There was no warmth to his expression then, no softness. Like he wasn't looking at *me*, but someone else. Someone who hadn't kissed him mere days ago.

I found myself walking toward him even though his expression said *stay away*, feeling as if lead had been strapped to my ankles.

Vincent didn't lift his gaze from his locker as I stopped two feet from him, not daring a step closer. "Good morning," I said, straightening my spine as much as I could. Feigning nonchalance, even though my insides were quivering. "Thank God for that snow day, huh?"

He didn't answer, but his hand stilled in his locker.

When I realized he wasn't going to speak, I cleared my throat. *Probably time to start apologizing.* "Listen, about Tuesday night, I'm so sorry for how everything played out—"

"It shouldn't have happened," he said. There was a stiff set to his shoulders that made me worried, made me want to reach out and smooth out the tension there.

"I know," I said immediately. "It shouldn't have. I shouldn't have put you in the middle of everything with my mom. I can't even begin—"

"Not your mom." Vincent finally, *finally* turned to look at me. There wasn't a trace of warmth in his gaze, and his lips were pressed into a hard line, his jaw firm. "All of it. None of it should've happened."

All of it. None of it. The words bounced around in my

brain, each ricochet losing more and more meaning. All of it. None of it. "What...what are you talking about?"

"We've got our own issues that we don't need to mix together. You don't need mine and I don't need yours."

I flashed back to crying on his front porch, and him pulling me into his chest, hand smoothing my hair. But the bluntness in his voice made that memory fade into the background. "Is this about what I told you? About the accident?" I dropped my voice to a whisper. "About my dad?"

"Why didn't you tell anyone about me?" He shut his locker door and faced me, expression impossible to read. "Why was it some big secret? Were you embarrassed?"

"No!" I said loudly, and then inwardly cursed myself. Gentler, I said, "Of course I wasn't. I just...I didn't want people thinking—"

"What? Didn't want people thinking *what*?"

I opened my mouth, but I had no answer sitting on the tip of my tongue. I hadn't told about Vincent was because I was afraid of what they'd think. So it *was* about Vincent. A sick sort of feeling twisted my gut, as if someone had reached inside and wrenched it tight.

"You just thought you could kiss me on the down-low and it wasn't a big deal?" he went on, but no longer looked at me. Something else had snagged his gaze in the hallway, something he refused to look away from. "I let myself entertain the idea that this could work. That our history wouldn't get in the way. That we could be honest."

"We can—" I tried to object.

"Can we? Why'd you tell your mom that I was Stella's boyfriend, then? Why'd you use my name like a curse word the other night? Why'd you always duck your head, getting into the truck? You might've kept me a secret, Adeline, but I never kept you one."

Shame poured its way through me. I *had* done that. Spoken his name because I knew it would cause her to react, even though I hadn't been aware of it in the moment. Kept our friendship a secret to everyone important to me. I'd never meant for him to find out, never meant to carry it out for so long. And yet...

Here I'd been playing the kiss on repeat, and Vincent had been thinking other things. Completely different things.

"Vincent," I tried one last time, my voice sounding so small. "I'm sorry. I just—I just didn't think about what I was doing."

"I know." Hope flared in my chest—maybe I could make him understand—but he quickly added, "Neither did I." And with that, Vincent walked right past me, leaving me frozen in the spot behind him.

I stood in the middle of the hallway for what felt like an eternity, unable to turn my head to see him walk away, too afraid to. The trembling in my fingers became so bad that I couldn't hold my grip in a proper fist.

The breath in my chest felt like it had solidified, crumbling off the walls of my lungs. It made perfect sense that Vincent would be hurt by everything, especially when Mom had come to the truck. Even in the moment, I'd known that was what I was doing. *Vincent Castello*, I'd said, knowing the last name would evoke her rage. *I was at Vincent's house watching a movie.*

Maybe he needed time to cool off. I could give him time. I could show him I was sorry. I'd have to plan how, but I could do it—I was a planner. I lived and breathed planning. After everything, there was no way could it all be over.

When I got to psychology, dragging into the room like a zombie just as the bell rang, I didn't even glance at the boy in the back corner. Mr. Walker called the class to order, asking everyone to turn in their peer interviews. I barely registered pulling my paper from my folder, unable to look at a single word of it.

Mrs. Keller got a phone call midway through last period. It was Principal Martinez, asking me to stop by her office after school. Immediately, my pulse and thoughts went into overdrive. Was she calling me down there because I'd accidentally slept in on Tuesday? Was she going to grill me about skipping? I steeled myself, preparing to rapid-fire her questions with answers that sounded legit.

I was super sick, I'd say. *Home with the stomach flu. Barely out of the bathroom all day, it was the worst. Have you ever had the stomach flu, Principal Martinez? Not fun.*

Maybe I could leave the bathroom line out of it.

However, when I walked into the office, I instantly knew something was off. The secretary looked at me with pity, sending me straight to Principal Martinez without hesitation.

"Come in, Adeline," Principal Martinez said with a polite wave of her hand, beckoning me to one of the empty seats in front of her desk. "Mr. Walker will be coming any moment."

Whoa, wait. Mr. Walker? Last I'd checked, my grade in psych was great.

"Am I in trouble?" I asked, but not out of fear—more out of confusion. I had no idea what I'd be in trouble for, but it seemed strange that I'd gotten a first-class ticket to the principal's office.

"Not at all," she answered with an uncharacteristic smile. "We'll discuss more when he gets here."

It only took Mr. Walker another two minutes to make his way from his classroom to the office. "Sorry," he excused himself, coming to sit at the chair beside me. "A student had a question about their exam tomorrow."

"Adeline, we recently heard something that gave us pause," Principal Martinez said, launching straight into the conversation, her formal speech making this moment a thousand times weirder. "Something about you."

"It made us *concerned*," Mr. Walker clarified, and I realized that he was holding a collection of stapled papers in his hands, keeping the front page turned away from me. "You've gone through such a tragedy recently, but we're concerned about how you may be handling it."

I blinked, twice, completely thrown off guard. "This is about the accident?" I guessed that explained the overly sympathetic expressions that were mirrored on their faces.

Mr. Walker began to look majorly uncomfortable, and shifted in his seat. "Today, the peer interviews were turned in. And there were some things touched on in your paper that made us concerned."

It took me a moment to find the words as I mentally scanned my report. "What about it? I didn't think I wrote anything bad in it."

"Not your paper," Mr. Walker said. "The paper *about* you."

Everything was suddenly crystal clear. *Vincent's paper.*

Principal Martinez leaned forward over her desk. "Adeline, is it true that you haven't spoken to a professional about your loss?"

"Is that really any of the school's business?" I asked, my tone coming off clearly as defensive. I folded my arms across my chest, making sure I glanced between the two of them evenly.

"We're allowed to make inquiries if it's regarding your health and safety," she replied.

Health and safety? What was that supposed to mean? When had I ever been unsafe at school? In fact, these past few weeks since had school resumed, I thought I'd kept up my façade had quite well.

After I spent another moment rifling through my thoughts, feeling confused and shocked and highly irritated, Mr. Walker lowered his voice. "Is it true that you are suffering from panic attacks? That you'd jumped out of a truck?"

My gaze dropped to the papers in his hand as the room stilled. My breathing stilled. My body stilled. The papers were turned away from me, but I could picture the scrawl written on it. Beautiful—more beautiful than I'd anticipated, the looping scrawl neater than my own writing. *He swore*, I thought to myself. *He swore not to talk about the accident.*

But that wasn't about the accident, not really. Just a side effect of it.

"If it's true, Adeline," Mr. Walker went on, "it worries us. Your safety is important, and talking to a professional is a *good* thing. Having someone there to talk to can help us sort through things. Sometimes it's too hard for us to do on our own."

"Meeting with our high school guidance counselor can also help," Principal Martinez interjected. "Miss Tilly? She's a wonderful listener."

I needed to get out of this room. Out of this room, out of this school, before I started screaming. "Thank you for the concern," I told them, not looking them in the eye. "I'll talk to my mom about it."

"We've already left her a message," Principal Martinez told me, a clear way of saying *no way you're getting off the hook that easy.* "We just want you to know that Greenville High is here for you in any way you may need. We'll always lend a listening ear."

I shoved to my feet without a response, desperate to get out of this room, and Mr. Walker stood with me. "Don't be mad at him," he said, because even though he hadn't named any names, we both knew who he was talking about. "From the writing, it's clear he's coming from a place of concern as well."

Somehow I doubted that. He'd been coming from a place of *anger*. He wanted to hurt me like I'd hurt him, wanted to take all of my fears and nerves and lay them bare for everyone to see. Or at least for Mr. Walker to see.

The whole conversation with Mr. Walker and Principal Martinez had lasted less than five minutes, so short that there were still a lot of people gathering their stuff from their lockers, but it had been all I needed to lose my mind.

It was probably a good thing I didn't see Vincent at his locker, even though I'd hurried down the hallway hoping to. Hoping to see him so I could yell his ear off. He wasn't supposed to write about that stuff. I hadn't written about his family life. I'd left his mom, his dad, and even Frankie out of it. And yet he thought he could write about all of *that*?

And of course, I had no idea what else he'd put into that stupid paper, except that he'd included me jumping out of his truck. Had he written about my meltdown in his front yard, my soul-eating guilt, too?

Standing in the hallway, fighting for normal breaths, I was torn between frustration and wanting to burst into tears.

twenty-four

I kept it together during the Snowflake Dance meeting, plastered on a smile so phony that I felt sick to my stomach. It was eerily reminiscent of the smile I'd worn when I came back to school the first time. It convinced everyone, even Mrs. Keller.

When I got home, though, all of it burst out. I threw my backpack into the corner of my bedroom, watching my books spill out, uncaring if any were dented. I wanted to rip them all to shreds. I wanted to launch them out of the window and into the snow.

The tie at my neck was choking me, and my fingers slid against the fabric, desperate to tear it off.

Vincent's whole speech about being honest with each other was such a load. I'd been open with him, honest. For the first time since the accident, I felt free to talk about anything. To be myself. It felt like he cared and understood.

And none of it mattered to him in the end. None of it.

It felt like a monster had been unleashed inside me, one that couldn't settle on one emotion. Anger. Hatred.

Sadness. Despair. Everything seemed to hit me at once. All those fights with Mom. Vincent walking away, writing all those things. Dad...dying.

If he'd never gotten in that car, things would've been so different. Mom and I wouldn't be arguing all the time. Even though toward the end he drank too much, he seemed to be the glue that held us together. No matter what, he knew how to make us laugh—I couldn't even remember the last time I heard Mom's laugh. If he'd never gone driving that night, I wouldn't have let the guilt suffocate me for so long. I never would've thought twice about Vincent freaking Castello. Sure, we might've still gotten paired together, but it would've unfolded so differently. I wouldn't have avoided being home. I wouldn't have gone to Crushed Beanz. I would've gotten the information I needed and been done with it all. Been done with him.

Each breath I drew in tore through my throat, to the point where I wanted to scream and never stop. I looked around my room, desperate for the next thing I could throw, could break, so my surroundings matched my insides.

"Addy?"

I whirled around to find Mom standing in the doorway, and as I stared at her, I realized just how fast I was breathing. Nearly hyperventilating. Her eyes were wide, a little cautious. "I got a call from the school today. They left a voicemail."

Ugh. Seeing her, though, dulled some of the monstrous feeling. "Can we not talk about this right now?"

Apparently, that was code for *please, come inside,*

because Mom walked further into my bedroom. Her steps were tentative, unsure, and it was clear she didn't want to have this conversation any more than I did. But that didn't stop her. "We've never...talked about anything. Related to the accident, I mean."

There's a reason for that, I wanted to tell her. Whenever I thought about her and the accident, I could only remember her falling to her knees, letting out a soul-shattering scream.

I sat down on my bed, gripping my fingers tightly. "I don't *want* to talk about it."

Mom ran her palms over her scrub pants, drawing in a steadying breath. "I know that it wasn't Mr. Castello's fault. I've always known that. It was easier to think that than whose fault it really was." But her next words weren't nearly as strong, quivering, about to break. "It was mine."

My eyebrows shot up, frustration immediately evaporating. That was the last thing I expected she'd say. "Mom—"

"It was so snowy," she said, but she wasn't looking at me. She spoke to the alarm clock on my nightstand. "And I planned to be driving the convertible until December. But that snowstorm—it came out of nowhere."

It had. The weatherman projected a slight dusting if that, but on the morning of the big storm, we'd already gotten four inches. From there, it just kept packing.

"Your father suggested I sleep in one of the extra rooms that night," she said softly, her words beginning to lose their steadiness. "They would've allowed it, of course. They were already offering that to some of the other nurses. But I didn't want to. I didn't want to be stranded there, so I asked him—" There was a catch in her voice, one that made her pause. "I *told* him to come pick me up."

All at once, I knew where she was going with that. "Mom. It wasn't your fault."

"Do you want to come with me?"

"No."

His voice echoed, a shadow listening in. "It's not your fault," I repeated, this time making sure my voice sounded stern. "It's neither of our faults."

All at once, the air *whooshed* from me, sucker-punched out from the words I'd just said. *Neither of our faults.* It'd fallen so effortlessly from my lips, and I realized I believed it. It wasn't her fault, but more importantly, it wasn't mine. Vincent's words had burrowed their way into my heart, changing my beliefs. Grief was still there, but the guilt was dampened. It wasn't my fault.

Dad dying...it wasn't my fault.

Mom's forehead furrowed. "Why would it have been your fault?"

"He asked me to go with him. I was so mad at him, and I didn't want to. So I said no." I drew my knees up to my chest and wrapped my arms around them. "I should've said yes—when I knew he'd been drinking, I should've driven instead. I shouldn't have let him leave. If it's your fault, then it's mine too."

"He hadn't been drinking, Addy." When Mom finally looked at me, her eyes were full of tears. I felt a pang punch through me. It'd been so long since she looked me in the eye —I almost forgot how beautiful her brown eyes were. How vivid and deep and warm they were. Looking into them alone made me feel like I could cry. "Oh, sweetheart, you thought that? He hadn't been. It was the first thing I asked about after...but he...he was sober."

I blinked at her, my thoughts stumbling over each other. "He was?"

But he seemed...he seemed...

This entire time, I'd been thinking he'd knowingly driven drunk. This entire time, I'd been so *angry* that he would do that. So angry at *him*. This entire time, I'd blamed myself for not stopping him, but he was never... A rock lodged itself behind my ribcage as the realization settled over me, as cold as ice.

Mom reached over and laid her hand on my knee, her fingers digging into the blanket that was draped over me so I could feel her touch. "Of course it was never your fault, Addy. I was always so afraid you would blame me," she whispered. "That you would think it was my fault that he was out in that storm."

I remembered what Vincent had said, about how Dad made his own choices. Dad decided to walk out of the house, decided to go on the road. But that was a hard pill to swallow. If I had stepped in, things would've been different. If Mom had agreed to stay the night at the hospital, things would've been different. If, if, if.

I didn't blame Mom, though, not one single bit. Much like I didn't blame Mr. Castello for driving too fast, or so Vincent claimed. Though I still held a bit of resentment for myself, I was inching closer and closer to accepting the truth.

Maybe it was the distance that helped me realize it, maybe I just needed someone to guide me through it. Vincent had been the one to introduce the truth—the one that I took so long understanding.

It was just an accident.

The pressure in my chest loosened, like an elastic band snapping, and I drew in a sharp, shaky breath.

"I wasn't there when you needed me most," she went on, squeezing my knee. "We were both pushing down everything. Me especially. I've been sleeping in the guest bedroom, for crying out loud."

"Are you up here because the school called?" It was the most logical reason of why she chose *now* to have this conversation. Not that I was complaining, but I was curious.

Mom gave me a small, sad smile. "I shouldn't have needed someone to tell me to talk to my daughter. I'm so sorry for that." I couldn't even guess what Mom had been going through, all on her own. Creating an idea seemed impossible. "We never really talked about everything, Addy, but I think we need to."

"You mean, talk to someone else about it?" I guessed, reaching up and swiping a palm across my cheek. I didn't even realize I'd been crying until my skin came away wet. "I'm not sure I want to."

"Me neither. But we need to."

Mom watched me for a second longer before she leaned forward, wrapping her arms around me. Though it felt strange and rare, I felt myself settle into it immediately. The last time we'd hugged, it hadn't really been a hug. It'd been me holding onto her tightly, her screams and sobs wracking her body. That hadn't been a hug, but this was.

One never really forgot the feel of their mother's hugs, and my body instantly relaxed at her touch. It reminded me of the times she'd been there for me in the past. Like when I failed my first test. Or when one of my ideas for a dance during my freshman year had been shot down. She'd held me just like this, comforted me with the mere embrace. Her hand smoothed up and down my back, and I never wanted her to let go.

My chest ached again, but almost in a good way. I felt like crying, but half of the tears would be from relief. Relief that Mom didn't blame me, relief that we weren't fighting anymore, and relief that this was finally all out in the open.

When she spoke, I felt her voice vibrate through me. "I may have judged Vincent a bit too quickly, but to be fair, you *were* wearing his clothes."

I laughed, but it came out a bit strangled, the tears in my eyes and throat clogging the noise. "It *so* wasn't what it looked like." Well, it wasn't *entirely* what it looked like.

"Well, you can tell me," Mom said, pulling back and pressing her palm over my cheek. "You can tell me about all of it. About Vincent, about anything. There are so many things I didn't notice, but I promise to listen. To *talk*."

What she was offering meant more than she could've possibly known. Or maybe she did know, because the light in her eyes was there, glinting. She seemed awake for the first time in what felt like forever.

I wrapped my arms around her again. "I miss Dad," I told her, voice muffled by the fabric of her scrubs, muffled by the suppressed tears. But they weren't so suppressed anymore; they were free and falling down my cheeks. "I miss his milkshakes and the sound of his footsteps when he came home from work. I miss the way he used to make us laugh."

Mom drew in a halting breath, one that sounded littered with tears, squeezing me back tighter. "I miss him too, sweetheart. So...so much. I miss how warm the bed used to be, how *safe* I used to feel with him beside me." She choked on a sob, her voice quieting to a whisper. "But...I'm so thankful you stayed home that night. I'm glad I've still got you."

I whispered back, "I'm glad I've got you too."

twenty-five

"You're missing a huge section of curl, Vesta. How can you seriously not see how you're missing that section?"

"I have naturally curly hair, Mollie," Vesta said defensively, angling the curling iron in a different direction. She stuck her tongue out in concentration. "I don't know how to use this dang thing."

Mollie's eyes met mine in the mirror in my bedroom, wide and desperate. "Can you please come and take over, Addy? She's going to burn my hair off."

I snorted, leaning into the mirror so I could put my teardrop earrings in. "She's not going to burn your hair off." My gaze snagged on the smoke wafting up from where the curling iron wrapped around Mollie's locks. "Well. Probably not."

"Vesta!"

"Here, dear, let me take over." Mom came into my room without an ounce of hesitation, plucking the iron from Vesta's grasp. "I haven't curled Addy's hair in years, but I think I remember a thing or two."

"Can't be worse than the job Vesta's doing," Mollie huffed, glaring at our friend in the mirror. Her eyes, though, were bright with amusement.

Vesta stuck her tongue out.

We'd been getting ready for the past few hours, and Mollie was the last to finish up. We already had our dresses on—Vesta wore her white one, which caused her hair to appear that much redder. It didn't have sleeves, and she left her hair down, her curls perfectly tamed.

Mollie's gold dress was a bit longer than Vesta's, flowing to the middle of her calf. She was the last to get her hair done, since she'd spent most of her time braiding mine back into a loose, low bun.

Mom gave me a gentle smile. "You look beautiful, sweetheart. You all do."

I glanced at myself in the mirror, at the way the blue dress hugged my waist. It had long sleeves, the sequins glittering in the light. My blonde hair was pinned up beautifully, with a few strands framing my face. Mollie had really nailed it.

"This seriously feels like a long time coming," I told them, sitting on the edge of my bed to slip on my flats. "It feels like we went dress shopping forever ago."

"So much has changed," Vesta said in a wistful voice, and I knew what she was thinking about. Bryce had asked her to the dance Friday morning—which was a little late, in my opinion, but he made up for it by bringing Vesta a bouquet of white roses. Of course she'd said yes. After everything, I would've kicked her if she'd said anything else.

We'd agreed to meet him at the dance instead of having him come here. Mollie and I were each other's dates for the night, since neither one of us had a guy to act as arm candy. A part of me felt fine with going by myself tonight—I'd have a fun time. The other part, though, couldn't help but wish Vincent...

No. Not going down that road.

"You could've had Jackson," Vesta had teased her, back before we'd gotten our dresses on.

But Mollie had shaken her head, giving a smile that was just a notch off of fully convincing. "I don't want to go with him. I want to go with you two."

Maybe one day Mollie would figure out what was going on with Jackson. I couldn't really gauge how she was really feeling about the whole situation. We'd talked about it a little, but it felt like that story was unfinished. Maybe Jackson would get bored and find someone new. Heck, maybe he'd go back to Trish. Whatever happened, Vesta and I would be there for Mollie. No matter what.

"You girls better get going if you want to make it on time," Mom said after she finished spraying Mollie's hair, making sure the hold was firm. "Let's go downstairs and we can take a few photos."

"Lipstick check," Vesta said to me, smiling wide enough to show teeth.

I couldn't help but smile back. "All good."

"You too. Mollie?"

She shook her head. "I just have gloss on."

Vesta grabbed my hand, stopping me from moving. "I know these past few months have sucked," she started, her voice low, eyes serious on mine. "But I want you to know I'm so lucky to have you as my friend."

I squeezed her fingers. "That should've been my line."

"We've been the worst," Mollie added, her teeth worrying at her bottom lip. "We should've been there for you more, been *open* with you more—"

"No should'ves, would'ves, or could'ves," I said, gently cutting her off. "Like Vesta said, these past few months have been hard. So hard. And who the heck knows what the next months have to hold? But I'm so glad I have you two to help me face it."

Mollie wrapped her arm around me first, Vesta following suit, and we once more joined our group hug.

I couldn't imagine living without these two. I hadn't known Mollie for a year yet, and I would've trusted her with my life. Vesta too. It was still funny thinking about the way everything with Bryce had turned out, but I'd meant what I said. I was happy for them.

Even if I didn't get my happily ever after.

Vincent and I had gone back to pretending that the other didn't exist, which felt wrong. Wrong to throw all of it away. All those feelings, all those memories. Ditching them felt...heartbreaking. Even if I was still angry about the paper, the way things went down between us made me feel so much worse.

"Have fun," Mom told me as she wrapped a scarf around my neck and handed me my car keys. "When you get back, maybe we can have a movie night."

The thought was so sweet that I found myself wanting to dig my heels in and stay home instead. "I'll hold you to that," I said.

Vesta turned up the radio loud as we made our way to the school, and even though she and Mollie weren't the best of singers, they sang along to each lyric, their happiness infectious. I tapped my hands against the wheel, careful to avoid any ice patches. It felt good that things were back to normal between us, that there were no more secrets between us.

When we arrived at the dance, I was surprised by how many cars were already parked in the lot. Vesta was bouncing in her heels, eager to see Bryce, eager to take pictures with him. Mollie had her arm wrapped around mine, huddling close to my coat, as if she didn't want to let go. I wondered if she was afraid of seeing Jackson, but thought better than to ask. Next time his name came up, it'd be from Mollie herself. I didn't want to keep pushing.

She might've been worried about seeing Jackson, but I wouldn't have to worry the same thing about Vincent. I knew for a fact he wasn't the kind of guy to come to the Snowflake Dance.

Mrs. Keller was manning the ticket booth, tucked beside the coat racks, and she smiled upon seeing me. Vesta and Mollie hooked their coats up while Mrs. Keller said, "You look lovely, girls. Addy, all of the committee's hard work paid off. Everyone thinks it's a dream."

"We'd never settle for anything less," I told her warmly, passing over our tickets. Once I shrugged off my coat, I allowed my friends to guide me toward the main area.

The double doors to the gymnasium were spread wide, and even though the inside lighting was low, I could still see the dance in its full glory. The entire committee had spent hours decorating today, hanging paper snowflakes from strings and laying blue fabric *everywhere*. We'd transformed the gym into a winter wonderland, with a photo booth, an archway, and a whole lot of fake snow.

Earlier while we'd been setting up, Mrs. Keller had gotten a ladder to hang the paper snowflakes from the rafters, much like she had last year. They turned and spun and glistened in the bluish lighting, just high enough above people's heads for them not to run into them.

To walk into the gym, we had to pass underneath the archway, and I couldn't look at it without my throat tightening. Memories flooded through me, so many, but I didn't try to force them down. Pretending things didn't affect me never worked—I wasn't going to try it again.

"It's so beautiful!" Mollie called into my ear, having to nearly shout to be heard over the music. "You guys did such a great job!"

I smiled at it all. The faux snow layered over everything, the columns in various spots off the dance floor wrapped with blue ribbon. The Snowflake Dance banner hung near the far wall, and even from here I could see the glitter. There was a tarp on the ground to protect the floors from our shoes, but I barely registered it. Everything else was so *wow*.

In that moment, I knew I'd done it: I'd checked off the last thing on my list. The Snowflake Dance was a success.

People were dancing, laughing, singing along with the music. I'd done everything I could, and it had paid off.

I hadn't realized I'd only come to see everything in its final form until it sunk in that I just wanted to go home.

"Vesta!" Bryce came around a group of people, his grin splitting ear to ear as he took her in. He wore a white tie, matching her perfectly. "You look beautiful."

Even in the low light, I could see her blush. "Want to take a picture?" Vesta turned to us. "Can one of you take it?"

"Mollie can," I said, all but shoving her forward. "I'm going to run to the bathroom."

Vesta was too caught up with Bryce to notice my expression, but Mollie didn't miss it. Her eyes lingered on me, as if wondering if she should say something. "If you want to go home, I can get a ride home with Bryce and Vesta."

I didn't deserve a best friend like her, and I knew it. My hand caught hers. "I'll catch up with you in a little bit, okay?"

Instead of waiting for her to respond, I turned around, heading toward the entrance. But as I turned away, my eyes fell on a figure in between a group of students, just standing there. *Jackson.* His height was the dead giveaway. The expression on his face was tender, almost like he was in awe. It almost felt weird to be witnessing it, especially when I had no idea what he was looking at.

When I followed his line of sight, though, I found it led to Mollie, who was walking with Vesta and Bryce to a brighter corner of the gym to snap a picture.

When I glanced back at Jackson to see if the look was still on his face, the crowd had shifted, obscuring him entirely.

Like I thought earlier, it felt like whatever happened between them was unfinished. Especially after seeing his face when he looked at her, not knowing anyone was watching. Maybe I'd been wrong about his intentions.

I just needed air, I decided. Maybe a breath of night air would help me feel a bit better. But the idea of dancing the night away didn't appeal to me, not when I couldn't stop thinking about something else that was going on tonight.

Untapped Potential played Fridays and Saturdays. That was what Vincent would be doing right now. I wondered what songs they'd be playing. I hadn't attended enough gigs to memorize their music, but I'd be able to feel the thump in my chest, like a second heartbeat. It made sense that I liked the drums the best in their songs. I liked their *drummer* the best.

I didn't bother putting on my coat, giving Mrs. Keller some lame excuse about leaving my lip gloss in the car. My heels clattered on the cobblestones as I made my way out the door, drawing in a breath of cool, icy air. The cold wrapped its fingers around my arms, snaking through the mesh part of my dress near my stomach and making me tremble.

A clear sky greeted me, absolutely free of snow clouds and the constant cover of gray that we'd been living under since winter officially began. No, they were absent tonight, and I tipped my head back to take in all the constellation of stars. They looked like the snowflakes inside, hung by a set of strings.

I didn't know how long I stood out there, allowing my soul to settle inside my body, to take a deep breath in and let an even bigger one out. Long enough for my toes to grow numb where they poked out of my heels. Long enough for the tracks to switch inside, for the DJ to start a slower song.

Long enough for most of the students to be inside already, even the latecomers. So that was why I noticed when a certain truck pulled up and parked in the lot, too far for me to make out exactly who was driving. I watched my breath fog in the air, not wanting to get my hopes up.

It only took a handful of moments for the person to hop out of the truck and head toward the building. Once the parking lot lights illuminated their face, I felt my heart kick-start, all of the butterflies taking off at once.

Vincent.

*I*t took an impossibly long time for Vincent to cross the lot, and he stopped a few feet away from me. He glanced down at himself almost nervously. "Don't laugh," he said immediately.

No chance of that. The black suit jacket was pulled over his chest and arms, the fit so perfect that it almost seemed ridiculous. Like he'd walked right out of a movie. He wore a white shirt accented by a bright blue tie, and the pop of color was so jarring on him that I had to fight the urge to laugh. His dark hair was loose, and he shoved it from his eyes as the wind caught at it.

Surprised wasn't the right word for how I felt, seeing him. *Flabbergasted* was more like it.

Despite everything, the mere sight of him spread warmth all over my body. However, my brain was still in control, and told my legs to stay put. "You look very handsome," I told him, hiding my shaking fingers by curling them into fists. "Got a hot date?"

"I don't know," he said softly. He held himself a little stiffly, as if he were uncomfortable. "I didn't actually ask her. In fact, I think I might've insulted her."

I inhaled through my teeth. "That's not good."

"It's because I'm an idiot who pushes people away," he explained. "It's something I need to work on."

I felt a small smile quirk at my mouth as I watched the snow fall behind him. The night was a shadow of black, and if the parking lot lights hadn't been turned on, he would've blended in well.

"You look very beautiful, Adeline." His gaze glanced over me before returning to my face. "Then again, what else is new?"

Another rocket of heat coursed through me, but I refused to give him a full smile, despite how badly the muscles in my face wanted to. As the shock of him standing in front of me began to wear off, everything between us came flooding back.

"Why'd you come to the dance? I would've thought Vincent Castello would've rather be dead than caught here."

It was his turn to smile ever so slightly, and I looked at his mouth, his lip piercing. If I concentrated, I could almost feel the metal pressed against my skin. He took one step closer. "Well, I was hoping you would be here so I could apologize."

"For which part?" I demanded, wrapping my arms tighter around myself. "For being such a jerk or for putting all that stuff into your report?"

He froze in his advancement. "Mr. Walker told you?"

"No, Mr. Walker and Principal Martinez told me they were concerned about me after hearing that I jumped out of a moving vehicle."

Vincent drew in a slow breath, something like frustration in his eyes. "So you didn't get to read the rest of the paper?"

"Nope." And after that little bit of information shared, I wasn't sure I wanted to.

Vincent came about a foot from me and paused, just watching. The silence that followed then didn't really feel like silence, not in the thick, unbearable way that I'd grown used to feeling. It was more charged, as if the brief pause were letting the tension simmer. "I swear, I didn't paint you in a negative light. I just described the answers to your questions, who you were on the inside."

"Oh? And who am I, according to Vincent Castello? A liar? A coward for not facing her father's death? A bad friend? You'd be right." I let out a sharp scoff. "I couldn't even tell my best friends what was going on in my life."

"I wrote about how deeply you care," he said in a low voice. "And how you're in pain, but you don't want to be a burden on anyone else. You keep things to yourself, put on a brave face, never want anyone to see the cracks."

I glanced down at my feet. "That doesn't sound like me."

"I wrote about how you like peppermint mochas and planning your heart out. I wrote how you like absolutely *garbage movies*."

Now I looked at him, gasping. "*Evil Killer Babies* is a work of art!"

His eyes lightened, lips twitching like he was about to smile, but then he hesitated. "I shouldn't have said what I did about the kiss."

"I didn't kiss you because I thought my mom would see," I told him honestly, feeling my cheeks heat. "Trust me, if I had known my mom was going to walk out, I would've made sure I wasn't all over you. Especially in your clothes."

"I shouldn't have said what I did," he went on, "because it's not like I didn't do the same thing that day. I knew hearing your last name would hurt my dad, and I said it anyway."

I shivered, feeling goosebumps rise on my skin. I forgot he'd said that. "So why'd you get so mad at me if you did the same thing?"

Before I knew what was happening, Vincent slid his suit jacket off and reached out to me, draping the heavy material over my shoulders. It left him in just his dress shirt and tie, and I had to admit, even that was stupidly attractive. "You know how you said that you felt like the accident was your fault?"

I felt my eyebrows pull together. "Yeah?"

"I never realized we had the same thought."

Shock fluttered through me. "So you thought it was my fault too?"

"No." He laughed once, short and swift. It almost sounded nervous. "We shared the same guilt. Both of us felt like the accident was our fault."

"Why would *you* feel guilty?"

"My dad was out driving in that weather, but I never told you why." Vincent looked beyond me for a long moment, at the school. He was quiet for so long that I wondered if he was even going to speak, until he drew in a quiet breath. "I was out at a party that night, and Dad told me not to go, but I didn't listen. It was Keith Richardson's party."

All at once, his words came back to me.

"What's one moment from this past year that you would change?"

"I wouldn't have gone to Keith Richardson's party."

"And I noticed that it started to snow heavier and heavier, but I was too..." He sighed roughly. "Too messed up to drive. I called Dad to come get me, and you should've heard his voice, Adeline. He didn't even yell, but I'd never heard him so disappointed in me."

I gripped the edges of Vincent's jacket tighter around myself, wishing the warmth would spread further. But as Vincent went on, the coldness stayed.

"It was a short drive, but he never made it. After a while, I figured it was some sort of lesson he was teaching me, and started to walk home. And not long after I left the party, I came upon the Ridge Road curve."

My eyes bugged wide. *Scattered glass, a car in the ditch.* The image I'd made up in my head, the one always on repeat—he'd seen it. "Vincent."

"I recognized Dad's car sticking out of the ditch, but not the other. And when I got there, they were...they were zipping up a body bag." His dark eyes met mine, guilt swirling in their depths. "And I...I prayed to anyone who would listen that it wasn't my dad in that bag. I *prayed* for it."

"Vincent," I said again, but he didn't stop.

"I hoped someone else had died so my dad would be okay." He spoke in a voice I'd never heard him use before, one so rough and tortured that I felt my heart tug. From where I stood, his green eyes looked electric, a sheen cast over them. "Because he would never have been out if I hadn't called him. He never would've been on that road."

My chest ached so fiercely that it almost felt like someone had punched a hole through it. I wanted to reach out to him, but I didn't know if he'd want me to. "You told me that I couldn't blame myself," I said, forcing my voice to be strong. Level. Even though I felt like crying for him. "You can't blame yourself, either. It's not your fault."

"When you told me you were the one who felt guilty, I wanted to *scream*." Vincent's gaze was so sad, and when he smiled, it was a bitter one, twisting up his face. "To know that you were feeling the same thing—to know that you'd been beating yourself up over it—I hated knowing you felt that way. That you were hurting because of me and my actions. I was the one who called my dad. I was the reason he was on the road that night." He drew in a shaking breath. "I hated knowing you felt that way and I hated that I couldn't do anything about it."

Without thinking about it for more than a moment, I pressed both of my palms against his cheeks. They were warm to the touch, and I forced his eyes to meet mine. "You did. You helped me see that it was just an accident. A horrible accident. Which means it isn't *your* fault either. If I can't take the blame, neither can you."

I tried to make my words as fierce as they could be, so that somehow they could burrow into his soul, so that he could believe me. Just like I held no ounce of blame for Mom or Mr. Castello, there was no blame at all for Vincent. We were all in the bubble of the being in wrong place at the wrong time.

It was funny how grief and guilt worked, how they burrowed their way into the soul. So many factors had gone into the fateful crash that night, so many people involved. But Vincent was right before. It *was* just an accident. No one could feel guilt for a situation they had no control over.

Vincent reached up and hooked his fingers around my wrists, not pulling my hands away but just touching my skin. "In the essay, I wrote about how even after everything, you were still strong. You didn't let your grief tear you apart. And even in those moments when you were crying over a popped tire or jumping from a moving vehicle, you still fought and came out on top."

"Did you really have to include the part about me jumping out of your truck? You were barely even moving."

"I could've left that part out," he admitted, letting his hands fall from my wrists, and I pulled my arms back. "But it just proves my point, is all. You're so strong—I admire you for it. Getting to know you these past two weeks has been more than I could've asked for, Adeline. Spending time with you, hearing your secrets—and finally letting someone glimpse my own. I...I wouldn't change any moment of it."

It felt stupid to hope. "Not a single one?"

Vincent reached out once again and placed his hands on my hips, and I took a small step closer, heart kicking into overdrive. "Maybe Tuesday night."

Stupid to hope.

"I would've kissed you before we left my driveway." His voice lowered to just a soft murmur. "No one would've interrupted us then."

I couldn't wait any longer. Not wasting another second, I pushed up onto my tiptoes and kissed him. The coolness of his lip ring seemed to zing my warm lips, a little shock working its way through me. His free hand came up to rest on my waist, and I could feel each one of his fingers press into my body through my sequined dress.

His mouth felt like a song against mine, the beat of the kiss moving me in a way that I'd never thought possible. It was an avalanche of feeling, and I wanted him to fall right along with me. I gripped him closer, lips slipping against his.

Vincent broke the kiss to lean his forehead against mine, swallowing hard. "I meant what I said, you know. It's not even funny how good of a kisser you are."

"You say that like it's a bad thing," I murmured, tracing the outline of his tie.

"Not a bad thing. Definitely not a bad thing."

I bit down on my lower lip, drawing in a honey-scented breath. "Aren't you supposed to be at Crushed Beanz?"

"Harry and Natasha agreed to do an acoustic gig tonight. They convinced me I was being an idiot."

"I should thank them." I thought about it, pulling him closer. "Later."

Vincent laughed, the sound barreling through me like a drumbeat. "Do you want to go back into the dance?"

Honestly? I wanted to stay out here all night, wrapped in Vincent's arms. Sure, it was cold, but we'd experienced colder. "My mom wanted to do a movie night when I got home," I told him, leaning back enough to peer into his eyes. "Maybe I can convince her to watch *Evil Killer Babies* 2?"

His eyes widened. "Good God, there's a *second one*?"

I laughed loudly, uncaring that the sound echoed in the night. "It's amazing. The CGI is almost believable."

"Will she mind? About me?"

I thought about Mom's words to me on Thursday, how understanding she'd been. Even though I'd told her that Vincent and I were probably never going to happen, she hadn't balked at his name like she had before. "I think she'll be okay with it. As long as you make the popcorn."

"Deal."

I needed to go back inside and grab my coat, to tell the girls that I was leaving—with Vincent—but I held back. At the last moment, I pulled him close to press one last kiss against his mouth. It wasn't quick, though, because as soon as our lips connected, I couldn't help myself.

"Thank you," I said, even though he couldn't possibly have known what I was thanking him for.

It was a myriad of things: for showing me it was okay to be my true self, for guiding me through the horrors of the past week and a half, for forgiving me for the unforgivable. For kissing me and being with me and choosing me.

For just being Vincent Castello.

"No," he replied against my mouth, and the word was a soft whisper on my skin, one that I felt shimmy down to the marrow of my bones. And even though I couldn't possibly have known what he was saying it for, he said, "Thank *you*."

epilogue

*J*onathan sat the peppermint mocha in front of me, the teal to-go cup hiding the deliciousness inside. "Admit it," he said, trying one last time. "Mine's better than his."

"I plead the fifth," I said, picking up the cup and pressing it to my lips.

Stella, who sat on the barstool beside me, snorted. "That's her way of saying that she doesn't want to hurt your feelings."

I nudged her, unable to keep from rolling my eyes. It was a Wednesday afternoon, one of their slowest days I'd seen yet, and we'd been talking for a little while now.

Stella's gaze dipped to my necktie, an unreadable emotion flitting across her face. "That's so pretty."

"Oh, thanks." My fingers drifted over the silk Gilfman tie, the one the stranger, Margot, gave me at the gas station. That jogged my memory about something. "Hey, do you have any siblings?"

"Two younger siblings," she answered with ease,

smiling at the thought of them. "Twins. They're ten. They gang up on me all the time. Why?"

Ah, so that girl *wouldn't* have been her sister. That was so, so bizarre—they looked so alike. I knew the chances of seeing the same stranger twice were slim, but if I ever saw her or Margot again, I seriously had to say something. Or take a picture to show Stella. Too, too weird. "You have a doppelgänger, did you know that?"

I didn't miss Stella's quick look at Jonathan, who met her gaze just as fast. "You don't say." She smiled, but it looked funny. "Hey, you need to come to the gig this weekend. I need someone to talk about boys with, and this one —" Stella jerked her chin at Jonathan, "—has no taste."

"It's because you're all gaga over high schoolers. Find a college-aged guy and we can chat until sunset." Jonathan winked at her, settling back against the counter.

I made a noise, swallowing a sip. "A certain singer isn't a minor, is he?"

A wide grin spread across Stella's face, but before she could answer, a loud slamming sound interrupted us, drawing our attention to the double doors that led to the kitchen.

After another bout of banging, Mr. Castello bumped through the swinging door, his wheelchair catching on the corner. He muttered a curse under his breath, waving Jonathan away when he rushed to help. "I've got it," Mr. Castello said, frowning with concentration as he wheeled his way behind the counter. "I've got it."

Jonathan lifted his palms up and backed away.

"Stubborn as ever," Vincent muttered as he followed

his father out of the kitchen, arms folded across his chest. When his gaze caught mine, the heat of the mocha finally hit me.

It'd been two weeks since the dance, since Vincent came by the house and we watched *Evil Killer Babies 2* with Mom. She had her hands over her eyes almost the entire time, but what really warmed my heart was how welcoming she was to Vincent. It took her a moment, but once Vincent offered to pop the popcorn, she was sold. "I really misjudged him," she'd said to me softly, guiltily.

"Addy," Mr. Castello said as he saw me, and I had to tear my gaze away from Vincent to look at him. "Good to see you. Have you finally thawed out?"

"Barely," I teased, lifting up the mocha. "This'll help for sure." Once the words were out, I looked back to Vincent, almost like my gaze was just magnetized to his.

"You know, I should restock the to-go cups," Jonathan declared. "We're getting low. Mr. Castello, do you want to help me?"

Mr. Castello glanced at Jonathan and then back at me. "With restocking?" he asked, but followed Jonathan anyway. This time, he didn't grumble when Jonathan held the door out for him.

"I've got to run to the bathroom," Stella said, pushing to her feet. She flashed me a knowing smile. "Make sure no one takes my drink, got it?"

Stella walked past Vincent, who'd been coming around the counter. "They're a little obvious," he said with a roll of his eyes, but came closer still, until he stopped directly in front of my barstool.

"What do you mean?"

Vincent glanced around the interior. "You didn't notice that they left us all alone?"

I let out a sigh of disbelief mixed with a chuckle. "I'm not complaining," I told him, reaching out and drawing him close. He stepped into the space between my legs. The height difference was still a bit much, since I was sitting down, but he didn't seem to mind. "Are you?"

"Of course not." For a long moment, he gave me a look so powerful and intense that it left me breathless, wondering what he was going to say next. "When's the day?"

I instantly knew what he meant. Reaching up, I slid my fingers into his hair, twisting the strands. "Saturday. The weather shouldn't be so bad."

"Are you nervous?"

"A little," I confessed, looking up into his eyes. So green. So beautiful. "But I'm glad you'll be coming with Mom and me. And Vesta and Mollie."

Vincent readjusted his hold on me, drawing me nearer. "We'll be there for moral support. Facing Ridge Road is a huge deal."

Mom had managed to get an appointment with our new therapist Monday, a miracle cancelation opening up a time slot for our first session. The therapist had suggested that we should face one thing that scares us, the one thing that hurt to think about. Mom's big trigger was her old bedroom—mine was Ridge Road. I was nervous and hadn't wanted to do it, but since Mom had agreed to try, so would I.

"I should probably pretend to be working when they get back," Vincent said in a lower voice. "But I just want one more kiss."

I narrowed my eyes. "Just *one* more?"

"So many more," he corrected, leaning closer, "as many as you'll let me have."

"You're lucky," I murmured against his mouth, unable to fight a stupidly wide smile. I didn't care about Stella probably rounding the corner at any moment, didn't care about Jonathan and Mr. Castello catching us. I didn't even care about a customer walking in for the free show. Right now, I didn't care about anything in the world, about anything except his lips, that freaking lip ring, and *him*. He was all I needed. All I wanted. "I could do this all day."

Thank you for reading!

If you enjoyed this book, I would so appreciate if you could take the time to leave a review. It would mean so much!

There's more to come! Stella and Harry's paths finally cross, and Mollie and Jackson's story isn't over yet! Don't miss out!

WHAT ARE FRIENDS FOR?

What Are Friends For?

Who said falling for your best friend was a good thing?

OUT OF MY LEAGUE

Out of My League

Fake dating the captain of the baseball team is all fun and games until someone catches feelings.

IF THE BROOM FITS

If the Broom Fits

How do you move on from someone you never fell out of love with?

ACKNOWLEDGMENTS

I swear, this part of the book is always the strangest to write, in the best way. It means it's done. It's finished. The final steps are these—it blows my mind every time.

Of course, thank you to my amazing editor, Rachel, who always blows me away with the fabulous suggestions. My beautiful betas helped me as well, and I'm so stinking grateful for Brook, Nicole, Rachel, and Valerie! You all helped me through the spots that didn't quite work, and I'm so grateful.

To my parents, who are always encouraging me when my head hangs low. Writing this book was tough for me, because putting myself in Addy's shoes brought so much pain sometimes. I'm so grateful and lucky to have you two in my life.

Thank you to my family and friends who have relentlessly been there for me, celebrating each book launch and smiling and nodding when I talk book-y with them.

And, of course, thank you to the One who is never-ending. The One who guides my steps and knows the plans for my life. It all is because of You.